INDUCTION

A MIKA FINLEY NOVEL

BOOK ONE

INDUCTION

A MIKA FINLEY NOVEL

S.E. SHARP

S.E. SHARP
AUTHOR WRITER

For Hanna (Skully).
This story wouldn't exist without you.

induction (*noun*)

- the act of bringing about, starting, causing

Mika – pronounced "mee-kah"

Eiko – pronounced "EH-iy-kow"

Jager – pronounced "yay-gir"

Dorei – pronounced "doh-ray"

CONTENTS

CHAPTER ONE

THE ACCIDENT

A semitruck rounds the corner, headlights briefly blinding me. I stare at the white line on the right side of the road, using it as a guide. The monstrous vehicle and its trailer rumble past, shaking the SUV. My knuckles are white as I grip the steering wheel, my armpits sticky with sweat as I navigate the curves.

I hate driving at night. Especially this stretch of road. The darkness is endless. My headlights unable to penetrate the dense forest of pine and aspen. I have a looming, unsettling feeling that I'll be swallowed whole, disappearing forever.

With a breath, I release one hand, regrip, and release the other—only to resume a white-knuckle hold when another vehicle approaches. This one is smaller, a sedan. Headlights not as bright. But still.

I hate it.

My regret at volunteering to drive home adds to the

already stress-tight muscles in my neck, but I need the nighttime hours of driving to get my license. I only have three out of ten. It would be nice to able to drive myself to work, as opposed to riding my bike. Especially when winter comes. Imagine, riding through sleet in the early morning hours, just to serve people coffee.

Yeah, no thanks. I'll suffer the anxiety of driving a car at night.

With a glance in my rearview mirror, I'm reminded of the other reason I volunteered to drive home. My dad sits between my twin siblings, Anita and Aaron, nodding off even as he taps at his tablet. The glow illuminates strands of his salt-and- pepper hair. He and my mom helped chaperone over fifty fifth-graders for their summer carnival and assisted with setup and cleanup. They are exhausted after being on their feet for over twenty hours.

My mom has fallen asleep in the passenger seat next to me, her head resting against the window, her cardigan acting as a pillow. Her light auburn hair is pulled up in a haphazard bun.

Anita is asleep, too, curled up against Dad. Her auburn braids are loose and fuzzy from a busy day of riding each carnival ride twice, if not three times. Aaron peers out the side window, the light drumming of his fingers against the door's armrest offering a peaceful percussion.

His hair color matches Anita's, but he convinced Mom and Dad to let him shave it into a mohawk. The twins share Mom's upturned nose and smattering of freckles.

Our older sister Carol, Dad, and I all share the same sloped nose, dark brown hair, and hazel eyes.

I check my speed. Five under the limit.

If Mom was awake, she'd lecture me. "There's a speed limit for a reason," she'd say. "It wouldn't be forty-five if it wasn't safe to drive that at night."

And Dad would interject with, "Let her drive at whatever speed is comfortable for her."

My cell phone dings from the cup holder, signaling a text. The message is from my best friend, Vic, who is currently in France for some martial arts summer school. When the sun goes down here, it rises over there. He's either getting up to go on an early morning run, or he already went for one. Probably the latter. The boy puts early birds to shame.

He likes to send me pictures of animals he sees on his runs. So far, he's seen deer and raccoons, and a farmer with his cows. Lately though, he's been obsessed with some girl. The love of his life, he says.

I resist the temptation to take a peek at what news he's sent me and adjust the air vent for the AC, silently praising myself for relaxing a little. Even with the sun down, the temperature is still a disgusting ninety degrees Fahrenheit. July evenings in Colorado at their finest.

With my newfound confidence, and no other passing vehicles with blinding lights, I take a second to adjust the radio volume. The regular music isn't playing, as the DJ talks about a teenage girl from the area who's been missing for twelve hours.

I frown, biting my lip, eyes scanning the road and forest ahead, my mind already going to the worst place, wondering what happened to the missing girl.

Aaron gasps. "Whoa, do you see that?"

No sooner do I glance out the side window than something large leaps from the side of the road, right into the path of the SUV. My eyes shoot to the road, gaze locking on the reflective yellow eyes of a mountain lion—a mountain lion the size of a grizzly bear.

I slam the brakes. Tires squeal. The bumper clips the beast, jolting the vehicle. Then we're spinning. A scream tears from my throat. Glass shatters. A force punches at my face and chest, slamming my body hard against the seat. My vision blurs red. A horn blares, piercing the ringing in my ears. Sharp lights clutter my fuzzy vision. I catch sight of a chrome grille.

Smash!

Pain shoots through my spine and my head, throbbing in my nose. I'm weightless, flying through the air. For a second, I think I'm dead.

The vehicle hits the ground, slamming hard against the earth, jarring my bones. I black out and come to several times. Each moment is like an eternity and a single second. Soft sobbing lulls me from darkness. I'm not sure if it's my own or from my family. Maybe both. Movement hurts as if every muscle is being pinned down with sharp implements. The worst is the hot, stabbing pinch in my left shoulder.

Too scared to move, I try to focus on staying conscious. Each time my eyes open, vision unfocused and swimming, I attempt to talk. Ask if anyone is hurt. But I can't. My mouth refuses to move. It just hangs open and aches with a deep throb along my left jawline.

Something warm and wet runs down my face. I tell myself the liquid is just tears, not anything else. My head rubs against the roof when I try to turn my head to check on my family.

How many times did the vehicle roll? I only remember hitting the ground once. The memory twists my stomach in knots. Bile burns in my chest, threatening to erupt up my throat.

Stop thinking about it! I need to focus on checking on my family, figure out how to get out of this crushed vehicle.

I force my eyes open and somehow manage to keep them open. The left headlight is broken and dim, but the right one pierces through the dark, illuminating a massive animal form as it rises to its feet. I don't dare blink. I don't dare breathe.

The enormous beast has the round head and short muzzle of a mountain lion. A long, sleek predatory body with muscles boasting of insane strength under tan, matted fur. It turns its head, glowing eyes unfocused as they skip over me. Dark blood oozes from its nose. Jaw hanging open, it huffs, showcasing rows of sharp glistening teeth.

Its unsteady gaze finds me, and I freeze. A moment, a second, a lifetime passes. Its muscles bunch, shifting its weight. Is it going to attack? My heart hits hard. Once. Twice. Then the beast turns and limps away from the vehicle, quickly consumed by the dark of the forest.

The vacating beast is the last thing I remember when I wake up the next morning in the hospital with my dislocated jaw, three fractured ribs, fractured humerus bone, and concussion. I don't remember the couple who called 911 and stayed with us until the EMTs arrived. I don't remember being moved from the smashed SUV to the ambulance, or the ride to the hospital, or surgery, where they set my bones and relocated my jaw.

And I definitely do not remember them pronouncing Aaron dead on the scene.

CHAPTER TWO

STRANGE SIGHTINGS

Four Months Later

Beep. Beep. Beep.

I swipe my phone screen, silencing the 9:00 a.m. alarm, then return my attention to my laptop. Scrolling through the articles, from six months ago and later, on a forum called *Strange and Unusual Sightings*. Most of the posts are obscure and vague at best, despite the authors' conviction they'd spotted Bigfoot or a UFO.

I don't comment or interact with any of the posts. I'm here for answers, and if I start posting and asking my own questions on this forum, wouldn't that make me just as crazy as DeeDee87, who swears Bigfoot walked through her backyard?

The picture on her post is grainy and dark. She's circled in red what she says is the freakish humanoid, but the

7

"thing" resembles a powerline pole next to a tree. A streetlight down the way offers the glow of an eye.

I click off her post and scroll through a few more. I've read most of them. These people haven't seen anything resembling the beast I encountered. The closest thing to a mountain lion the size of a four-hundred-pound grizzly is an oversized wolf some guy saw, but that was up in Canada.

I'm starting to think maybe I do belong among these people.

With a heavy sigh, I type in my email website. The homepage has articles—most about politics, the rich and famous—but one catches my eye. Another girl has gone missing since last night. My cursor hovers over the article. What number is this one now?

A series of loud quick knocks rap against my door, and I clench my jaw. My heart thuds in a panic. God, I need sleep.

"Mika! Get up," calls Carol, my older sister. Her voice stern and words clipped. Her blatant irritation heightens my dread. "You still need to empty the trash from last night."

"I'm up." My voice breaks with fatigue. I sigh, trying to ease the weight that never ceases.

I click on the inbox icon. Third in the inbox is an email from Vic, which came shortly after 3:00 a.m. when I first checked my email after I gave up on sleep and fell down the rabbit hole of the *Strange and Unusual* forum.

Vic's in Peru right now for a school trip and doesn't have cell service, so he's reduced to sending emails when he can. He's attached a picture, and a small smile tugs at my lips. He stands next to a llama, the loose hair from his ponytail sweat-pasted to his forehead as he grins from ear to ear. The llama, on the other hand, looks less thrilled, its eyes squinted in annoyance and ears drawn back.

I start to type a response, asking if he got spit on.

"Mika!" Carol yells, knocking again.

"I'm up!" My voice doesn't break and my frustration builds. But I don't let it simmer. I can't. I'm the reason everyone is angry, and I accept that. A mountain lion the size of a grizzly? Not a real thing. Distracted drivers at night? That's a real thing.

Four months since the accident that killed my brother. I've healed from physical wounds. I've returned to work at Scott's Latte Stop, riding my bicycle since no one— including myself—wants me to drive ever again. And I research. I look for evidence of what I saw. Needing to prove that what I saw is real.

No luck so far. Just Bigfoot and werewolf sightings.

Another sigh and I sit up, the box spring squeaking. My left shoulder is stiff and sore, a constant reminder why Carol is irritated with me. I rub the muscles, trying to ease the tension.

I look around the bedroom. My work clothes—polo shirt with Scott's Latte Stop embroidered over the left breast, and black jeans—lie in a pile by the closet. My dresser's bottom drawer is ajar from when I retrieved my pajama pants last night. My journal on the bedside table is open to a sketch of the mountain lion. More of a doodle really. Unrefined lines, exaggerated triangles for teeth, scraggly fur, and angry circles for eyes.

This creature is the reason sleep eludes me, even with a dose or two of melatonin. It haunts my dreams. My nightmares. Along with my younger brother's scream.

I wince, shoving my fist against my mouth, biting down on my knuckle. Tears prick my eyes.

His death is my fault. At first, I blamed the beast, the giant mountain lion that no one else believes exists. No one saw it except Aaron and me. Not even the couple who'd called 911.

When I told Vic what happened, he said he believed me, but that's what best friends do, right? They stick up for each other no matter what.

I know what I saw, but doubt—heavy, bone-deep doubt—has me second-guessing. I did get a concussion that night, but I know I saw the beast before the crash. Aaron did too.

An animal that big had to leave tracks. I hit it with the SUV too; there should have been blood or fur on the bumper. I remember the dark, almost black blood leaking from its nose. But there was nothing. No evidence except of a distracted driver—me—spinning into the opposite lane and getting T-boned by a truck.

This has been related by my parents, Carol, and the

news articles—articles I've read over and over again that make it seem that what I saw is a work of fiction I made up to alleviate the guilt over Aaron's death.

My thought from earlier returns: I really do belong with the people on the *Strange and Unusual Sightings* forum.

When I force myself out of bed, my movements are slow and methodical. I brush my short, dark brown hair, working out the knots that formed in the few hours of restless sleep. Except, of course, for the side of my head where they had to shave my hair down to the skin to suture a laceration that looked worse than it was.

A four-inch-long scar mars the side of my head. The hair is finally growing in around it. If the hairstyle wasn't such a gruesome reminder of the accident, I think I would keep it. But the strands won't grow fast enough for my liking.

I glance around the room for my hoodie, only to catch my reflection in the full-length mirror hanging on the door. One wouldn't be able to guess the hell I went through just by looking at me—average height, average weight, and sixteen years old. Dark, baggy circles hang constantly below my eyes, but maybe that's just part of having a job. Between that, the dark clothes I wear and my punkish hairstyle, most probably figure I'm emo or goth.

I dress in a T-shirt and jeans. My hoodie is nowhere to be found, so I dig through my dresser and pull on the first long-sleeve shirt I come across.

On my way to the kitchen, I peek in the living room to

see Anita curled up on the couch, gaming controller in hand. Her headset is on, and every once in a while, she talks with the other players. I look at the screen, watching her swiftly maneuver her warrior princess through treetops and dodge arrows.

She's delved into the gaming world since Aaron's death. They likely provide her an escape. She suffered whiplash, a mild concussion, and a few cuts and bruises from the accident. She was the least injured, along with Mom. Dad broke his collarbone.

Going about my morning routine, I sense that familiar tightening in my chest. I prepare my breakfast in the kitchen: cereal and a glass of orange juice. I skirt around the island to the dining room and hunker down at the table, sitting in the corner. One little colorful loop at a time, I eat my cereal.

Carol's voice drifts down the hall from her room. "I've been carrying my bear spray. It's basically Mace." I listen, taking another bite. "Yeah… It's clearly a serial kidnapper. This is the fourth girl taken since July…"

Right. The fourth one. I focus on my cereal, not wanting to let my thoughts wander. I can't help but imagine who took the girls and what he's doing to them. I shudder, hunching closer to the wall, as if it could swallow me whole and I won't have to bother existing.

A shadow looms over me. I don't look up. From my peripheral, my older sister is standing at the end of the table, arms crossed and glaring down at me.

"I'll take it out on my way to work," I say, dipping my spoon in the milk, watching a certain piece of cereal that I will consume next. I stare at food a lot these days. I haven't looked my family in the eye since the accident, not needing to see what I can hear from their voices.

"Can you please take it out now?" she says. "We made chicken last night, and it stinks already." Her tone implies a command, not a polite request. My frustration rises again. I close my eyes, bite my cheek, and inhale slowly through my nose.

"Okay." I push my bowl to the side, take a sip of orange juice, then stand.

Carol retreats to her room, carrying a collection of animal anatomy and veterinary terminology textbooks. Considering she's always been better with animals than with people, she'll make an excellent animal doctor.

I pull out the bulging bag, wrinkling my nose and holding my breath, but not before catching the rancid stench of rotting meat. I tie the bag closed and replace it with an empty one that smells something like lemons and pine, an obviously artificial scent, but far better than the natural rotting chicken.

Outside, I take a deep breath of the frigid November morning. The odd mixture of autumn and winter in the air, dried leaves and fresh snow. Remnants of yesterday's snowfall dapple the yard, safe from the sun in the shadow of the eight-foot-tall, wood-paneled fence bordering the yard.

Our family's old black lab, Licorice, greets me with lazy tail wags, unbothered to actually get to her feet as she lies in a patch of pale sunlight. I set down the bag and walk over to her. Her tail wags faster, and she lifts her sweet, graying face to receive pets. I scratch behind her ears, massage her back, then rub her belly. At least, she's happy to see me. Dogs are cool like that.

I kiss her head, then resume my trash duty. At the gate, I struggle with the latch. The darn thing has been sticking over the past couple of weeks. I keep forgetting to mention it to my parents.

Or, to be accurate: I feel I can't mention it to them.

"Should fix this stupid gate myself," I mutter. You can learn anything from the Internet.

Except if grizzly-sized mountain lions are real.

I lift the latch, and the gate swings open away from me. Bordering the south side of my home, the forest stretches in an expanse of pine and aspens. Part of the forest is state-owned, a small portion is public land, and a good mass of it is private. I don't know the owner.

My siblings and I have come up with different ideas about who owns the land—it's actually a game we'd play, to see who can come up with the most nonsensical ideas.

A thing of the past now.

I toss the bag in the large bin and drag my feet as I head back to the gate, examining the scuffed toes of my shoes.

A low growl rights my attention. Licorice stands at the gate, head low, staring toward the forest, her hackles raised. Her lips twitch with a warning snarl.

"What do you see, Lick?" I whisper. Goosebumps break across my arms, and a tight, tingling feeling runs down my spine. I glance in the direction the dog is staring, and do a double take. My breath catches in my throat. "Oh, my god."

At the edge of the forest, maybe five hundred feet from my house, surveying the sparse grass and loose gravel, stands all four hundred pounds of predatory muscle.

The mountain lion.

CHAPTER THREE

STUPID GIRL

I race inside, yelling for my sisters, hands desperately patting my pockets for my phone, coming back empty. I must have left it on my bed.

I find Anita in the living room. She's pulling off her headset, face crunched in concern.

"What is it?" She eyes me warily.

"The mountain lion is out there! You have to come see!" I reach out to grab her arm, intending to drag her outside with me.

Carol appears, stepping between us and glaring hard. "Mika, stop it!" She knocks my hand away.

I stare at her, words stuck in my throat. My attention returns to Anita. She's shying away, eyes wide, lower lip sucked in. I pull back, flexing and curling my hands in an effort to wrangle my excitement.

"But the mountain lion beast is real!" I cry. "It's right out—"

"There is no mountain lion." Carol's eyes are as hard as her words. "Never was."

I snap my mouth shut and glare at her. "I'll prove it to you!"

First things first, I get my phone. It's sitting on my bed where I left it. I clutch the device tight, like a lifeline. *I'll show them I'm not crazy,* I think. *I am not crazy.* The mantra is a steady beat in my mind, fueling my already racing pulse, making my body start to perspire.

On my way back outside, I glance at them in the living room. Anita gives me a solemn look before putting her headset back on and continuing her game. Carol continues to stand between us, hands on her hips. She shakes her head, opening her mouth to say something, but I turn away.

I can prove it to them now. They won't be able to stay mad at me.

The screen door slaps shut behind me. Licorice still stands at the open gate. I scold myself for leaving her alone, for not closing the gate to keep her from chasing after the mountain lion. But, like a good dog, she stayed put, protecting her territory. I pat her head, gaze lifting to where I saw the beast. Heart skipping a beat when I don't see it.

Ah, there it is! Retreating into the forest.

"No." My hope sinks as it disappears into the shadows of the trees. I can't let it go. The need to prove myself not crazy overrides the stupidity of what I'm doing next.

I pull Licorice back, telling her she's a good girl, to stay put, before I push the gate closed. I give it a yank to ensure the latch is engaged. I don't try to convince myself that this is a monumentally bad idea as I race across uneven ground, up a slope, and enter the forest. All I know is: the mountain lion is real. I am not crazy. Aaron didn't die because I suck at driving in the dark.

~

Leaves crunch underfoot, my pace slowing. I lean against a tree, panting for breath. I glance around the forest of ponderosa pine and aspens. The trees are towering and dense, even in the thick of autumn. I rub my arms to ward off a feeling of panic.

I'm lost.

An aspen's cream-colored bark is smooth against my back. It would be difficult to climb to get a vantage point on my surroundings. To my left, the rough, brown-orange bark of the ponderosa looks promising, but none of the branches are low enough for me to grasp. The orange-yellow leaves of the aspen, and the thick, long needles of the pine sway in the breeze. Their limbs stretch tall and long, disorientating me the longer I stare up at them.

"Good job, Mika," I mutter to myself. Numbness creeps into my muscles.

Then I realize—something as big as the beast probably left tracks.

My gaze drops to the forest floor, scanning among the

brown, fallen leaves and pine needles, pinecones, and brush overgrowth. I forget I'm lost, and I don't think about heading home.

Tracks! There's a partial paw print the size of my face in a thin layer of snow that hasn't melted away yet. And another one! A full-sized print, several feet from the first. The stride length of this beast illustrates its massive build.

I kneel, stretching my shaking fingers over it. The paw print is almost bigger than both my hands together with fingers spread to their full width. My heart thuds, and I swallow hard.

I retrieve my phone and click the camera icon—noting the lack of cell service. I roll my eyes, thinking, *Typical*, then hold my free hand up next to the paw print for scale and take a picture.

Proof. I have proof. Excitement swells in my chest. I almost want to cry with relief. I survey the tracks, wondering where they lead. A short debate with myself, whether I should follow them to find my way home or continue into the forest, to see where the beast is heading.

Since I'm a one hundred percent rational human being, I follow them deeper in the trees, farther away from safety—with no cell phone service, and no real jacket, just the long-sleeve I pulled on this morning, which I'm starting to regret. The cold I didn't feel before, because of the adrenaline, is now starting to stiffen my fingers and wrists, numbing my cheeks and the tip of my nose.

I return my phone to my back pocket and rub my

hands together as I walk, telling myself over and over to turn around, but I'm on autopilot. I want more proof than a paw print picture.

My heart seems oddly loud, though it's no longer racing. Maybe the anticipation of—

Snap!

I glance down at my feet, then over my shoulder. I gasp and fall backward to the ground. At the edge of a clearing looms the beast, its head lowered, menacing, hungry eyes locked on me. I scramble backward. My back slams against a tree, my fingers curling into dirt and leaves. Dried needles prick my palms with sharp pain, proving I'm awake, that this isn't a dream.

This can't be happening. But, of course, it is. This is what a stupid girl gets for wandering into a forest after a predatory creature.

The beast's tail flicks from left to right. Its jowls open to reveal its unnatural, sharpened rows of teeth. Too many teeth. Its eyes darken and intensify. Not unfocused like the night of the crash.

If this is the same one. A terrifying thought. There could be more than one.

It lifts one of its giant paws, exposing thick, pointed claws, surely meant for grabbing and pinning down prey. It lowers into a position I know well from watching kittens play. It's preparing to pounce. Gaze locked, muscles rippling and bunching with strength.

My breath is stuck in my throat, where my heart races

with an effort to escape without me. Spittle gleams on the beast's teeth. My skin tightens and—

I am going to die.

The beast springs. Letting out a yowl, deep and guttural. I let out a strangled whimper and tumble to the side, scrambling behind the tree. Sharp pain digs in my arm as the knife-like claws graze me. A scream rips from my throat. I clamp my hand around the wound. Warm and wet, blood seeps through my fingers.

Go, go, go!

The forest is a blur. I'm running. In its thudding pursuit, the beast closes in. I'm not fast enough. A sob constricts my throat, and I plead with the universe, with God, that this isn't my end.

Something grabs my uninjured arm. I scream, trying to yank it from its grasp. The grip tightens, and a voice next to me yells, "This way!"

I'm pulled to the side, and I'm running with someone in dark clothing, with something like a ski mask over their head. *What the heck?* But I don't stop running until they place a gloved hand on my shoulder and push me to the ground. The masked face appears before me, putting a finger to their mouth—*Shhh*. They run away, brandishing a long, thin sword from a sheath on their back. The blade a sheen of cobalt in the sunlight.

Mouth agape, huddled low in the brown, dying brush, I stare at my rescuer as they race to join two other figures in black clothing—much like the ninjas in Anita's video games. Black, loose, pajama-like clothing. Faces covered save for a single slit for their eyes.

Swords raised, they all rush at the beast.

Ninjas and giant mountain lions. I must be dreaming. But they're real. The sharp, burning pain in my arm is proof that I'm awake and alive. Even with the odd, terrifying sight in front of me, I glance at my arm. My gorge rises. Blood seeps from the claw marks, the metallic scent heavy in my nose.

Shouldn't have looked!

A bloodcurdling yowl jerks my attention to the fight. The ninjas slash at the beast's legs. One of them manages to leap and climb up on its back, raising their cobalt sword for a killing stab. The beast bucks, spinning with a snarl. The ninja is flung across the forest before crashing into a thick aspen tree.

"Hey!" One of the ninjas lets out a war cry, raising a red garnet sword, and runs toward the beast, who spins to face them. The other ninja jumps in the fray. Their emerald sword slicing the back of the beast's legs.

With the beast distracted by freaking ninjas, I find the sense to push myself up from the ground and run. I don't look back. I run until I can't hear the shouts of ninjas and yowls of the beast. I run until I find myself on my knees at the edge of a creek, sucking in air with giant, heaving gasps.

My gaze jumps around the forest, expecting to see the beast leaping out at me, ready to tear me apart. If not for that, it would be beautiful out here, just me with aspen trees, their leaves yellow and orange falling to the ground, the pines with the breeze whispering through their needles, and the trickle of the creek. I reach for my phone, wanting—needing—to call for help. My hand fumbles against an empty pocket.

"No," I whimper, tears blurring my vision. I grab at all my pants pockets, then at the forest floor. No phone within sight. Gone. "No!" I shake with a sob.

I'm aware of all this: tears streaming down my face, snot draining from my nose, blood getting sticky between my fingers, jeans soaking up the damp, cold earth where my knees connect with the ground, but I can't manage to get myself under control.

I did almost die, I remind myself.

My sobs quiet to soft whimpers, chin trembling.

I almost died, but I *didn't* die. I grab at the water, the icy liquid biting my flesh, making me gasp, but I continue to wash the blood from my hands in relentless, stiff movements. Biting the inside of my cheek, I pull my sleeve up past the wound on my bicep.

The pain deepens. I wonder if my family would think I just cut myself for attention. I can imagine the bored, annoyed expression on Carol's face, the sad and helpless expression on Anita's. No way would they believe me about the monster, even with the gaping wounds.

I mean, *I* wouldn't believe me.

I blink hard, fighting back the tears.

"Are you okay?"

I jump to my feet, almost tumbling into the creek. Water seeps into my shoe, but I don't move, staring at the ninja now standing a couple of yards away from me. Raising their hands in that supposed calming gesture.

"Whoa. Easy now." The voice is lower pitched, male, the words calm yet quick, as if their coming out faster will settle me. "I didn't mean to scare you."

My brow furrows, and I continue to stare at him.

"Right," he says. "Hold on. Just promise me you won't freak out."

I huff. It's a little late for that request. I'm already freaked out. I'm bleeding, and cold. I've been attacked by something that shouldn't exist and rescued by something that shouldn't exist. At least not here.

Ninjas. Nowadays the mere word sounds fake. Silly.

"I want to help you. That looks bad." He gestures to me. "I like your shirt."

I glance down at myself. I'm wearing a shirt that features a band, *One Times Three*, that I used to be obsessed with when I was twelve, thirteen. I guess that's his tactic to calm me down, get my mind off the reality of what happened, because I'm a deer in headlights, frozen and staring.

"What—" My words cut short when I look up at him. He's removed his mask. My mouth bobs as I realize I recognize him. His typically straightened hair is bunched into natural, tight, dark curls. But it is him. The younger version of his sun-kissed face is on my shirt. One of the brothers/members of *One Times Three,* Devon Stehn. The oldest brother, he was fifteen at the time of their short-lived fame; now he's nineteen.

I must be dreaming. Ninjas and monstrous giant cats I can handle. But my childhood band showing up—as ninjas—is a whole other thing.

My gaze sweeps over him, trying to comprehend. Maybe the pain in my arm is just phantom pain from when I broke my arm in the car accident.

Except, it's the wrong arm. And I smell the blood.

It is most certainly Devon Stehn. Instead of his usual outfit of a striped V-neck shirt and skinny jeans, he's wearing loose, slightly baggy pants. I imagine it's for ease of movement while fighting. His top is long-sleeved, sort of wrapping around the torso and held with a thick belt full of pouches and small knife sheaths. A stark contrast to the colorful, studded belts he'd wear in music videos. A strap over his chest holds the sheath to his back for his sword, instead of a bass guitar.

He nods, offering a small smile. "Okay, you're handling this well, I think."

He takes a slow step toward me. I take a step back. He steps again, raising his hands in that inane, coaxing gesture, and I step back again.

"You should've kept your mask on, Dev," says a smooth, female voice behind me.

I spin, trying to scramble away, but a hand clamps my

shoulder. Gentle and firm at the same time.

"Yeah, I'd run away from a mug like that too."

I can hear the smile in her voice. Her calm tone somehow keeps me from trying to bolt again, and I glance at her. Another ninja, judging by her black attire. I don't know this one, even with her mask removed. She appears to be a couple of years older than I am. Eighteen or nineteen. Smooth, golden skin. Dark-chocolate hair pulled back into a braid that reaches past her elbows. She's about my height, but slighter in stature; less broad in the shoulders and hips.

Her round green eyes are kind as she applies slight pressure to my shoulder, saying, "Sit down. Let's take a look at your arm."

When I'm on the ground, she glances over at Devon— bassist, good at piano, decent at hacky sack, loves sorbet—

"Go meet up with Jo," she says. "He's about a mile back, east. Our blades didn't do a thing to that cat, dude."

He snorts. "Which is ridiculous."

I stare at him. How did I not recognize his voice right off? I'd been obsessed with their music, listening to only their songs for hours and hours. And I've seen all their interviews and behind-the-scenes for the music videos.

"The blades couldn't be more blessed," he adds, putting his hands on his hips and pressing his lips together as he watches us. I frown at him.

Blessed blades? Who are these people?

"It's not the blades," she says under her breath. She pulls bandages and wet wipes from one of her pouches. Her eyes meet mine for a second. "This'll sting." She wipes the wound, and around it. I wince and take a sharp breath. More tears prick my eyes that I force away with rapid blinks.

"The cat's skin is fortified by something. Jo will need help scouring for samples. Our swords had to have done something." She gives him a stern look. "Go."

"Okay, okay. Geez." He casts me an apologetic look before pulling on his mask and running off.

"Sorry about him." She sighs, shaking her head. "My name is Elizabeth."

"What's going on?" I keep my eyes on her, watching to see if she's going to brush off my question or lie to me. Not that I'm an expert at detecting lies, so I guess that doesn't matter, does it?

She pauses her work on my wound, pressing her lips together. Her wide-set eyes lock with mine. She may only be a couple years older than I am, but there's a maturity in her face that surpasses her physical age that I recognize in my own face. She's lived through tragedy like I have.

"I'm sorry, but your world just got a lot bigger, weirder, and a whole heck of a lot more terrifying." She takes a breath, eyes searching my face, almost like she's trying to place me. I shift under her gaze.

Her attention returns to my arm. "I'm not sure how my mentors will want to handle this, but if you are who I think you are—"

A loud screech pierces through the forest. I cringe and clamp my hands over my ears. Elizabeth does the same, head swiveling as she searches the forest. I try to ask her what's happening, but the sound intensifies. I crumple to a fetal position, gasping, vision going red as the screech stabs into my eardrums, trying to force my eyeballs and brain out of my head.

The sound stops. I wither on the ground. I can taste blood. *This must be what hell feels like.* Why would I be allowed into heaven after getting my brother killed?

Two boots come into view—black combat boots. One of them nudges me. I don't have the strength or energy to respond. A mewling whimper is all I can muster.

"Huh. Pitiful," says a monotone, bored voice.

A sharp, warming prick in my arm. Nausea quickly follows, the forest floor wobbling. My eyelids weigh down to a close, reminding me of the sedatives and medication from my time in the hospital.

CHAPTER FOUR

CAPTIVE

My world is dark. Pain is my only company. I'm trapped again in the car, meeting eyes with the monster who stares back at me with hunger, with anger, and instead of limping away, it stalks toward me—

Frigid water smacks against my face and body. I inhale sharply. My eyes shoot open. Panic wracks my body. Everything aches, my arms and head most of all. The inside of my mouth is sticky and metallic. I go to grab my head but I can't move my arms. Each breath comes shorter and quicker than the last. My chest tightens, the world blurring at the edges.

"Mika, calm down. You'll be okay."

The sound of my name jars me. I glance around, trying to focus on something, anything to show me that I'm not still in my nightmare, trapped in a car with my dead family. I'm greeted with dark granite walls on three sides and floor-to-ceiling metal bars in front of me. Not the crushed metal and smashed glass of a car.

Oh, god, what is this place? It seems I've traded one nightmare for another.

Dim lights overhead illuminate my cellmate off to the side. The girl from before. What did she call herself?

Elizabeth.

She's suspended from the ceiling, wrist-bound by metal cuffs. Her ankle shackles clank as she dances on the tips of her toes, straining to touch the ground. Veins pop out on her forehead and neck from the effort. Her nose is bleeding, her face red. She's stripped of her ninja garb and weapons, wearing only a black, sweat-drenched sports bra and leggings.

"Take a deep breath. In through the nose, out through the mouth." Her instructions are calm, even though the words are strained and quiet.

I inhale through my nose, only to gasp as I assess myself. Chin quivering, I realize why my arms and head hurt so much. I'm restrained as she is, arms pulled up overhead, cuffed at the wrists and ankles. The only difference is my feet fully touch the ground.

"Wh…what—" I choke out the words, unable to finish my question because I don't know what to ask. Breath coming in short, shallow bursts.

"Deep breaths, slow and easy," she repeats.

I clench my teeth, pulling in air through my nose. Despite my better judgment, I swing my gaze around the room again, water flinging from the ends of my hair.

There is a drain in the floor to my right, where a thin stream of water trickles down from where I hang.

My breath resumes in short, whimpering bursts as the worst-case scenarios run through my mind. I'm chained up in a room that has drains in the freaking floor! The nausea builds, and I fight it, shifting my attention to a bald man standing outside the prison cell. His eyes are void of emotion, his expression blank. His jumpsuit and combat boots as drab as the walls. He holds a thick black hose that's connected to a reel mounted to the wall. Water drips from the nozzle.

Oh, god. My gaze returns to Elizabeth. Not sweat. Water. What is going on?

"Deep breaths. Yes, this is all real," she says, speaking quickly. "Mika, whatever happens, you're stronger than you think."

"Wha—"

"You EONs are all alike," a monotone voice interjects. "Handing out motivational quotes that are nothing more than bland, stale fortune cookies."

The feminine voice is familiar, sending a shudder through me. The speaker is the one from before, when we'd been paralyzed by that ear-bleeding shrill sound. Whoever those combat boots belonged to. Claiming that I, or someone, was pitiful.

The *click* of a lighter breaks the silence. A deep exhale follows, as does the acrid scent of a cigarette. Tendrils of smoke enter my vision from outside the cell. A slight shadow is cast across the floor where the speaker stands just out of view.

"This is bold. Even for you," Elizabeth says. "You know they're coming for us."

There's a short, bitter laugh. "Oh, I know. They wouldn't want to make that mistake again."

Elizabeth sighs, lowering her head. "Elle—"

Another laugh. This one angrier than the last. "You don't get to call me that anymore. Especially you." Another long puff of smoke.

My stupid, panicked, confused brain starts to connect the pieces. These two share a history I've been dragged into. And all I wanted to do was prove a giant mountain lion exists. Stupid me.

"I'm not—" Elizabeth lets out a huff. "Elle…"

"It's Sahara. You lost the right to address me as anything else."

"Look, if you want quality time, you didn't have to go this far. We can talk."

I glance at Elizabeth, unsure what to think. She's gazing toward where the speaker hides, a solemn expression on her face.

"Don't. Patronize. Me." The speaker's words are quiet, but the anger in them has me feeling small.

This is all a bad dream, right? I'll wake up at home, and the worst thing happening to me will be running late for work. But no, I'm trying to utilize the deep-breathing method to keep my heart from jumping out of my chest.

I remain quiet, trying to be as invisible as possible.

"I don't think you realize the gravity of the situation." Elizabeth spares a glance in my direction. "You've kidnapped a civilian. This isn't a game."

The speaker steps into our view, wearing a blood red button-down blouse, gray tactical pants, and familiar black combat boots. A sheathed knife is strapped to her hip. The bald man returns the hose to its reel, then steps forward, unlatches the door and holds it open for her.

I stare at the young woman like a gaping fool, then turn my eyes to Elizabeth. They're almost identical: same wide-set eyes, nose, chin, lean, athletic build. The only physical difference is their hair. Sahara has the same dark brown color, but her locks are cut into a sleek bob, unlike Elizabeth's long braid.

The evil twin eyes us, a cigarette loosely held between her middle and index finger. She first stares at Elizabeth, an unspoken threat hanging in the air. Then she turns that burning hatred to me. I can't help but flinch.

Her lips twitch. Next thing I know, she's beside me, pressing the burning end of her cigarette to my neck.

Fire spreads under my skin. I scream. Elizabeth yells. Chains rattle. Through tears I see the evil twin staring at me, the corner of her lips twitching with a sadistic grin as she takes in every shudder of pain with cold amusement. She straightens when my screams become whimpers, then saunters over to Elizabeth.

"I don't think *you* understand the *gravity* of the *situation*," she says, anger underlying her threat. "This was never a game. You should know that best of all."

She turns on her heel and strides out. The cell door slams closed.

CHAPTER FIVE

SECRETS

Waves of tremors wrack my body, and the burn on my neck throbs. I choke on my sobs and runny nose. All I want to do is shrivel up in a ball, but I can't move. The shackles dig into my wrists. Elizabeth is talking, trying to soothe and reassure me, but my horrified imagination of what can and will happen obliterate all hope of rescue.

They're both right about one thing. This isn't a game. There are no checkpoints to restart if I die. There are no extra lives like in Anita's video games. This is real. The pain is real. The hate in Sahara's voice is real. The threat of death is very real, as is the threat of torture.

"Mika, do you hear me? We're going to get out of here."

Snot and tears run down my lips and chin. "How d-do you know m-my name? I never t-told you."

"We have a…mutual friend. It's a ridiculously small world."

I scoff. "I'm b-being tortured by your evil twin, and you can't g-give me a straight answer? That's nice."

"You're right. You don't deserve stupid answers." She inhales sharply, then says, "I know Vic."

My head shoots up. Pain bites down my spine, making me wince. The quick movement causes the walls to blur together. I don't believe I heard her correctly.

"Yep. Victor Jager Choi." She laughs half-heartedly, her face contorting into a grimace. "He didn't really win in the name game. Jager. Who names their kid that?"

"It was his grandpa's name." I stop myself from defending him and get back on track. "How? Is he a…ninja too?" Saying the word out loud is weird. Ninja. I'd laugh if I wasn't going through a whole ordeal right now.

She tilts her head, eyes drifting closed. "That's not my secret to tell."

"So, he is?"

If there was ever a good candidate for a ninja, Vic would be one. He's proficient in Tae Kwan Do and hapkido and various other martial arts—with trophies to prove it—and dabbles in parkour. Not to mention he's proficient in several languages, useful for all his overseas travel. But no. He can't be a ninja. He would have told me. No way that boy hasn't told me he's a ninja. This secret would be too much. I'm his best friend.

Right?

She opens her eyes to peek at me. "You figured it out.

I didn't tell you. If he ever asks. He's been wanting to tell you for years."

I can't wrap my head around this. I stare at the floor yet see nothing. My head's already exploding from the pain-building pressure. First, I discover that my childhood band members are ninjas, and now my lifelong best friend is one too? Maybe I am in a coma, and it is still July, which would explain why everything hurts—because I was in a car accident. That would make more sense than this.

"So, Devon…all the members of *One Times Three* are ninjas?" It's been a while since I was obsessed with that band. For some reason, it's easier to rationalize them being ninjas than Vic.

"Again, you figured it out for yourself. Actually, you can blame Devon for that. Please do."

Although she's trying to keep the situation light, the fatigue is stark in her voice. Each word strained. I glance at her. Her eyes are closed again, head resting against her arm, rotating her wrist. She almost looks peaceful, but every couple of seconds, she trembles.

"And…Sahara, she's…"

"My sister. Twin sister." Her voice is tight with sadness and grief.

"You really think we're getting out of this?" I know I'll get the same answer she's been giving me, but I need to hear it again.

"I don't think so. I know so." The look she gives me sends a chill down my spine. She takes a deep breath and lets it out, muttering, "This is going to put me out of commission for a while." Another deep breath.

My eyes widen as she heaves herself up by her wrists until the shackles restrict her. Her arms are outstretched in a T-shape. My pulse spikes as I wait, unable to look away from her. Her body trembles. The breath she'd taken pushes out through her lips. She inhales again through her nose. Her eyes lock on something across the room, determined, then her face goes blank. I want to ask, but I don't have to.

In the blink of an eye, she lets herself drop.

CHAPTER SIX

ELECTRICITY

A crack. A thump. Chains clatter. A yelp and gasp of pain.

My skin tightens and my stomach jolts. Elizabeth is slumped on the ground, one arm free from the cuff. She shoves her face against her shoulder, teeth biting into her flesh, her body shaking. I catch sight of her free hand: bloodied, the skin ripped off, revealing the white of bone. My head starts to swim for the hundredth time since waking up in this dungeon.

Should I be impressed or horrified? Is it possible to be both? Either way, I'm going to pass out or throw up. Or both. With being chained up, at least I won't wake up in my vomit. Ah, yes. A silver lining.

She casts a glance at me, then gasps, "It's…not as bad…as it looks."

"I'll take your word for it."

"Good idea." She attempts a laugh, but it comes out as a whimper.

After a couple of shaky, deep breaths, she reaches up with her damaged hand. My heart pulses hard in my head. Is she going to rip her other hand loose? Oh, I am going pass out now.

But she does nothing of the sort. She pulls something from her braid. Her hands shake as she uses that item to pick the lock, freeing her other hand.

"I can't believe you did that." I let out the breath I've been holding. No wonder I feel like passing out.

"I told you, we're getting out of here."

She works on the cuffs around her ankles. I turn my attention to the cell door, realizing for the first time that the bald guard isn't standing by the hose anymore. He's nowhere to be seen.

I listen for any sign of someone coming to discover her escape. *Our* escape. I twist my own wrists in their restraints, hoping to pull my hands free and trying to ignore the mental images of ripped flesh and exposed, bloody bone.

Heavy footsteps sound from down the hall. I hiss a warning to Elizabeth. Another tall, bald man appears in the doorway. Or he's the same one from before. I don't know. He sees Elizabeth, and his lips press in a tight line.

I start to wiggle and tug my wrists. If I can just get one hand out...

"Prisoner loose," he calls over his shoulder. Words easy, casual. Not a true note of concern in his tone. He unlatches the door and walks in. I stare at the open door—

they didn't lock it. I guess when your prisoners are chained up, what's the point in locking the door?

The oversight is going to bite them in the ass. We're getting out of here. Elizabeth raises her chin in his direction as she stands to her full height. My hope shrinks when I see how huge he is compared to her slight frame. While her arms are corded with muscle, they're lean. His arms are three times the size of hers. He towers over her, the top of her head just level with his shoulder.

She just watches him, jaw set, eyes alert.

He reaches out to grab her. She shoves his hand away, then punches him in the throat. As he stumbles back, she grabs his shoulder, yanking him toward her before kneeing him between the legs. He crumples to the floor, gasping and moaning.

Mouth open, words nonexistent, I stare at his withering form, wanting to laugh and cheer at the same time. A girl half his size just kicked his butt in mere seconds.

Any time for celebration is short as Sahara enters the cell, crossing the distance between her and Elizabeth in long, quick strides. I don't have a chance to call a warning. The evil twin swings a metal rod, jabbing the end into her sister's chest. An electric spark sends her flying across the room, slamming against the wall before falling limp to the floor.

I crane my head to look at Elizabeth. Her chest lifts and falls with shallow breaths, but there's no movement to indicate she's conscious.

"Defective." Sahara clicks her tongue, shaking her head at the downed guard. She stabs the end of the stick against his head. A buzz of electricity and his body tenses, trembles, then goes limp. Dark, gray, blood-like liquid oozes from his nose.

My chest tightens. The stench of burnt meat is the final blow to my system, and I heave, spitting up bile and what little I ate this morning. The liquid runs down my chin and neck. Eyes and throat burning, aching.

I avoid looking at the psycho in the room. She just killed one of her own people, and possibly killed her own sister. I don't even want to think of what she intends on doing with me.

Combat boots appear in my vision. Hot metal touches my chin, forcing my face up. My chin trembles as more dreaded tears build, clouding my vision, but I can see Sahara staring at me, using her electric prod to direct my attention.

"And I thought I could use you. A simpering child." She shakes her head as she looks me over, clicking her tongue in disgust and disappointment. "I'm sure we can find some purpose for you, though." A wicked grin further contorts her face.

She lets my face drop and crosses the floor to Elizabeth. I glance at the dead guard, then at Sahara and at the prod in her hand. She's going to kill her sister, isn't she? I need to do something. Anything!

"Le-leave her alone!" My scream comes out stuttering and broken, the words ripping from deep in my lungs and throat. I yank on the chains, twisting them, willing them to break.

"Oh, please," Sahara mutters. "Don't be ridiculous. I'm not going to kill her. Unlike you, I can use her." She looks at me with a thoughtful expression. "Unless you're born into it, the OSE only recruit the best. How is it you wound up with them?"

I blink. OSE? Recruit?

She turns from her sister and walks back over to me. "Perhaps you're a brain. You're definitely not an EON."

EON. That's the second time she's mentioned that. I begin to wish I'd kept my mouth shut, because she pokes at my arms with the electrical rod, then places the end on my abdomen, staring intently into my eyes, waiting for an answer.

I try to speak, but all that comes out is a hoarse moan. My vocal cords strain with effort, but I can't form any words. I don't know what to say. I don't have an answer for her. But the prod is pressing into the soft tissue of my belly. I need to give her some sort of reply.

I try again, mouth opening. A shout rings out down the hall. Sahara's lips pull into a deeper frown; she steps away from me and leaves the cell, neglecting to close the door behind her. Not that they lock it in the first place. And Elizabeth is presumably still passed out.

Joke's on them, I hope.

"Hey," I croak. I clear my throat and try again. "Elizabeth…"

My throat feels like I gargled sand.

The shouts continue down the hall, along with clangs of metal and muffled *thumps*. Someone barks out orders. Footsteps—running—draw closer. I don't dare breathe, or hope. I watch as two men race past, identical to each other and to the dead one in my cell.

"Took them…long enough," Elizabeth says.

CHAPTER SEVEN

DON'T FREAK OUT

My heart leaps. *Oh, thank god!*

I look at Elizabeth. She's getting to her feet, injured hand clutched to her chest. On her way over to me, she stoops down and picks up a thin piece of metal—what she had used to pick her restraints. She casts a wary glance at the dead guard as she steps around him, skirting the pool of odd gray blood around his head.

Her hands shake but she still works in quick, easy movements to unlock my own restraints. When she gets them open, she guides my arm down so it doesn't drop.

"It's going to hurt a bit as the blood rushes in," she warns, in a gentle tone.

She's right. Directly after the relief of having my arm no longer elevated, prickling and pinching set in. I focus on the fact that I'm free. That's what this pain means. Freedom. My other hand is free, and it reacts the same way. But I'm free.

Once she's done with the shackle around my ankles, she puts a hand on my shoulder and guides me out. My shoes drag along the cement with each step, as if my legs had started to atrophy.

Hell, I hadn't been hanging from the chains like Elizabeth had. Which leads me to wonder what kind of training she's been put through. How does one prepare for this? Plus, she came prepared to pick locks. Who *are* these people?

We pass empty cells, an unpleasant distraction from my thoughts. They're identical to ours, down to the shackles on the ceilings and floor, a thick black hose on the wall outside each cell, and a drain in the floor within the cell. I don't want to stare, but I do.

How many others has she chained up in here? Dark splatters stain the floor in a cell at the end of the hall. A large, dark reddish-brown stain below the chains on one side of the cell is the scene that finally forces my gaze away. My stomach keeps churning.

Don't think about it, don't think. Which, of course, makes me think even more about the horror these walls have seen.

Cries and grunts from a fight down the hall only add an eerier soundtrack.

"I guess they finally approved it." Sahara's voice comes from behind us. "The trackers. A couple years too late, don't you agree?"

Elizabeth keeps her hand on my shoulder as we both

turn to face our captor. Sahara stares at us, finger tapping the metal rod in her hands. The fight continues down the hall, out of sight.

"Run!" Elizabeth whispers.

I look at her, starting to argue, but I catch myself. How am I supposed to help? I can barely stand on my own two feet; one arm aches furiously from the mountain lion's scratch, and I can't feel my other arm, save for its tingling.

Clenching my jaw, I turn on my heel and push off on numb feet to run. A snarl sounds behind me. I glance over my shoulder. Sahara hurls the electrical prod through the air like a spear, directed at me. I stumble, hands out to catch myself. Pain flares through my arms when I hit the ground. I scramble, knees scarping concrete, expecting to be electrocuted.

Nothing hits me. I look up to see Elizabeth swinging the rod in a fluid, easy movement, blocking a blow from Sahara. They perform a series of moves, each anticipating and blocking the other's strikes.

"You forget, we had the same mentors and teachers." Sahara cocks her eyebrow as she pulls a long knife from the sheath on her hip.

"Yeah, yeah. Except I—" Elizabeth lunges, swinging the rod in a low arch, aiming at Sahara's side. The rod connects with a bone-jarring *thwack*. "—didn't drop out."

Pain flashes in our captor's eyes, but she growls and grabs the rod. She jumps, twisting in the air and ripping the rod from Elizabeth's grasp. In the same second, she slashes out with the knife, the blade inches from her sister's face.

Elizabeth's hands fly out, knocking the knife away. Her other hand grips Sahara's throat. She slams her against the wall. The crack of her skull hitting concrete makes my own head ache.

I push to my feet just as Elizabeth releases her grip from our captor. She rips the knife from her twin's hand and knees her hard in the stomach, doubling her over. Then Elizabeth runs toward me.

"Go, go, go!" she shouts. Her injured hand is on my shoulder, pushing me along, her other hand white-knuckling the knife.

Just ahead, a masked figure appears around the corner—racing toward us, a black sword held low.

"Took you long enough, Elvis," Elizabeth shouts with annoyance, but the words are heavy with relief.

The figure continues running toward us, then passes us. I glance back to see them pulling something from a pouch on their belt. Elizabeth nudges me, making me pay attention to my running. All I need is to trip and get recaptured.

Seconds later, the figure—Elvis—is racing along the other side of me. Their hand touching my back, keeping me moving forward.

"Don't freak out," they say in my ear. Voice male— and my stupid brain is trying to place it. Do I know this ninja too? *Who cares?* Reason shouts at me. *Focus on the escape.*

A loud blast erupts behind us, hot air shooting past us. I flinch at the cacophony, but I don't freak out. Connecting the dots. This new ninja laid some sort of explosives to help our escape, to slow down the bad guys. I hope it made glorious art of blood and brain matter across the walls.

We round a corner and race into a vast, open space. The room stretches before us, cement flooring almost endless until it slopes upward and disappears under a granite doorway. Steel structural beams lead up to the high ceiling. Bold, circular LED lights illuminate the area.

Tall, thick-barred cages line the stone walls on both sides, some of them empty. Two of the beasts, identical to the one I encountered, are in their separate cages, pacing their too small enclosures, hungry eyes watching us. One of them yowls, sending a chill down my spine.

Well, that answers the question of whether there's more than one. At least I know that I am without a doubt not crazy. The monsters are real. And I'll forever have nightmares. I swear I'll never enter another forest again.

If not for the ninja's hand on my back keeping up my momentum, I would have collapsed, and that would have been the end of me. But they keep me moving, toward what I hope is the exit.

"Circe. ETA seven minutes," the ninja says, holding his hand to his ear.

We get to where the floor starts to tilt up and out. I can

see light. Cool air, with the scent of dirt and dead leaves, breezes in.

"Savanna!" A guttural scream.

We all look back. Sahara stands in the hallway, rod in her hands. A coating of dust and dark smudges on her face and clothes. She's breathing hard, glaring as if she could kill us with a look.

"We've got to go. This isn't the place for this," the ninja says, giving me a push up toward the exit and gesturing for Elizabeth to follow. The ninja reaches into his pouch and tosses small, round objects to the floor. They roll fast down the slope.

A pained look crosses Sahara's face that only deepens right before we turn our backs and run up and out of the lair. A single word follows us, echoing, before being obliterated by an explosion.

"Traitor!"

CHAPTER EIGHT

NINJAS AND BOY BANDS

The blast from the second explosion feels like an eternity ago, though only a few seconds have passed. My leg muscles are already burning when we reach the top, emerging from the underground lair to the forest. Tall pine and aspen trees cast long shadows from the evening sun, and cold air nips at my exposed skin. It's surreal and disorienting after being surrounded by bland gray stone.

A hand on my back pushes me forward, not giving me a chance to regain my senses. We continue running. Through brush, over logs, across streams, until my sides ache and a sharp pain pings in my shoulder. My throat is tight, my lungs scream for air, and we continue racing away. Somehow, I haven't tripped. Yet.

"Circe. We're thirty seconds out," the ninja says, his words easy, like he's not running for his life. He's not the one who almost died, though. Elizabeth and I are. But she's also not gasping for air like I am.

A chopping sound of a helicopter thrums in the distance, the first sign of normal civilization since we emerged from the dungeon. We burst into a clearing, a meadow of winter-browned grass taller than my knees. The clearing stretches a couple hundred yards before deferring to the forest again. The ninja and Elizabeth come to a stop. I bend over, hands on my knees. Through hacking coughs, I try to catch my breath.

"Stand up straight, hands on your hips or your head," Elvis says. "You'll breathe easier that way."

I peek up at him as he stands next to Elizabeth, wondering if his name is really Elvis. I don't recognize his voice, but it has been years since I've listened to *One Times Three*. Voices change with puberty. But who's to say he *is* one of the brothers? He could be unrelated to the band, for all I know.

Elizabeth leans against an aspen, skin as pale as the aspen's bark, and nods at me. She holds her injured arm to her chest and Elvis eyes her injury with concern. I straighten but leave my arms hanging at my sides. I cough a couple more times, my lungs unaccustomed to such aggressive cardio.

"Don't freak out," the ninja says to me again.

What's he going to blow up this time? Is he going to pull off his mask?

Elizabeth gives him a look. "Stop it. She doesn't need your stupid warnings."

"It's protocol." His words are clipped, and his

attention keeps returning to her injured hand.

Elizabeth rolls her eyes, but before either of us can interject, I hear the helicopter again. Closer. The chopping of its blades, the rumble of its engine.

"That's for us," she says, grinning tiredly.

A rush of wind blows past us. A shadow passes overhead. My hands press to my ears as I watch the helicopter lower into the middle of the clearing, wildly tossing the grass and our hair.

You've got to be kidding me! I can't take my eyes from it. This isn't real. Now I really am in one of Anita's video games.

As soon as the skids touch the forest floor, the two guide me to the helicopter. Instinct has me ducking my head as we approach, though with how the helicopter is built, I can stand fully upright and not get my head sliced off.

A gloved hand appears in my view, and I look up into yet another masked face. My heart beats as rapidly as the blades. I take their hand as I'm helped into the flying machine. They buckle my seat belt for me and slide a headset on my head, adjusting the mic close to my mouth. The din of the engine and rotor instantly recedes.

I sit across from the ninja who helped me in, and next to Elizabeth. "Elvis" sits across from her, leaning forward to assess her wounds.

The pilot is a slight woman with black hair cut to her sharp jawline. She's wearing a baseball cap, sunglasses, and a form-fitting T-shirt. Her left arm is a sleeve of tattoos all the way to her knuckles. A slight southern accent spurs her speech: "HQ, this is Circe. ETA five minutes. Medical attention is needed."

She then asks us how we're doing. The question isn't stupid or awkward, like when friends and family asked after Aaron died. *We've just been through a traumatic event. How do you think we're doing?* The question is more calculating, like a doctor trying to assess our pain level.

"It's been a day," Elizabeth answers, eyes closed and head leaned back against the seat. "Elvis" is examining the hand she ripped from the shackles. Even with his mask on, I can see the pinch of concern in his brow. Her hand is swollen, purple and black bruises peek out from under dried blood.

"Sahara was there," he says, not taking his eyes off her mangled hand.

Silence hangs like a fog in the air; not even the sound of the rotors can diminish the sadness and loss of those words. I may not have any connection to Sahara, but I've experienced loss. We don't have to share the same reason. Loss is loss.

The ninja in the front seat pulls off his mask, revealing familiar tight curls—Devon.

"Uh," someone says.

"She's already seen my face, chill," Devon says, as he readjusts his headset.

"Huh. Cool." The ninja in front of me pulls off his

mask. His dark hair is cut in a faux hawk fade—buzzed on the sides, a couple of inches longer on top. Not the longer, shoulder-length hair I'm used to seeing on all the posters I used to have. Without a doubt in my mind, I know he is Jonah from *One Times Three*. The second oldest of the brothers. He waggles his thick eyebrows at me.

I blink, looking away. Not sure where my head is at. A pounding in the back of my skull spreads to the rest of my head. My eyes ache.

"This is not protocol," the ninja with Elizabeth says, focusing on her hands as he shakes his head.

He doesn't have to take off his mask. Two out of three brothers have revealed themselves. This concerned-with-protocol ninja is Adam. He's the youngest. I'd be lying if I said he wasn't the one I crushed on the most. Maybe because he's closest to my age, or because of his alto voice, or for his love of pineapple on pizza. The one thing we have in common. I was into a lot of things when I was thirteen that I don't pay much mind to anymore.

"She knows who you are, A—"

Adam flashes his brother a dark, warning look.

"Whatever." Jonah throws up his hands.

The tension is heavy, and the awkward silence is deafening. I keep my attention directed out the windshield. A mansion comes into view, nestled on the hillside and surrounded by trees. The building's neutral earth tones keep it from popping out like a sore thumb, even with the elegant pillars and vast backyard swimming pool. In the front sprawls a cobblestone courtyard with a circular fountain.

Despite the fog and warbling in my head, I recognize that mansion. I've seen it from below, on the road leading to the highway. The tall, peaked roofing and the turret-like thing at the entrance.

It takes me a moment, though, to realize the mansion is our destination. On the side of the building is a large concrete helipad. The pilot lowers the helicopter, keeping it steady.

A stone pathway leads from the platform to the mansion. A middle-aged, suntanned man and a young Black woman stride down the path with taut, grim expressions. The man's strict military buzz cut speaks of authority, and he is clad in dark khaki pants and a black T-shirt that strains against the brawn of his barrel chest and shoulders. The woman's hair is done up in dozens of braids, pulled in a knot on the top of her head. She wears a blue long-sleeve shirt and leggings that hug her curved, muscular body.

Being back on solid ground is weird. As smooth as the helicopter ride was, my stomach starts to churn like the fog in my head. My jaw tightens. Saliva rushes into my mouth. I stumble from the platform, fall to my knees, hunch over, and spew bile, coating a bush that lines the path to the mansion. Never mind the needles and little pieces of gravel digging into my palms and knees. My head throbs, my body aches. I sit on my knees, trembling, staring at nothing.

CHAPTER NINE

AFTERMATH

"Let's get you cleaned up," the Black woman says softly, her hands coaxing me to my feet. She has high cheekbones and hawkish eyes, sharp and keen. Despite the intensity in her gaze—and the fact she's a total stranger—I trust her.

Even though my legs feel like Jell-O, I manage to stand and lean against the woman as we head up to the mansion. Ahead of us, the military-style man and Devon help Elizabeth ascend the stairs. I don't know where the other two brothers are. Maybe helping the pilot with the helicopter. Beats me. This is a whole new experience I'm convinced isn't real.

The man is shaking his head while Elizabeth talks, her voice carrying down to me, but too soft to make out the words. He pulls her into a hug and kisses the top of her head. Is he her dad? There's a pang in my heart when I think of my own dad. My throat gets all tight, but I grit my teeth.

"My name is Jacqulyn. I'll help you get cleaned up and take care of your wounds, okay?" The woman's voice is reassuring, and I get the sense she does this a lot. Calming and guiding scared people.

"Thanks. I'm Mika," I say with a nod, words quiet, getting stuck on the gunk in my throat as we ascend the steps.

Smooth cobblestone stretches before me, constructing a courtyard boarded by creeping juniper. The shrubs' slender branches choke the ground between clusters of tall, golden grass. A large, three-car garage stands on one side of the courtyard, across from a two-car garage not attached to the main house save for a bridge to the upper level of the house. The driveway leads out under the bridge.

We enter the attached garage, pass two SUVs, and head to the door at the back where the man who walked with Elizabeth talks with Devon. The girl is nowhere to be seen, but the two males glance at me, the man's brow furrowing. We don't stop to talk with him, though, and he doesn't stop us.

Jacqulyn leads me into a room, pulling the door closed behind her.

Two adjustable chairs sit in the center of the room, like what you'd see in a dentist office—the kind that lean all the way back into a flat position. Warm LED lights attempt to make the room appear cozy, but the drains in the stained concrete floor and the stainless-steel countertops and cabinets reflect the opposite.

My expression must be one of horror because Jacqulyn reassures me, "You're safe." She's going to help me get cleaned up now. I let her lead me past the chairs to a room with tiled floor and walls. There's the familiar cadence of a running shower. Lockers with benches line the wall on one side. Across the room is a full wall mirror and sinks.

"Do you have any allergies to medications?"

I shake my head. The woman nods, then asks me to wait a moment as she grabs an unmarked bottle from one of the benches and heads to the back toward the showers.

Alone now, I brace myself with a shallow breath and face myself in the mirror. For a moment, I fail to recognize my reflection, then am overcome with dismay. Those are *my* hazel green eyes staring back. The few freckles I have are covered by streaks of blood and vomit. I lean closer to the mirror, tears welling as I examine the cigarette burn on my neck. With quivering fingers, I poke around the wound. The skin, an angry red color around the seared black mark, asks to be left alone.

Jacqulyn walks back in, and I pull away from myself. She hands me two small, round pills and a small white plastic cup filled with clear-ish liquid. I stare at the pills for a moment before I recognize them as ibuprofen, then give the contents of the cup a quizzical look.

"Coconut water," she says. "Do you have any food allergies?"

I shake my head again. "Why coconut water?"

"Electrolytes."

Ah, of course. I swallow the pills, chasing them with the liquid. She takes the cup and discards it.

I grimace at my long-sleeve shirt: the large bubble font of *One Times Three*, with the brothers' faces below the band's name. I peel the shirt off with Jacqulyn's help, and without too much pain.

We both examine the wound I sustained from the mountain lion. The gashes aren't leaking blood anymore. Under the dried and crusted blood, blue-purple bruising is visible.

"Not deep, and clotting really well." She tentatively touches around the wound. "Doesn't look like you'll need stiches."

"I'm just glad I still have my arm," I say.

She chuckles, nodding. I wasn't trying to be funny. I *am* glad I still have my arm.

We enter the shower room. Tiled floor and walls, chrome knobs and showerheads. Shower spaces with their own curtains held off to the side with a chrome hook. Only one shower has the curtain pulled with rising steam. Likely where Elizabeth is.

I'm led to an already-running shower. Jacqulyn hands me my own unmarked bottle.

"It'll sting at first," she says, "but it'll help disinfect."

After removing the rest of my clothes and setting them off to the side in a neat pile, I step under the water and pull the curtain closed. At first, the warm water makes me tense and shake, and I realize how cold I am. The liquid stings as it touches my wounds, but soon eases the tension of my body. Washing away the sweat, snot, bile, and blood in brown and red swirls down the drain.

Under normal circumstances, I might relish the warmth, but I am too conscious of the fact that I'm in a strange house, a strange shower.

It stings, the transparent brown contents of the unmarked bottle. Far worse than the water had. A pitiful whimper escapes me. Eyes misting from the vinegar-like scent alone, I carefully lather it on my wounded arm and neck.

Minutes later, I'm rinsed off. My clothes aren't where I left them, but a black towel hangs on a chrome hook. Jacqulyn appears just as I wrap myself up in it. The shower across from me stands empty, drops of water clinging to the nozzle.

"I've brought you some clothes," she says, gesturing to the locker room. "The sizes are probably a little big, but I think you'll be comfortable."

She heads past me, collecting the unmarked bottles from Elizabeth's and my showers.

"How long have I been gone?" I ask quietly.

"About six hours."

My eyes widen. "Six hours…"

I'm not sure what to think about that. It felt much shorter, and way longer, than that. Time flies when you're unconscious and running for your life. I remember the sky when we emerged from underground, the evening sun casting long shadows from the trees.

Six hours. I wonder if my family have any clue I'm missing, or if they think I'm at work.

Work. Crap. They've likely tried calling me. I almost start patting myself down to check for my phone when I remember I'm wrapped in a towel, and the device is missing in the forest. Unless…

"You guys didn't happen to find my cell phone in the forest, did you?"

Jacqulyn shakes her head. "I don't think so. I can ask the boys."

"Okay. Thanks." I regard the floor. I'm still trying to wrap my head around everything. This mansion. I rode in a helicopter. The beast is real. Ninjas are real. My childhood band members are ninjas. Vic, my best friend, is a ninja. And he didn't tell me. How could he not tell me?

Against protocol, my mind interjects, inflecting Adam's tone.

In the locker room, I get dressed in sweatpants and a T-shirt Jacqulyn set out for me. I stare at my reflection in the mirror, and the bold letters spelled out across the shirt:

OSE.

Underneath, in smaller font, are the words: Knowledge. Courage. Integrity.

"O. S. E." I frown at the letters. Sahara had mentioned the acronym. What was the other one? "E. O. N."

What ABC organization have I stumbled upon?

The helicopter pilot appears in the doorway, no longer wearing her baseball cap and sunglasses. Her short black hair is pulled back into a ponytail. She offers a small smile.

"I'm Nelly," she says. "If you'll come with me, we'll get you bandaged up."

CHAPTER TEN

ACRONYMS

Back in the first room, the one with the adjustable chairs, Nelly has me sit in one. I only hesitate a moment before taking a seat. I glance at Elizabeth, who's sitting in the other chair as Jacqulyn works on her hand.

"All right, we'll start with you, Sav." Nelly takes the wrapper off some fresh bandages.

Who's Sav?

Then Elizabeth starts recounting the day's events, starting with them finding the beast as it pounced for me. It hits me then: Sahara had called her Savanna, screamed at her, calling her a traitor.

Not for the first time in so many hours, I find myself questioning what I've gotten myself into.

"Ah, that explains why you look so familiar," Nelly interjects, bringing my attention back to the present. She's careful as she checks the burn mark on my neck, concern creasing her brow. "Victor talks about you a lot."

Cool. A whole room of people who know me, but I don't know them. I'd almost rather face the beast. The gash on my arm throbs.

Okay, maybe not.

"I'm sorry for the loss of your brother," Nelly adds, tone soft and full of compassion.

I nod, avoiding eye contact. I still don't know what to say to that. For as many times as the words have been said since Aaron's death, I should have a response, right?

"Um, what is the OSE?" Changing the subject is always a good way to go. Plus, it would be nice to know what kind of crap mess I've gotten myself into.

"The OSE," Nelly pauses, securing a bandage on my neck. "Is the Okada School of Excellence."

That's not a fancy boarding school name at all, nope. All sarcasm intended.

Then it dawns on me. Okada. The name of Vic's school. This is Vic's school. My mind starts to swim, and I move on to another question, as if it'll keep me afloat. "And what's an EON?"

The woman pulls back, wiping her hands down with a disinfectant wipe. "Eiko Okada Ninja or Ninjas."

"And you guys fight monsters," I say.

"Monsters, demons, things that go bump in the night."

What else did Sahara say? "And a brain, what's that?"

"Ah." Nelly chuckles but casts me a wary look. Perhaps she's wondering how I know that term. "That's part of our science division."

I raise my eyebrows and huff out a breath. "With another ABC name, I imagine."

That gets a laugh from everyone in the room. Even from Elizabeth, who's been grimacing since I entered the room.

"It's true." Jacqulyn chuckles, nodding. "We do love our acronyms."

There's a knock on the door, interrupting any further information. Which I am a little grateful for. I want to know what's going on, but the ibuprofen hasn't kicked in yet, and my head will likely explode. They'll explain more later, right? I don't know what modern ninjas do. Or what ancient ninjas did. Not really. Paid assassins, aren't they? So, unless I have a price on my head, I'm safe, right?

You're overthinking it, I tell myself, and yet, that thought doesn't settle the unease.

"You can come in, Devon," Nelly calls to the door, then returns her attention to me as she starts to collect discarded bandage wrappers. "We'll discuss this subject in depth, I promise."

She winks at me and continues her cleanup. Devon enters the room and sits on the stool that Jacqulyn had been occupying, next to Elizabeth. His dark curls glisten wet under the lights. He wears regular clothes, T-shirt and sweatpants, looking more like the guy I know from band posters.

He takes Elizabeth's uninjured hand in both of his. They share a long look before she shakes her head and closes her eyes. She leans her head back, tears streaming down her face. Devon presses his lips to her hand, murmuring words I can't hear.

I turn away, focusing on my own hands as I try to wrap my head around this whole thing. Ninjas. Acronyms. Monsters. Demons. A shudder runs through me at that last thought: *Things that go bump in the night.* I'm taken back to my research on the *Strange and Unusual Sightings* forum— maybe, just maybe, those folks on the forum aren't crazy.

None of these are comforting thoughts.

Another knock at the door and in comes the muscular, broad man who'd walked Elizabeth from the helicopter. Bustling around him is a stout woman with graying black hair, heading straight for Elizabeth. Her tongue clicks as she looks at the girl's bloodied and torn hand.

"Going to need an X-ray," she says, a slight Spanish lilt to her tone.

"Dr. Castillo, I'd like you to give Mika a quick look-over as well," Jacqulyn says, gesturing to me and mentioning the wound on my neck and the gashes from the beast on my arm. She says something in Spanish, but since I almost failed Spanish last year, I'm at a loss.

The doctor's attention turns to me, and she raises a thin eyebrow. "You faced down *el gato* and lived?" A kind smile plays on her lips. "Impressive."

"I guess," I mutter.

She says something else in Spanish, making Jacqulyn chuckle. The man, who continues to stand in the doorway, is assessing me. His expression betrays nothing, causing me to squirm in my seat.

"I'm sure you'd like an explanation for all this," he says finally, gesturing to nothing in particular with his tanned arms. Forearms solid with muscle and coated with dark hair.

I nod, remaining silent, a million questions racing through my mind, jockeying to be the first.

"After," Dr. Castillo says, looking between me and the man in the doorway. "The Q and A can wait until after I check her over."

CHAPTER ELEVEN

FOMO

Dr. Castillo deems me healthy, despite my cuts and bruises. No stitches required, but she gives me some mild painkillers, a bottle of antibiotic ointment, instructions on how to clean the wounds, and tells me to get plenty of rest.

I'm not sure if I'll be able to achieve the latter request.

Now, I'm sitting in the burly man's office. He introduces himself as Hogan, Nelly's partner. He wastes no time having me call my boss. Long story short, I'm not fired for not showing up or neglecting to call out, but I have to work the opening shift tomorrow.

I should have said no, but did I? Cue laughter that turns to sobs. Nope, I'm going to work. The bike ride is going to be cold, long, and painful.

Shelves of framed pictures and trophies line the wall behind the circular desk, where Hogan sits, typing on his computer with rapid keystrokes. His eyes never leaving the screen.

I scan the pictures on the wall, finding one of Vic and his straight-toothed grin. He's wearing his martial arts garb—loose pants and robe-like top—in the photo, and he stands next to Nelly. They're both holding up a gold trophy. The same trophy from the picture sits next to it, polished and shiny.

My heart drops. *He kept this from me.* I stare at his stupid, perfect grin that took three years of braces to achieve. He's in several photos, some with Nelly, some with other people I don't recognize. I guess this is what FOMO feels like. Or would it more accurately be termed SIMO? Sad I Missed Out.

Freaking acronyms.

There are other pictures without Vic, of course. Some of Elizabeth—maybe some of her twin, unsure on that— Jacqulyn, Devon, Jonah, Adam, and people I don't recognize. Each trophy has some sort of side-kicking martial arts figurine on top.

Nelly enters the room, and I hold the cell phone out to her. She shakes her head. The crow's feet at the corner of her eyes crinkle as she smiles, and I notice a faint scar leading up from the side of her eye and disappearing under her hairline.

"Keep it for now," she says. "We'll need it to keep tabs on you."

I rest my hands in my lap, smoothing my thumbs over the darkened screen. "That isn't creepy at all."

Hogan looks at me over the top of the computer monitor. He stops typing. "Yes, well, when you venture into the forest after a bloodthirsty animal, you need someone to keep tabs on you."

"Touché." I lower my gaze.

"Mika, what we do here…" Hogan starts to say, folding his hands on the desk. "You'll need to keep an open mind. The kind of danger out there in the world that people don't know about, and refuse to acknowledge. Danger that we train our students to deal with, in order to protect humanity."

Students? Right. They are a school. A school of excellence. Sahara had said they don't just recruit anybody. She didn't believe I could be one of the ninjas, so she assumed I was a brain.

I pick at the edge of the phone case. This place is well out of my league.

"You've seen the giant cougar-like beasts," Hogan continues, his expression stoic. "You don't need convincing. But it goes deeper than that. Scarier. Supernatural."

"So, like, vampires and werewolves are real?" I keep my voice even. I don't know what their plans are for me, if they'll "recruit" me, or send me on my way. But I get an itching feeling that I need to be here. I need to learn.

"To the extent of our knowledge, no. Vampires and werewolves don't exist." Hogan frowns before adding, "At least not how they're portrayed in popular media."

"The things out there…" Nelly shakes her head, a haunted expression crossing her face.

"I'm exposed," I say, glancing at the phone in my hands. My reflection on the dark glass stares back at me. Eyes swollen and sad, yet lit with defiance. I won't let them keep me in the dark. "I need to learn how to deal with it. All of it. Unless you wipe my mind, I'm going to keep looking until I die. If I don't go insane from looking over my shoulder first."

Like Hogan said, I've seen the "giant cougar-like" beast. The cause of the accident that killed my brother. Not only do I have the physical proof they exist by the scratches on my arm, I've seen freaking ninjas fighting one.

And it's not just the crazy, oversized mountain lions. I've met Sahara. She's disguised as human. She burned my neck and hurt her own sister—and killed one of her own men—with no hesitation or remorse.

The images of the other dungeon cells flash into my mind, the bloodstains on the floor. Who knows how many more she has hurt?

The couple looks at each other, sharing a silent conversation. I watch, pulse a rapid staccato in my ears. An argument forms in my mind. Nelly tilts her head to the side, smiling a little, and Hogan lets out a deep breath.

"It won't be easy," he says. The intensity in his eyes is unnerving, but I try to ignore it. "Sessions, both physical and mental, can be brutal."

"I can do it," I say.

"You'll have to finish out your current semester with your school," he says, gaze moving to the computer screen, eyes moving as he reads. "You're enrolled in an online high school, correct?"

A grin spreads across my face as I nod. I had no idea I wanted this so much until now. "Yes. Easier for both my parents to deal with."

"Good. You can study here a couple days a week so we can start implementing our schooling. We'll need permission from your parents as well."

I slump in the chair, knowing full well that my parents will never agree to this.

Hogan's stone face softens. "Don't worry. This isn't my first rodeo."

I don't find reassurance in those words.

A knock on the door interrupts the meeting; then the door opens with a soft *swish*. I glance over my shoulder, only to do a double take at Adam.

CHAPTER TWELVE

STANDOFFISH

The third and youngest brother of *One Times Three* is clad in sweatpants and a loose black T-shirt with OSE in bold letters on the front. It matches the one I'm wearing. Dang. He does not look like a kid anymore. Dark brown, curly hair that used to be long and loose is now short and tight against his head. His once long, lanky arms are now lean and defined with muscle. I guess puberty—and ninja training—will do that to you.

He glances at me before he turns to his teachers—guardians?—and holds up some tablets.

"Reports are done. Elizabeth hasn't started hers, but you're aware of that." He enters the office and passes the devices to Nelly.

"Thank you, Adam. Would you take Mika to the kitchen?" She winks at me. "You need a good meal after what you've been through."

"Actually, I think I should head home." The words

spill out of my mouth. "I need to check on my sisters." Though I'm sure they don't care. Probably don't even notice my absence.

"I understand," Nelly says with a short nod. "We'll pack you some dinner to go."

"That's not…" I glance at Adam, his face as deadpan as Hogan's. "Not necessary."

She raises her hand to brush my objection away. "Oh, please. What kind of ninjas would we be if we didn't send you home with some food after this whole ordeal?"

"Uh… normal ones?"

Nelly chuckles. I think Hogan smiles a little. Adam does neither.

"You're not wrong," the woman says. "But, no arguments. You're not leaving without some of the best home-cooked food you'll ever have. Jonah should have gone to culinary arts school."

"It would increase his repertoire," Hogan agrees with a nod.

Nelly snaps her fingers. "All right, let's get this thing going. Adam, take Mika to the kitchen, have Jonah put together a to-go box, and—"

"Tell Jacqulyn to take her home," he interrupts. Another glance in my direction, keeping his head turned so as to not face me directly. I turn my attention to the phone in my hands, realizing I'm gaping like an idiot, and heat creeps across my face.

"You know what's up," Nelly says, her accent making

her sound more jovial than necessary.

"Of course." Adam sounds as thrilled as ever. Not.

"We'll see you tomorrow after you finish your shift, Mika," Hogan says. "While I think it goes without saying…"

I look up at him.

"You cannot tell anyone about this."

"I won't. You can trust me," I say as I stand.

"See you tomorrow, Mika."

After thanking them and saying our farewells, I follow Adam out of the office and into the wide hallway with its dark hardwood floor and soft green walls.

I do my best not to ogle him, but I'm so used to seeing him as a scrawny kid with a microphone and guitar—even if it was only in music videos and interviews—and now here he is. In person. His voice has deepened, and I can't help but wonder what his singing voice sounds like now.

He glances at me. "So, they're recruiting you?"

I clear my throat and say, "I guess so," following it with a deep exhale. I run my thumbs over the screen of the phone.

"Hm. Interesting."

Given his tone, I don't think he finds me being recruited "interesting" at all. Is it annoyance? Like, how dare I follow a beast into the forest and need to be saved? Getting one of his classmates and friends captured in the process and *again* needing to be saved.

But I can't blame him. He doesn't know me. If I were

him, I wouldn't be worried about some new girl revealing some secret ninja organization to the world. I'd be worried she'd babble about meeting *One Times Three*, blowing whatever cover he and his brothers have here.

Which prompts a question: how does a boy band end up as ninjas? Running through the forest, chasing down beasts, and rescuing stupid girls from certain torture and death?

I want to ask him and tell him I'd never share his and his brothers' secret. But I'm probably being paranoid about his disinterest and annoyance. He's allowed to be neutral. I don't need his gushing concern. Everyone else has done that tenfold. The nagging want for his attention would be the ol' fangirl in me. So I remain silent as I follow him to the kitchen, keeping my eyes on the hardwood floor.

He holds the door open and motions for me to go in. The glorious aroma of baked bread greets my nose. My stomach rumbles, reminding me I haven't eaten since this morning and that I puked up what little breakfast I ate.

"After you." He keeps his head turned to the side, not looking at me full on.

I meet his sideward gaze for a moment, a thank you on my lips though I can't quite get out the words. My throat is dry and I feel…I don't know, like I'm being intrusive. I hurry into the kitchen, a beautiful area with countertops constructed of dark gray granite with swirls of black. A lovely contrast to the white of the tile floor, the cabinets, and the drawers, with their brushed silver knobs and handles.

"Hey, girl!" Jonah beams at me, looking up from the oven, from which he's removing a tray of golden-brown dinner rolls sprinkled with herbs. "You are in for a treat tonight. I'm making—"

"She's not staying," Adam says, walking past me. "Is Jacqulyn back—" His words are cut short as the woman comes in from the adjoining door. "Jac, Hogan would like you to take Mika home. She's requested to return."

Requested? I frown at his word choice.

"I want to know that my family is okay. I need to see them," I say, shooting a look at Adam.

Jacqulyn gives me a sympathetic look. "Of course. I'm ready to leave when you are."

"Oh, bummer." A frown replaces Jonah's grin, but he nods. He opens a cabinet door and starts rummaging around. "I'll pack you something to go—"

"She's not hungry," Adam mutters. He exits through the door Jacqulyn had come through. All three of us frown at the door as it swings closed.

"The youngest child, am I right?" Jonah scoffs, resuming his search in the cabinet.

"Sorry, he's not usually that…" Jacqulyn tosses a nod at the door that Adam left through . "Standoffish."

I open my mouth to reply, but words fail me. The day is finally starting to sink in. I pull my arms around myself, careful of my bandage, and lean back against the countertop.

Jonah rolls his eyes. "Don't defend him. He knows better than that." He gives me a sheepish look, holding a container with a bright orange lid in his hand. "You probably want to get out of here. I'll get this packed up for you. We'll be seeing you tomorrow, right?"

I nod. "After work, yeah."

"Oh, freaking dope, dude." Jonah sighs with a dreamy expression as he places two dinner rolls in the glass container. He arranges a piece of wax paper around them. "A job. You're making money in the real world."

"Oh, please," Jacqulyn says "You'll be making thousands in royalties until the day you die, so shut up, Mr. Singer-songwriter-superstar." She moves over to the stove, and examines the dinner rolls and inhales deeply. Her eyelids flutter a little.

"Yeah, a job in the real world isn't all it's cracked up to be," I say quietly. The fatigue is a growing pressure behind my eyes. I peek at the phone Nelly let me borrow for the time being, and withhold a sigh. I'll be lucky if I get enough sleep tonight.

I'll be lucky if I even fall asleep.

CHAPTER THIRTEEN

LATTES AND SURPRISES

It's the start of the noon rush at Scott's Latte Stop. Tables fill with people on their lunch breaks. A few patrons from the morning still linger at tables near the back, their earbuds in as they type away on laptops or read books while nursing their beverages.

I queue up the afternoon playlist the coffee shop owner put together and brace myself for the horde of humans I'll be serving. I tug at the collar of my polo shirt; the cigarette burn itches, as it has all day. A pale bandage, a shade darker than my own skin, covers the wound. An injury I told my family happened at work. And at work, I tell them I burned myself with a curling iron, even though I don't own one.

Last night, Jacqulyn made sure I had everything before we left to take me home: a small, reusable bag with extra bandages, antibiotic cream, a travel size bottle of ibuprofen and Dr. Castillo's written instructions for wound care. Along with a dark gray, zip-up hoodie with OSE embroidered in small font on the left breast.

They also returned my clothes from the day, washed, dried, and folded neatly. A nice gesture, but I promptly threw them into the trash when I got home. Goodbye, embarrassing *One Times Three* shirt.

My sisters didn't notice my disappearance, believing I'd been at work. Neither of them questioned me about the mountain lion. Anita glanced away from her game long enough to say hello and ask how my day went, not noticing I wasn't in my work clothes.

I gave her the short answer and returned the question. She gave a short reply as well. I wanted to ask her what game she was playing and delve into the magical world with her, but I couldn't bring myself to approach her.

Presently, a tall, lean woman in a sleek business suit looks down at me through thin-rimmed glasses. She taps her credit card against the countertop. "I'd like a non-fat, double espresso latte, please," she says. "In the biggest cup you got. And, you know what, add an extra shot of espresso. One of those days, you know?"

"Sure do." I nod, pulling my lips into a smile, crunching my eyes a little to make it appear real. I poke at the tablet screen to place her order. "That'll be $7.28."

She flings her card to me as she digs inside her purse. I swipe the card and pass it back, my shoulder, biceps, and forearm protesting at even that mild stretch. My undershirt's long sleeve pulls against the bandages on my arm.

Why did I come into work? I almost died yesterday.

"Thanks, kid," she says, snatching her card back with short, manicured nails. She drops a dollar bill and a couple of quarters into the tip jar, then marches to the end of the counter where she takes a seat on one of the barstools to wait.

I grit my teeth against her "kid" comment—I've been called worse—and I greet the short, stocky man who steps up to the counter. "Welcome. What can we make for you today?"

The stocky man stares up at the menu behind me, lips pursed in thought. "Uh, do you…have…any…" He continues to stare at the menu, squinting. The person behind him rolls their eyes and crosses their arms.

This is my penance for my brilliant idea to follow a beast into the forest.

Could be worse, I suppose. I hold back a sigh. My eyes flick to the digital clock across the shop. I only have an hour left before I can leave. It was a long, cold bike ride here, and it will be a long, cold ride home. Well, to the OSE. According to the weather gauge on the clock, the temperature's risen five degrees since four thirty this morning.

The man finally orders: "I'll take a medium black coffee and one of those little twisted bread…thingies."

"A croissant?" I point to the one in the display, my abs and arms aching. Thanks, body.

"Yeah, that'd be great." He grins, handing me a twenty-dollar bill.

He drops the change in the tip jar, then goes and sits down at a table next to the entrance. The businesswoman is exiting, latte in hand and phone pressed to her ear.

The impatient man orders a green tea.

With no one else waiting in line, I help Brittney, my coworker—also the assistant manager—fill orders from the drive-thru. Her gorgeous black hair is always up in a fancy braid, and her porcelain skin puts a vampire's complexion to shame. At twenty-five, she's got a bachelor's degree in creative writing, working towards her master's, with a side-gig as a freelance beta reader and proofreader. We fill several orders over the half-hour, and my mind drifts back to last night.

When I got back from the OSE, Carol noticed my container of food but didn't ask about it. She was on the phone. I didn't hang around long enough to catch what the conversation was about, but school seemed to be the topic.

I wanted to sit down and talk with her about school. I wondered if she was getting close to interning at a veterinary hospital. She's been volunteering at a local animal shelter/ranch and working weekends at a hotel for pets. But I knew she would say she didn't have the time. She's very busy. None of my family wants to talk with me anymore after what happened. And I don't blame them a single bit.

So, I put the container in the fridge and shut myself

away in my room, where I curled up in a ball on my bed and sobbed until I passed out.

I should be dead.

I woke up a few hours later, so hungry I felt queasy. I warmed up the dinner Jonah so graciously packed for me, ate it—it was some of the best food I'd had in a while—took another shower, redressed my wounds, and went right back to bed. Nightmares made for a restless night of tossing and turning.

I should be dead.

"Excuse me," says a voice. "I'd like a fat-free, sugar-free, soy-free, dairy-free, vanilla latte with extra foam."

The voice brings me back to the present. I turn around from placing two black coffees at the ready for Brittney, expecting to see someone tall, lanky, and wearing a beanie with a pop culture T-shirt.

The customer is tall, sure—almost a foot taller than my five-foot-four self. His dark brown hair is pulled back in a messy ponytail, free-flies framing his face. He's wearing a black T-shirt with a sport logo on the left breast and black joggers. As per usual with this guy.

"Or whatever people order these days," he adds, grinning broadly.

"Vic!" I squeal. I scurry from behind the counter, my muscles objecting with every step. They can't stop me, though. I wrap my arms around my best friend, burying my face in his chest.

"Ah, that burnt coffee smell," he says, returning the

embrace.

"When did you get back?" I pull away from him to look at his stupid face, ignoring the glances from the lingering patrons.

"About two hours ago. How are you?" His gaze travels over me, pausing on the bandage on my neck, before meeting my eyes again. His expression stark with concern, grin disappearing.

"I've been better, but I've been worse too." I shrug. "So, you know."

"We've got a lot to unpack, don't we?" His smile is a guilty grimace.

I glower and tap his shoulder with my fist, but I can't be mad at him right now for keeping this secret from me. I'm grinning again and hugging him tight.

He chuckles. "Anyways, I thought I'd surprise you and offer you a ride home. It's freaking cold out there. Is it supposed to snow?"

"Uh, I have no idea. Maybe. I haven't looked at the weather forecast. I've been preoccupied." I pull away so I can check the clock. "I have less than half an hour left on my shift. Wait." I frown at him. "When did you get your driver's license?"

He's been traveling a lot, which doesn't allow him much time to get his hours in. Or so he says.

"I didn't. Jacqulyn is driving. Oh, she would like a black coffee, please. Medium." He holds up a ten-dollar bill. "The blackest coffee you have, she said."

I return behind the counter and ring up the order. "Would you like anything?"

He puffs out his cheeks, widening his eyes. "No. I'm already on three and a half energy drinks." He holds up his hands, showing the tremor wrecking through them. "I need to wind down."

I give him a look. "Dude. That's disgusting. You're going to get kidney stones. If you don't die of a heart attack first." I place the change in his shaking hands, which he promptly drops in the tip jar. "I'll get you a water. I think we even have coconut water."

As I'm preparing Jacqulyn's coffee, my other coworker—Carter—comes in from the back. He always works a closing shift. He's twenty-three with short blond hair styled in unruly spikes and takes college courses in the morning and afternoon. He greets me with a nod as he ties on his apron.

I pass the coffee and a bottle of regular water to Vic, letting him know they can wait inside if they want.

"Mika, register," Carter barks at me.

Vic casts him a look but says they'll wait in the car. I go over to the register and log out.

As Carter's logging in, he asks, "Is that your boyfriend?"

"No," I answer after staring at him for a moment. "He's my brother."

My go-to defense for whenever someone assumes Vic and I are dating. Though the only resemblance we have is dark hair—he has his Korean father's tan skin, cheekbones, and laid-back demeanor, but his German mother's height—people seem to believe we're related. They don't question it, maybe assuming we're half siblings, or something. I don't know. I don't care. As long as they leave me alone about it.

Carter raises his eyebrows at me. He glances at Vic exiting the shop, then back at me. His gaze flitting to my neck for a short moment, he might be questioning my bandage. "Hm. I thought your brother, you know, died."

"Carter," Brittney snaps, staring hard at him, mouth agape. She holds her hand over the drive-thru mic, even though no one can hear unless she has it switched on. "That's insensitive." She gives me a sad look before turning back to her duties.

He mumbles an apology, or something along those lines. I swallow a lump in my throat and let out a slow breath. If I breathe, maybe I won't cry. This is going to be a long fifteen minutes. I glance at the clock, withholding a groan.

Twenty minutes.

CHAPTER FOURTEEN

MOMMA'S BOY

Jacqulyn and Vic stare at me as I unlock my bike from the rack next to the coffee chop. She's wrapped up in a puffy blue jacket with a matching knit scarf and gloves. I'm in my street clothes: T-shirt, jeans, fading brown jacket. Vic's not even wearing a jacket.

"You did *not* ride your bike here. From your house. In this freaking weather." Jacqulyn pauses, her lips pressed in a thin line. "With the injury to your arm."

"It was either brave the cold or get fired, and I like making money." I coil the chain and put it in my backpack. "It is what it is."

Vic leans around me to grab the bike, muttering, "Even though you and Carol aren't speaking, you should have asked her to drive you." He gives me a look before he carries my bike over to a large blue SUV.

"Or called in sick. You're either hardcore or crazy, girl," Jacqulyn says. She presses a button on the key fob and the SUV's hatch pops open. "And I thought EONs were nuts."

Vic sets the bike in the back and touches a button on the hatch, which lowers and clicks as it settles back into place. We get in the vehicle. Vic lets me have the front passenger seat. He sits in the middle seat in the back.

"You're going to learn about some pretty freaky stuff," he says, propping his arms up against the front seats.

"Freakier than giant, mountain lion beasts?" I watch the cars pull up to the drive-thru, spreading my hands on my jeans. Or a psycho who tortures their own sister. My skin tightens and stomach roils at the memory. *How am I not dead?*

A human being with no regard for human life is about as scary as it gets. One who thrives on torturing others, watching them wallow in pain. The mountain lion beasts are just animals. Killing things for food is what they do to survive. Cats play with their food. They don't distinguish right from wrong; logic and reason aren't things they possess.

Humans, though, humans know better. And yet...

"I'm sorry, Mika. That I couldn't tell you about this." Vic leans forward to catch my eye. "After the accident, I wanted to—hell, I almost did tell you. I had a whole speech and PowerPoint prepared." He glances at Jacqulyn. "Don't tell your dad."

She shakes her head with a dismissive wave.

His eyes search mine. "I was fighting the rules to tell

you, especially since the accident was caused by a monster that we EONs are sworn to fight."

While he knew the mountain lion beast existed, Vic never shut me down about it, never said it was some play of my imagination, trying to justify my role in my brother's death. I bite the inside of my cheek and turn to watch the world blur by.

"This is not the way I wanted you to find out," he says. "But alas, life." He taps his fingers on the center console. "You don't hate me, do you?"

To my relief, I laugh. The lump in my throat dissipates, as do the tears in my eyes. "I couldn't hate you."

"Yeah," Jacqulyn interjects, looking at Vic in the mirror and giving him a wink, much like the winks Nelly gives. "Now you can argue that if you had been able to tell her after the accident, this whole mess wouldn't have happened."

"Oh, you're right! Ha!"

"Don't tell my dad I gave you that idea. Either of you."

Vic crosses his chest, grinning. "Secret's safe with me."

After a moment of silence, listening to the heaters blow warm air and the tires crunch along the icy road, I ask, "So, who's your dad, Jacqulyn? Some big EON hotshot?"

Saying the acronym is very odd.

The two glance at each other. Did I ask too personal a question?

I'm ready to retract my question when Jacqulyn says, "Hogan is my dad. Obviously, not my biological father."

She runs a hand along her arm, her skin a dark espresso contrast to Hogan's and Nelly's suntanned skin. "He and Nelly adopted me when I was four months old."

Vic nods. "No clue as to who her biological parents are. She was left at a fire station as a baby."

"And I don't care to know who they are." Her words come out nonchalant, but I hear something in her tone, or maybe the stiff set of her jaw makes me believe she's livid about her birth parents giving her up. "Nelly and Hogan are the only parents I've known, and they've done a damn good job at raising me, and that's all that matters."

I don't know what to say to that, so I change the subject. A skill I should put on my résumé, honestly. "So, Victor, do your parents know about this? What about Rick?"

He shakes his head. "They don't. And they never will. You imagine how much my mom would freak? She's stressed out enough that I do martial arts and travel in general." He rolls his eyes and scoffs, but he's picking at his nails—something he does when he's pretending to be not as bothered as he really is.

"Right. She is a bit intense," I say, recalling how his mother never goes to his competitions, or join the conversations about his travel or martial arts. She's not dismissive, just apprehensive, I think. Like, talking about it will make it real to her. That her little boy is growing up. That's how I see it, anyway.

"And Rick is such a momma's boy," Vic continues,

"he'd tell her in a heartbeat. Plus, he'd want to join, and that'd really give Mom a heart attack."

"You're both momma's boys." I chuckle, thinking about his younger brother. Four years younger than me, at twelve. When my mom was in labor with the twins, we stayed with Vic's family. His little brother, age two at the time, hid behind his mother for the day and a half we were there. With the little art projects his mom gave us to keep us preoccupied, Vic would always show her the finished results before his dad.

"Ugh, please don't." He slumps back in his seat.

I crane to look at him. "Your dad seems like he'd be cool with it." Mr. Choi is a laid-back man with an easy smile and always ready with a joke, with thousands upon thousands of puns to tag on. He'd easily kept Carol and I entertained while our mother gave birth.

"Yeah, but that's an awful big secret for him to keep from Mom." He's picking at his nails again. "And like the stuff we face, both my parents would lock me away. Especially Mom."

"See?" I grin at him. "You are a momma's boy."

Jacqulyn and I both giggle. Vic groans, muttering in Korean.

CHAPTER FIFTEEN

SOME ANSWERS, MORE QUESTIONS

I pinch myself as we pull up to the mansion. I'd only ever seen it from the main road before yesterday. It's hard to believe this is all real. My siblings and I used to come up with stories about this place, much like the private-owned land around our property.

There's a pang in my gut when I think about how Vic kept this secret from me. He was—*is*—going to a school basically right down the street from my house. I thought we were best friends. I tell him everything.

I shake my head. I can't think like that. This isn't just his secret he's keeping. He's also keeping the secret of several other people. Including *One Times Three*.

Oh. My. God. I have to face them all again today. My stomach flips. I can't decide if it's from fear or excitement. In this case, it's likely both. Devon and Jonah were nice enough, but Adam…he was aloof, and I hate that it bugs me. Maybe years of preteen me dreaming of the perfect meeting of *One Times Three* has me a little deflated. They say never meet your idols.

Funny how I'm more scared about seeing the boys again than I am to learn about the monsters of the ninja world. I don't think my priorities are straight.

"I'd like to check your wounds, Mika, before we do anything else," Jacqulyn states, glancing at me as she pulls the vehicle in the garage. "Vic, you have reports to fill out, and you better do them now before Dad realizes you haven't done them."

"I'm sure it can wa—" His objection is cut short with a glare from Jacqulyn. Vic groans, casting me a grim look. "Being a ninja isn't all it's cracked up to be."

We go our separate ways. I shed my jacket and sit in one of the adjustable chairs in the medical room. Jacqulyn starts undressing the wound on my arm.

"You do this a lot?" The silence rings in my ears. I need some conversation.

"I'm a trauma nurse at the county hospital when I'm not here bandaging up my fellow EONs." She smiles a little, but her attention is on my arm, touching around the bruised, swollen areas.

"Wait, you guys have jobs outside of being ninjas?" I give her a quizzical look. "Jonah made it seem otherwise."

She chuckles. "That's because Jonah is Jonah. You'll soon discover. But yes." She applies ointment to the wound and starts bandaging it back up. "We do work outside of the organization. Encouraged, actually.

Especially if it's a job where we can gain more experience in our particular field. Working in the trauma center gives me valuable training and skills. Plus, I love it."

"And you can keep your ear to the ground for activity that the…" The acronym escapes me, though she just said it. "The ninjas may be interested in. Like, strange animal attacks."

"Exactly. And other things. You'll learn about those." She stares at the wound on my neck, the furrow in her brow deepening.

"Is it bad?" I ask, paranoid it may be infected.

"No," she sighs with a slow shake of her head. "I just can't believe she did this." Then her faces morphs into a reassuring smile. "The burn is healing nicely."

"Okay." My voice is quiet. "What… How…" I pause, trying to figure out how to ask about Sahara.

"What's her villain origin story?" she asks for me, voice soft and eyes somber. "I guess you could say we failed her."

Of course, I don't have a chance to ask her to elaborate because Nelly enters the room.

"Hello, Mika. How are you today?" greets the older woman.

I mull over my answer for a second. "I'm ready to learn."

"I bet you are. There will be plenty of time for that. First though, you need an official tour of the place—" She's interrupted by a jingle from her phone. "Oh, Jac, do you think you could give Mika the tour?"

"I have work in a half hour." Jacqulyn finishes applying the new bandage, then moves to clean up the bandage wrappers and used antiseptic pads.

"The boys can give her the tour," Nelly says. She nods at Jacqulyn, then leaves to answer her phone.

"I'm sure Jonah will trip over himself to show you the place," Jacqulyn says. "He gets excited for new blood. The opportunity to brag about being a ninja doesn't happen often."

I nod, saying, "Oh, that makes sense," in the calmest voice I can muster as my insides are flip-flopping. Nerves clash with excitement. Any more questions about Sahara are pushed to the back of my mind. I take the subtlest deep breath I can manage.

It's not a big deal. Nope, not a big deal at all that *One Times Three* is going to be giving me a tour of the ninja school.

CHAPTER SIXTEEN

THE TOUR

Jonah stands in front of me, a broad grin on his face. Looking like a kid who's been given the best gift ever on his birthday. "So, would you like to start with the most exciting part or the least exciting part of the tour?" His grin falters. "Well, you've seen the helicopter. You've *ridden* in the helicopter. That's usually where I start tours."

"You've never given a tour," Adam says under his breath. He's leaning against the arched entryway that leads to the living room from the foyer. His arms are folded over his chest, and his jaw is set as he avoids looking at us. Both brothers are clad in black sweatpants as well as long black-sleeved shirts with OSE in bold writing on the front.

Jonah ignores his younger brother's comment and peers around the building. "Let's start with the boring stuff first and work our way to the exciting stuff." He turns to me with a smile. "What do you think?"

I shrug, trying to be nonchalant, but my heart is racing.

Every time he looks at me, my stomach does a flip. I need to calm down.

"Honestly, it's all pretty exciting," I say, a grin overtaking my blushing face. I can't help it.

Devon and Elizabeth come from the dining room, the door swinging closed behind them. They're not wearing any OSE attire. He's in a green T-shirt and khaki pants, and she is wearing gray sweatpants and white sweater. The hand she ripped from the restraints is wrapped in a light blue cast. Her long hair is pulled into braid.

"Hey." She grins at me. "Heard you were getting the official tour. Thought I'd join."

"Cool. I don't need to be here, then," Adam says, punctuating his statement by leaving.

Watching him go, the nerves twist in a different way, bordering on guilt as opposed to anxiety. Is he mad at me? He doesn't even know me, and yet…

"He is so salty," Elizabeth says, narrowing her gaze at his retreating form.

"He shouldn't have taken that test. Ignore him." Jonah shakes his head, then claps his hands. Grin restored. "All right! Let's head downstairs to the schoolroom."

He says the destination with distaste, a twisted facial expression to match. He pivots, then waves for us to follow.

"We don't let Jonah be in charge much," Elizabeth whispers to me. "So, when we do, he gets a little…"

"Extra," Devon finishes with an eyeroll to the heavens,

like he has to wrangle his younger brothers far too often.

I smile, the discomfort fading. Jonah recounts tales of riding couch cushions down the stairs as we descend a wide staircase with a solid wood railing. He points to a dent in the wall that wouldn't have been noticeable if he hadn't revealed it. He claims his elbow struck the wall there during one of the couch-cushion excursions.

"So, how long have you lived here?" I direct the question at both Devon and Elizabeth. Jonah continues on, clearly loving the sound of his voice. He hasn't noticed the three of us fell back.

"The brothers' parents are, like, second gen EON," Elizabeth says, smiling at Devon. "The lucky ducks were practically raised here. Their father is on the international OSE board of directors."

Devon gives her a fond look.

"And your mom?" I ask him.

"Uh, she's around." He rubs the back of his neck and keeps his eyes forward.

"I see." I don't pry, figuring she's on some sort of secret mission he can't elaborate on. We reach the bottom of the stairs, entering a long, well-lit hallway. Jonah carries on about something, then disappears around a corner.

"And you weren't raised here, Elizabeth?" I turn my attention to her. I'd assumed Hogan and Nelly were her parents.

She shakes her head, her expression solemn and guarded. "Nah. We weren't introduced into the ninja world until we were, like, eight. We—my sister and I—were, uh, attacked by these little, creepy things called imps." She offers a smile that doesn't reach her eyes. "Found out our parents were a whole hell of a lot cooler than we ever knew."

"And your parents, where are they?" As soon as I ask, I wish I could take it back.

Sadness breaks into her guarded expression, and she blinks hard. "They died about a year ago."

"Oh, I'm so sorry." My heart hurts. "I didn't mean—I'm sorry."

"It's okay." She places a hand on my shoulder and offers a gentle, reassuring squeeze. "Sucks to talk about it, but it won't get better if I don't, right?"

"Yeah." But I don't truly agree with her. Maybe I should talk about Aaron's death, and how messed up my emotions are, but who do you go to for that? It's not like they can slap a bandage on it and call it good.

Jonah pokes his head out from around a doorway ahead. "Hey, are we doing a tour or not?" He steps into the hall as we get closer. Then, with arms outstretched, he adds, "Welcome to school." Promptly punctuating it with a short, gagging noise.

Devon shakes his head with another eyeroll to the heavens, gaze lingering on the ceiling. Elizabeth chuckles. I stare at the darkened room. Jonah reaches around the corner, and the lights slowly illuminate the large, conference-like room with tan walls and gray carpet.

Eight tall, wide desks, each with two chairs, face a large projector screen at the front of the room. While there are sixteen places to seat students, only five places have a laptop. Makes sense, with only five students: Elizabeth, the three brothers, and Vic. But soon, there will be a sixth laptop.

I step into the room and run my fingers along the desk closest. Smooth and cool under my fingers. I can see myself sitting here, with my little laptop, taking notes on whatever beast or monster we're studying.

Learning how to defeat them. A shudder runs through me. Can I do this?

"This is where we learn all the boring things like math, science, history, languages." Jonah leans back against the desk where I stand, his lips pursed. Oblivious to my awe.

"I guess it also serves as the operations room for missions, but mostly school." He pushes off, striding from the room. "Onward to the weapons room!"

"And we learn about the things we're going to have to fight," Devon says with a sigh, shaking his head. "Whose idea was it to let him lead?"

"He's doing okay," I say, feeling a little heat in my cheeks.

Elizabeth chuckles. "I'm surprised he showed you the schoolroom, to be honest. He resents having to learn 'mundane' things."

Devon turns off the school lights as we leave. "He gets good enough grades to continue competitions and go on missions, but he won't apply himself more than that. But I guess if he wants to be a career EON, it doesn't matter."

We continue down the hall, Jonah nowhere in sight.

"Do you two want to be career EONs?" I ask in a quiet, hesitant voice, hoping I'm not prying. I really did a number by asking them about their parents.

Devon shrugs. "I haven't decided. This girl on the other hand—" he drapes an arm over Elizabeth's shoulders and grins proudly—"is going to be one of the best brains the OSE has ever produced. She not only loves math, but is crazy good at it. Been taking college courses in calculus and physics since tenth grade."

"Yeah, yeah." She blushes at his praise but doesn't pull away from him. "Not sure what I'll do when I graduate this spring. The AIO isn't looking for calculus or physics majors."

"Oh, please," Devon counters. "Physics—"

"Hi-ya!" Jonah bursts from a room with a long wooden sword, swinging it in a high arc over his head. He brings the blade to waist level before balancing up on one foot, raising the weapon over his head again, then moving into a low lunge. He presents the wooden weapon to me.

"And this is one of our most important training tools. It is called a bokken." He straightens and regards the sword with an affectionate look on his face.

"We'll leave you two alone," Elizabeth says, eyeing Jonah warily, motioning for me to follow her.

We skirt around him as he continues his lovestruck

trance with the sword, then step into the weapons room. One wall is lined with swords of various lengths. Some blades are chrome-shiny, some are dark gunmetal, a select few range in shades of the rainbow, and some, of course, are wood. Wood of various types and colors.

I peer closer at the curved blade of an elegant short sword, recognizing the swirling, almost wood-grain-like metal of Damascus steel. The hilt is composed of a dark red-brown wood, with accents of some kind of black stone. I run my fingers along the grip, inhaling deeply. While I'm not really a weapons person—at least I don't think I am—I can't deny it: the sword is gorgeous.

"All of the blades, metal and wood, are blessed," Jonah says, sidling up to me, "since everything we come across has some demon essence. Whether the monster is organic or fabricated by humans."

"Blessed?" They'd said something about that in the forest, when I first met them. "Like a priest threw some holy water on it?"

The three of them laugh, and Elizabeth says, "Something like that. They're forged with the elimination of evil in mind. The blades, the hilts, the stone accents all have properties that help expel the demon."

"But the user still has to do all the work," Devon says. "The blessings are just there to help banish the demon essence."

"I see." Though I'm not quite sure that I do. But a blessed blade kills demons—how much deeper does the knowledge need to go? So, I move on from the swords.

The section at the back showcases the ninja garb. I realize they wear a sort of malleable, bulletproof vest—probably a smart piece of gear to have. There are also smaller items: thin discs about the size of my palm, some golf-ball-sized objects with six sharp points projecting from them, and small black orbs the size of a quarter in diameter. All of which, Jonah informs me, are explosive devices. The latter I recognize from the rescue—Adam had used them.

The wall opposite from the swords features rows of drawers about hip height, above which are other weapons. Some I recognize, like the nunchucks, bō staffs, and throwing stars, but the rest I haven't even seen in video games. Like the spear items and the weird chain thing with short, curved blades on the end. I can picture myself losing a finger. Or something more vital.

"This is…" I gaze down the long room, trying to take it all in.

"Beautiful. Gorgeous. The most incredible thing you've ever seen. Yeah, it is." Jonah takes a deep breath, leaning against the bokken.

"Ookay," Elizabeth says, giving Jonah a wide-eyed grimace. "Let's move on."

We all exit, except for Jonah.

"We'd be in there all day if it were up to him." Devon glances back at his brother.

"I think I'd spend a good amount of time in there," I

say, "just getting to know what's what. I didn't recognize half the things in there. You guys really use them all?"

They both shake their head. Elizabeth answers, "Some of the odder items are paying homage to past EONs who used them. It's hard to find teachers who know how to use all the weapons. So, we stick to the classics. Katanas, short swords, daggers, and throwing knives and stars."

I give a flabbergasted scoff. "What? No nunchucks?"

Devon laughs. "Adam's decent with them. I know a lot of other EONs who are proficient. It's a popular weapon. We're just more into swords here, I guess."

"So, is the AIO the science division?" I recall the acronym Elizabeth mentioned earlier.

"Uh…"

"Oh…"

Their hesitation makes me realize my foot is way too comfortable in my mouth.

"The AIO is the Arcane Intelligence Organization," Devon explains while Elizabeth leads the way for the rest of the tour. "When one graduates from the OSE, they have the option of becoming a career EON. There are many divisions."

"Special Ops, Intel," Elizabeth lists off. "Education, Investigation. Along with the science division—the SD— those are the top five."

"Though, EONs get the lovely title of 'brain' when they join the SD." Devon is giving Elizabeth another adoring look. "That's where you're headed come spring."

She rolls her eyes. "We'll see."

We head up a different staircase to the dormitory area at the end of a T-shaped hallway, toward the back of the mansion. Sixteen bedrooms line the corridor, eight on each side, all with shared bathrooms.

The only people who don't stay in the dormitory are Jacqulyn—she has a room next to the garage, since she keeps odd hours as a trauma nurse—and Hogan and Nelly, who have a room on the main floor.

We emerge into the living room/game room. It boasts of two large couches with fluffy pillows, and two armchairs centered around a smooth, redwood coffee table. A book-reading nook is nestled in the wall, with a large window overlooking the pool, which is somehow not an eyesore with its earth-tone cover. I don't notice it until Devon points it out.

The game room side has two huge TV screens, a long couch stretched before the screens. The room is complete with a Ping-Pong table tucked in the back that, according to Devon, is a huge hit when they have guests over and has been known to destroy friendships. They have various gaming consoles, including a VR setup and a cabinet full of video games.

"My little sister would be drooling right now," I murmur, glancing over the titles. I don't find anything I recognize. But then again, it's not my forte.

We continue upstairs to the training room, where grunts and little war cries, punctuated with the *thump* of something hitting the ground, greet our ears.

CHAPTER SEVENTEEN

SPARRING

"Sounds like training," Devon says.

"Guessing Adam and Nelly," Elizabeth says, picking at her cast. "He's been beating himself up over that test."

"What test?" I glance between the tour guides.

Devon lets out a long sigh, but Elizabeth answers with, "The instructor test."

"Instructor test? Like, teaching others how to fight?" I give a slow blink and the two nod. "But isn't Adam a little young?"

They share a glance before saying in unison, "Yes."

"But he is two levels above Devon in sparring and techniques," Elizabeth adds. "He's got skill. He just doesn't have teaching experience. Which is hard to get when most new EONs already have a background in martial arts."

"Huh." I purse my lips and murmur, "Hard to get experience when they don't let you do the thing you need experience in."

"Right on." Devon raises his hand for a high five, and I oblige.

We round the corner. It takes a second for me to take in the massive room. On one side is something resembling a jungle gym, only much bigger than what little kids use. There are no slides, but there are monkey bars, swinging rings, a maze, gymnastic uneven bars, ledges with at least a twelve-foot fall, and four ropes anchored to the ceiling.

Along the back wall are several punching bags—thick, tall ones, some shaped like the torso of a human without arms, and some a little smaller than a volleyball—that hang from a bar on the wall.

Off to the side is regular gym equipment: rows of free weights, three weightlifting benches, two rowing machines, three treadmills, and those are just the ones I know the names of.

Across the room is a large mat, black fading to gray from years and years of use. Two people are sparring, throwing punches and dodging kicks. It takes my brain another couple of seconds to process who they are. The short, curly hair of Adam and the messy ponytail of Vic. Nelly stands off to the side, tablet in hand as she observes. Her eyes flicker to us for a split second, but otherwise her attention stays on the sparring boys.

"Ten bucks on Vic," Elizabeth whispers as we tiptoe into the room. We sit on the floor, our backs against the wall.

"I can't take that bet because I also bet on Vic," Devon whispers back. "Adam's been off his game. Depressing."

Elizabeth looks at me. "Vic is a level below Adam in sparring and technique, but considering that he hasn't been an EON for very long is super impressive. He's got a knack for this work, and not just the fighting."

I nod, unsurprised. "I expect nothing less from him."

He's been in martial arts since he was a little kid, and he took gymnastics for a couple of years before he started getting into parkour. What came first, I wonder: the parkour or the ninja thing? He and I need to have *the chat*. The chat about how he wound up here.

Maybe thirty seconds have passed since we entered the training room. After a series of kicks from Adam, Vic grabs his leg and pulls him off balance, pinning him in a headlock. A couple more seconds pass, and Adam taps Vic's arm. Vic lets him go, rolling back out of the way and onto his feet. He bounces on his toes, arms raised like a boxer.

I watch him with a heavy weight in my chest. Hating that he hid this from me, but understanding why he did.

But he could have told me.

"I'll buy us lunch the next time we go out," Devon says, voice quiet.

I glance at him, noticing his fingers are interlaced with Elizabeth's.

"And breakfast will be on me," she agrees in the same quiet tone. "Vic's improved so much since France."

France? I make a mental note to ask him about France. He and I never talked about France much, since he'd been there around the time Aaron—well, around the time of the accident.

"I can take that punk." Jonah saunters in and throws a nod at Vic, who grins and rolls his head.

Nelly motions him over. "Well, come back up your smack talk." Her southern twang makes the comment sound more like a challenge.

Continuing his boxer bounce, Vic throws a couple of punches, attention locked on an invisible target. There's something mature about the focus he gives during the wait between sparring matches. Adam is walking off the mat, unwrapping the white gauze-like tape from around his hands. Jonah taps his shoulder as he passes, his hands already wrapped up and ready to take on his opponent.

"Who are you betting on this time?" I try my best to ignore Adam as he walks past.

Devon stretches his legs out in front of him and crosses his ankles. "Vic. All the way."

"I don't know." Elizabeth purses her lips and leans against Devon's shoulder. "He did have to go through Adam. He's tired. I'm going with Jonah this round."

"You're on. Mika?" He glances at me. "Thoughts?"

I raise my eyebrows, watching Vic bounce on his toes. "Eh, he's my best friend, so I'm biased."

"Ten on Vic," Adam says, slumping down beside Devon, water bottle in hand. "He's just getting warmed up." He leans to his older brother and talks to him in a hushed voice. Devon laughs and Adam pulls away grinning, taking a swig from the bottle.

I feel myself smiling, then turn my attention back to the match. I tell myself that my increased heartrate is from the anticipation of watching another sparring match with Vic. He is my best friend, after all, and I'm concerned for his safety. Yeah, that.

Of course, I'm rooting for my bestie. I clench my hands tight in my lap as I watch Jonah approach, a serious expression on his usually dopey, grinning face. Both boys look to Nelly, who shifts her eyes from the tablet to them. She nods.

Jonah doesn't hesitate. He attacks right away, coming in with several kicks and punches. Vic dodges and blocks. A swirl of movement faster than my racing heart.

"What level is Jonah again?" I ask in a breath as Vic ducks under one of Jonah's kicks, dancing away from another flying leg.

"Same as Vic." Elizabeth keeps her eyes on the fighters, as entranced by the match as I am.

Vic gets a few blows in, but Jonah is fast. He kicks him in the chest. I inhale sharply, eyes going wide. Vic grabs his leg and pulls him to the ground. A scuffle of movement, a scramble to get back on his feet, but Vic pulls Jonah in the same headlock he had Adam in earlier. I see his lips move next to Jonah's ear, a smile tugging at his lips.

"Told ya," Adam says, pushing to his feet.

Like a pathetic, lovestruck girl, I watch him leave, then return my attention in time to see Jonah laughing and tapping Vic's arm several times. When Vic lets him go, Jonah rolls on the floor, holding his stomach as he laughs. Vic is bent over, hands on his knees. Also laughing.

I bite the inside of my lip, hating the empty sort of clench in my chest. Seeing my best friend having a good time with his other friends, me being outside whatever joke they're having.

"Good work today." Nelly brings the boys to attention. They face her, bow their heads, and she returns the gesture before dismissing them with a wave and turning back to her tablet.

"That was more intense than any of the competitions I've seen you in," I say to Vic as he approaches. I stand to meet him.

He grins. "Because the last comp you came to, I was eight years old."

"Yeesh." I make a face. "Has it really been that long?"

"Yeah, remember how your parents reacted when you said you wanted to beat people up for fun too?"

I laugh. "Oh, dude, that's right!"

Then a realization dawns on me. My gaze falls to the floor along with my grin.

"What? What's wrong?" Vic gives me a worried look. "I know it's intense, but you don't just learn how to throw a punch. You learn how to take them and how to fall so you don't hurt yourself even worse."

I heave a sigh and look up at him. "It's not that. My parents will never agree to this."

Vic regards me, one brow lowering. He takes a breath, then puts an arm around my shoulder. "Don't worry about that. Hogan has dealt with some crazy parents. He's been dubbed the parent whisperer."

As we walk from the training room, he continues on, telling tales of nightmare parents now no longer a worry.

CHAPTER EIGHTEEN

OKADA SCHOOL OF EXCELLENCE

It's the end of the day and Hogan is here in my house, going over the details of my "scholarship" with my parents. The last time I sat in the same room with both my parents at the same time was at the hospital after the accident. A fact I avoid thinking about while we sit at the dining room table.

How did Hogan convince my parents to be home at the same time on such short notice? I have no clue. Maybe because it's the weekend? Or because neither of them have work tomorrow?

Or perhaps, like Vic said, he's the parent whisperer.

I keep my hands in my lap, playing thumb war with myself as Hogan talks about the different programs: martial arts for self-defense and discipline, traveling for learning languages and culture, advanced classes for college courses. That last one makes me stiffen with dread. I get decent grades, mostly Bs with a few As. But I don't think I'm ready for advanced classes.

My parents listen and nod. Dad, his glasses perched on the end of his nose, only frowns a couple of times. Mom, who is still in her scrubs, her radiology ID badge clipped to the pocket, appears to be thoroughly reading the brochures.

Both my parents seem to like the idea: a full ride scholarship to a private school—the same private school Vic attends—and Mom is always commenting about the "opportunity for growth" the school provides him. Even when Hogan mentions it'll require me to live at the school, neither one bats an eyelash. Granted, by letting me attend and live at this school, they're getting rid of the constant reminder of why their son is dead. A bonus for them.

I clench my hands so hard it feels like my skin will rip apart at the knuckles.

Hogan finishes talking, intertwines his fingers, and rests his hands on the table. The pause gives my parents some silence to mull over the offer. They look at the papers detailing what I'll learn, where I'll be traveling, all the tame stuff. Nothing that describes fighting monsters or beasts.

My parents look at each other. An ever-so-subtle nod from my mom. Dad turns to me, a smile pulling at the corner of his lips. The hope I feel is nauseating.

"This does sound like an incredible opportunity, boo," he says.

I nod, relaxing my hands and setting them on the table.

My leg starts to bounce. "Yeah. I mean, I wouldn't have bothered you guys otherwise."

My mom reaches across the table for my hand. "Oh, hon, you're not a bother."

I could literally cry right now, but they haven't said yes. Are they trying to play up to the big fat "no" they're about to give me? Like smiling and acting nice will soften the blow.

"You sure absolutely want to do this? Says here…" My dad taps a paper. "Your GPA can't drop below three-point-oh. It has before."

I roll my eyes and groan. "Daaaad! That was at the beginning of high school."

The bounce in my leg is about to go supersonic.

"I know you've always loved to travel," my mom interjects. "This is definitely an amazing opportunity, and we have a couple of months to prepare."

That's the downfall, having to wait until almost mid-January—the tenth, to be exact—to start regular classes and move into the OSE, but the wait will be short. The anticipation will make it seem like forever—

—Oh, wait! My leg stops bouncing. My line of thought is interrupted by the realization of what Mom said. *We have a couple of months to prepare.* That sounds like a yes to me.

"Thank you! Thanks!" I grin, blinking back embarrassing tears. I want to hug them, but I don't dare for the fear the illusion will break and they'll refuse to let me go. Instead, I squeeze my mom's hand.

"Well, let's get the paperwork over with," my dad says.

Fifteen minutes later they're walking Hogan to the door, talking and laughing like old friends. I stay at the kitchen table, looking over the papers detailing the schooling at the OSE.

Knowledge. Courage. Integrity. Okada School of Excellence, founded by Eiko Okada in the late 1800s. The year 1895 to be exact. A black-and-white photo of her is next to a short bio.

She's about thirty-five in the photo, if my math is correct. Her sleek black hair is pulled back into a high bun. Her expression speaks of no nonsense, all business. Her dark eyes are focused and hard. Born in 1860 in Japan. Orphaned at four years old. Adopted by a Dutch couple at five years old, only for them to be killed when she was eighteen years old.

She had a child at thirty-two, lived to see her first and only grandchild in 1923, then died at seventy-five in 1935 from natural causes. The school is now run by a board of directors. Her great-great-grandson Isao Tanaka is the head of the board. I note that Mathias Stehn—Devon, Jonah, and Adam's dad—is on the board as well, as Elizabeth mentioned earlier.

What monsters appeared in Eiko's life? Losing her birth parents, then her adopted parents, somehow must have driven her to build a school that secretly teaches people how to fight monsters. Not to mention other useful skills that could lead to prominent careers.

Languages, math, science, history, world culture, and martial arts. I let out a deep breath, running my fingers over the picture of a student in the martial arts garb. An odd sensation fills me as the realization of *That's going to be me* starts to settle in.

Another odd sensation tugs at me in the back of my mind, heavy and draining. I slump against the table, tracing my finger along the wood. *I don't belong at this school.* My GPA? Just making it into the 3.0 range. My ability to speak other languages? Slim to none. I can count to five in Spanish. Understanding equations and formulas in algebra? Forget about it. Retaining information for understanding how the world works from a biological and sociological perspective? In one ear and out the other.

I'm not a brain. I'm not an athlete.

"So, you're moving away?"

I look up at Anita. She walks over to the table, her gaze drinking in the brochures before resting those sad brown eyes on me.

"I won't be far. I'll visit as often as I can." I put emphasis on the last sentence, but I don't know how often I'll be able to uphold the promise.

She looks away, face scrunched in thought. Then she hugs me. My heart freezes. I stare down at the top of her head, throat aching with a sob.

"I'll miss you," she says, her voice tight and small.

My brain stops misfiring. I hug her back, holding her tight, swallowing hard to keep the tears back. Why did it take my leaving for this to happen? A reconnection.

"But only because you won't be around for me to kick your butt in racing games," she says, pulling away from me and giving me a challenging smirk.

"Right," I scoff. "You mean because *I* won't be around to kick *your* butt."

"Go off," she says, following it with a mocking laugh. She gestures to the TV. "Care to defend yourself?"

I raise my eyebrow in retaliation. "It's frowned upon to make babies cry."

"Don't cry, then," she says with a stoic expression that would put Hogan to shame.

I push to my feet and join her. Both of us knowing I'll lose.

CHAPTER NINETEEN

QUESTIONS, CAROL, LIFE

The next day, I sleep in. I don't mean to, but playing video games late into the night—until Carol commanded for the sixth time that Anita and I go to bed—had been draining. Draining in the best way possible. Reconnecting with my younger sister led to the most restful night I've had since the accident. No melatonin needed.

When I wake up, I do my chores, finish some school assignments so I don't have to do them Monday, then study the parent-approved brochures for the OSE. I'm not going into the school today, as I have to work late. Which I don't mind. It gives me some time to process.

I sit down on my bed and open the Notes app on the cell phone, typing out questions I want to ask.

Who is Eiko and what happened to her that led her to create the OSE?

Did she also create the AIO?

I stare at the screen for a moment, then tap the top of

the note and type out the acronyms.

AIO = Arcane Intelligence Organization. Not mentioned in the brochure, as I'm sure parents would say "hard no" on fighting monsters.

OSE = Okada School of Excellence.

EON = Eiko Okada Ninjas. Also not mentioned in the brochure.

Demon essence: what is it and how does it work?

Blessed blades: what is the process of making a blessed blade? Who blesses them?

What else? I tap my thumbs on the edge of the phone as I read over what I typed out. I spot the clock in the screen's upper right corner and let out a short curse. My shift starts in thirty minutes.

~

Lucky me with the closing shift, but tonight, I don't mind. The countertops and creamer/sugar station are clean, restocked, and organized. The display with kitschy greeting cards and knick- knacks is rolled to the back of the shop. The methodical task of putting barstools and chairs up on the tables gives me time to think.

My life has gone from me losing my mind and scouring forums to joining a school to learn how to fight the thing that caused the accident. From thinking my best friend was just a parkour nerd, to discovering he's a ninja who slays monsters. I should be mad at him.

Fortunately, I'm done cleaning the coffee shop for the

night. Another five minutes alone with my thoughts could lead to simmering anger toward Vic. He knew the beast was real, and he didn't tell me. He never denied it, but he never confirmed it either.

I triple-check that the doors are locked and the machines turned off. With all my distracting thoughts, I don't want to leave only to find out I neglected to do something.

Backpack secured to my back, I grab the two bulging trash bags and head to the back door. I punch in the alarm code, brace for the cold, then exit. My teeth start chattering as the cold nips at my cheeks.

From the corner of my eye, I glimpse my family's SUV beneath the parking lot light, and I wave before fishing the keys from my pocket to lock the door. I mutter to myself to move slowly and purposefully, so I don't drop the keys.

My dad gave me a ride to work. He said he'd pick me up at the end of my shift, so I don't have to fend for myself in the dark and cold—which is maybe another reason I didn't completely dread today's closing shift.

Has the prospect of my leaving snapped them all out of the grief haze? I feel good, but what have I gotten myself into?

A question on repeat. Which I answer the same way.

The mountain lion beast flashes through my mind's eye, followed by Sahara—specifically, the memory of her burning me with a cigarette. I touch the bandage on my neck.

I know exactly what I have gotten myself into. And this is not a choice I'm taking lightly.

After locking up and disposing the garbage, I jog over to the SUV and fling open the passenger door. My greeting sputters when I recognize my older sister in the driver's seat instead of my dad. She looks up at me from her phone, eyelids droopy with boredom.

"Oh, hey." I fumble with removing my backpack and set it on the floor before sliding into the seat. "Wh-wh-" I clear my throat and try again. "Where's Dad?"

"I needed the car." She puts her phone away and buckles her seatbelt. "I taught a class tonight at the ranch. Said I'd pick you up."

"Oh, right." A silent moment. "Thanks."

She doesn't respond, just stares out the windshield as she maneuvers the vehicle from the parking lot. I adjust the heat vents. She has it on the highest heat setting, but blowing on the lowest setting. I hold my hands in the warmth. At least the heat is on.

"Dad said you're going to a fancy school. That must be nice," Carol says. The way she says "nice" doesn't reflect the meaning of the actual word. Like with the limited amount of heat I'm getting from the vents, I'm going to have to accept the fact that this is about as "warm" as Carol is going to be toward me for the rest of my life.

Whatever. Another thing I can shove to the back of my mind and forget about when I leave, right?

"Yeah…" I clear my throat again and trace a stain on

the knee of my pants. "It'll look good for college. How's, uh, how's college going for you?"

"Good."

"Are you, um, interning yet?"

"Nope."

And not another word muttered, mumbled or murmured. I trace the stain the whole ride home.

When we walk in the front door, Carol right behind me, I frown at the empty couch. Usually Anita is there, playing video games. A game is up on the screen, but it's paused.

I step to the side to kick off my shoes when a voice comes from the kitchen, talking about being spit on by llamas. Anita and my parents erupt with laughter. I recognize the voice right off.

"Victor!" Carol says, entering the kitchen ahead of me. "It's been too long, dude!"

I step into the warm light of the kitchen in time to see her pull him into a hug, and I sit on a barstool at the kitchen island.

"Your hair is freaking long," she says. She reaches up and runs her fingers through his hair, which is loose from the typical ponytail he sports, the tips of which barely brush his shoulders. Carol's just able to reach the top of his head. He's almost a foot taller than I am at six-foot-three, and I'm around six inches taller than her four-foot-ten.

"I could say the same about you." Vic tussles her

brown locks. "You had the pixie cut thing going for a while."

She did. It worked for her, in a "speak to the manager" kind of way. Only she would never ask to speak to the manager. She'd have her death glare on lock until her victim squirmed themselves to death. Now, her hair is long enough to pull back into a ponytail, as she has it now. Loose strands frame her elegant face.

I watch from my perch as they all continue to chat and laugh. They're *laughing*. There hasn't been this amount of joy in the house for a long time.

Noticing me, my dad pats Vic on the back. "Hey, look who's back from Peru." He turns to Vic. "Say, you know she's going to be joining that fancy school of yours?"

"Oh, yeah?" Vic gives me a surprised smile. It appears authentic. I smile back ignoring the questions his act brings to mind.

"God, this is the last thing the world needs." Carol widens her eyes, but she's still smiling. She gives Vic one last hug. "It was good to see you again. You need to come over for dinner, share your wild stories. Right, Mom?"

"Oh, of course," my parents say, almost simultaneously.

"That reminds me." Vic's grin turns somber and sympathetic. "My parents want to invite you guys over for Thanksgiving dinner. They understand if the answer is no, but the invitation is there for you all."

"Thank you, Victor." My mom smiles, kindly. "And tell

your parents thank you. We'll consider it."

She glances at my dad, who nods solemnly.

And with that, my family disperses. Carol goes to her room, my dad goes to the living room with Anita, and my mom goes to her room. Vic rounds the kitchen island, heading straight to the fridge.

"You want anything?" He opens the fridge door, scanning the contents.

"You're so weird. Being a host in my own home," I say with a sigh. He's done this for as long as I can remember. I guess my mom would always tell him to help himself.

"But do you want anything—ooh! What's this? How old is this?" He pulls out a pie plate, a pie that looks to be some sort of berry flavor.

I shrug. "Can't say." And I really can't.

He peels the lid off and inhales deeply. "Looks good to me. Smells even better."

"Thanks for coming over. They needed a goofball moment."

He pauses his search for a plate and fork to look at me. "What are friends for, right? And like Carol said, it has been way too long."

"This is the happiest I've seen them since..." We both know since when.

He nods. "Healing takes an incredible amount of time. Especially from this kind of thing." He returns to his search, gets his pie, puts the rest back in the fridge, then takes a seat next to me. "Hogan told me everything is taken care of. Come January tenth, you're an OSE student, on your way to becoming an EON."

I lean my head against my hands. "You'll need to tell me how you wound up with them. Wait!" I sit up. "How did you get here?" He doesn't have his driver's license. I wouldn't put it past him to run here, but he'd also have to run back to the OSE.

"Jac dropped me off on her way to work. Nelly will pick me up in about an hour on her way back from town." He takes a bite of pie, followed promptly by another bite.

"So…?" I reach over and jab his shoulder with my finger. "Spill."

He glances toward the living room, full of the animated and lively sounds of Anita's videogame.

"Tell me!" I prod in a whisper.

"It was two years ago. I was out for a morning jog," he whispers back, his gaze flitting back to the living room. "Eh, this isn't the place." He chuckles under his breath and gives me a sheepish look. "Been dying to tell you since this all began, and now I'm hesitating."

"Let's go outside," I say.

Despite the dropping temperature, I'll face the chill for his story.

CHAPTER TWENTY

REDCAPS

We both bundle up. I tease Vic about actually wearing a jacket, and he teases me about always having to wear one. We walk down the road a bit, the breeze to our back.

"Now, spill it!" I jab my finger at his shoulder. "You were out for a jog, two years ago…"

"Actually, at this point, it's more like two and a half years ago."

I roll my eyes, though in the dim moonlight, fighting to peek out around snow-laden clouds, he can't see my face. I groan to make my point known. "And you were out for a jog."

"It was one of my long jogs. The route I take across the park that goes past that sketchy strip mall."

I nod and hunch my shoulders against the cold. I've ridden my bike with him on a couple of his jogging routes. "And you end up going around the lake and back home. Or to that juice place."

"Yeah, only I never made it to the lake. Never made it past the strip mall that day." He rubs his hands together. The movement is slow, absentminded. "It was early, dawn starting to break. A scream, like a terrified, wounded animal, sounds as I'm passing the strip mall. I stop running, trying to figure out where it came from. Maybe I can help.

"The scream comes again from the alley up ahead." He runs his hand through his hair, sighing, looking over at me. "I had no freaking clue what I was running into. Fourteen-year-old me, thinking I was going to be some hero and save someone."

We stop walking about two hundred feet from the house. He leans against a stop signpost at the crossroads. I peer up at him, trying to make out the expression on his face.

"But you can't save someone if they're already dead. She was dead. Her attacker crouched over her, blood everywhere. It saw me and took off running. I don't know why, but I ran after the thing. It looked…human. But when I caught up with it—when it *allowed* me to catch up—I realized it wasn't human."

"Wh-what was it?" I stare at him, eyes wide.

"The OSE call them redcaps. They don't look like much. Kinda like a stout, disgruntled, scraggly-haired old man. But they're strong and quick on their feet. And their teeth aren't human. They have vampire-like fangs. They drink the blood of humans. They prefer females, but they won't discriminate against males for a meal."

He clears his throat, idly rubbing his hands together. "He hid, waiting for me to run past, then attacked. I would love to say I held my own against him, but I was freaked out, dude."

He huffs a humorless laugh, pulls his phone from his pocket and activates the flashlight. He has me hold it while he rolls up his sleeve, showing a scar I'd seen before on his forearm.

"I told you it was from a parkour accident, but now you know what really happened."

"Geez." I poke at the scar, remembering when he'd told me about it, and now I'm getting the real story behind the two round, puncture scars, trailed by several ragged lined scars. As if the redcap bit down and dragged its teeth across his arm.

I don't ask how many other things he's hidden from me. There's another time for that. "How'd you get away?"

"If Elizabeth hadn't shown up when she did, I'd be dead." He leans his head back against the post, smiling, teeth flashing white in the faint moonlight. "I had a pretty big crush on her for a while after that."

"I can imagine," I say. "The first ninja you meet happens to be someone who can kick serious butt, you're bound to be smitten."

The thought reminds me of earlier this summer, when Vic had been obsessed with some girl. "Is she the 'love of your life' you were going on about in France?" After I ask,

I realize the timeline doesn't add up. Not even a little bit.

He chuckles, a sad and awkward sound. "No, no. That was a completely different girl. Completely different. A thing of the past." He starts picking at his fingernails.

"Well?" I ask, waiting for him to elaborate. Something I never got the full story on because it hasn't been on my mind since, you know, the accident happened around the time. If she's an EON, maybe Vic can't talk about her. But I know about that part of his life now.

He stays silent. The way it hangs in the air has me peering at him, trying to make out what little I can see of his expression, his eyes. Maybe his jaw is working, and he's not looking at me.

"Dude, what's wrong?" I gently poke his shoulder. "Why won't you tell me about her?"

He shrugs, a big movement as he hunches. "Because I'm not proud of myself for how it ended. It doesn't matter how I tell it, I'm the asshole in the story."

"Okay…" I say slowly. "But you should talk about it."

"Yep. Kinda like how you should talk. To your sisters, to your parents. See that they don't actually hate you."

"I liked it better when we were discussing the love of your life," I say in a curt tone. "Or the lack thereof."

"First of all, rude." He looks up at the sky. A moment of silence follows, filled with a breeze carrying tiny snowflakes. "Anyway, you can go ahead and yell at me."

I scrunch my forehead. "What? Why would I yell at you?"

"Seriously?"

"Uh." I shake my head, trying to think of why I need to yell at him. Maybe for being idiotic and almost getting killed? But that's par for the course with Vic most days. Parkour, martial arts. I can add chasing down monsters to that list.

"For meeting *One Times Three* and not telling you about it!" He taps my shoulder with on open hand. "Duh! Like you've had a crush on Adam since you were like twelve and—"

I crouch down, picking up a handful of leaves and tossing them in his face. I take off running back toward the house, giggling as I hear his feet thudding behind me in pursuit.

"You're lucky you're injured," he says, falling into an easy jog beside me.

I slow to a walk. "You and your legs." The short burst of rapid movement has my heart racing, leaving me gasping for air and my skin hot. The chill of the night is refreshing. "How did Hogan convince your mom to let you join the OSE?"

"I have no idea." He bounces on his toes then settles to walk with me. "The day after the redcap attack, I woke up to find my mom waiting for me, she gave me the brochures and told me to have an answer for the school by the next morning and that Dad was cool with it."

"Really?" I look up at him.

"Yeah, dude. It was weird." He shakes his head.

"Anyway, I'm sorry I didn't tell you sooner. Especially that the monster you saw was real. I should have found a way." He drapes his arm over my shoulders, and I wrap my arm around his waist.

"Don't worry about it." I feel like I might actually mean those words. Maybe.

CHAPTER TWENTY-ONE

MONSTERS AND DEMONS

Even though I'm not an "official" student until January, Nelly figures it won't hurt to teach me about the evils they fight. I won't be able to learn the fighting until I'm officially a student though. Something to do with liability and insurance reasons. I understand, but it bums me out. I'm looking forward to learning how to kick butt.

I'll just have to be satisfied with learning about the things they fight—as we are now, at nine o'clock in the morning.

Elizabeth sits with me at a front desk in the schoolroom, Vic on the other side of me, having pulled a chair over. Devon sits on Elizabeth's other side. Jonah sits at the desk beside us, Adam at a desk in the back.

Monsters. The three categories are as follows:

Earth Dwellers or EDs: organic monsters and demons that exist on the mortal plane with nothing done to them by a human. Redcaps fall into this category.

Hybrids: artificial, manmade monsters, created with whatever DNA of animal-human the creator fancies and bound with demonic essence. Usually, the essence of an Earth Dweller. The giant mountain lion beast and Sahara's henchmen are in this category.

Monarchs: demons of the netherworld. They exist on the immortal plane and sometimes cross over to cause anarchy, chaos, pandemonium. Choose your favorite mayhem word. I hope to never have the pleasure of meeting one, and lucky for me, encounters with them are extremely rare.

Nelly starts out with the giant mountain lion beast, classified as a GMP—Genetically Modified Puma. Puma being the genus in the Felidae family, as the GMP has puma/mountain lion traits, despite its massive size and fortified skin which even the sharpest blades have difficulty penetrating. They haven't been able to collect any useable DNA samples to help figure out how to defeat them.

I don't even try to comprehend how DNA is going to reveal the solution. I clipped one with a SUV, and it limped away with a bloody nose. If they can figure out how to kill one by looking at its DNA, more power to them. Maybe it has something to do with the potency of a blessed blade? Do blessed blades have "potencies" of being blessed? Another question to add to my ever-growing list.

At the bottom of the GMP profile on the projector

screen is a list of proven associates. Sahara is the only one listed.

"While she's always been adept in science, specifically biology," Nelly says, "she doesn't possess the know-how or equipment for merging and altering DNA and essence. Someone is working with her."

The OSE, or the AIO, have a few ideas of who could be assisting her, but they haven't been able to confirm any leads.

I take notes on my laptop with other windows open so I can look up any given definition or acronym.

Next on the screen are the macho, bald, identical henchmen from Sahara's lair. They're classified as Henchmen-S. The "S" standing for Sahara, as she is the only proven associate. The henchmen are clones, and their DNA is currently being analyzed by the science division. Devon and Jonah had been able to collect a sample while creating a diversion to rescue me and Elizabeth.

Henchmen-S are strong and agile, not too bright and a little cocky. Decent fighters. One-on-one hasn't been much of a problem, but fighting off two or more can prove troublesome because of their strength.

I recall Elizabeth taking down one of them in less than a second. The most badass thing I'd ever witnessed, second only to her destroying her hand to get free.

"We're starting with the things you have seen," Nelly says from her stool at the front of the classroom, remote for the projector in hand. "It should help lessen the blow of reality."

I nod, wanting to say I'm fine, but I don't really know. Not yet, anyway. What could be worse than a human being burning my neck just to be sadistic?

The henchmen picture flicks to a picture of Sahara. Elizabeth stiffens. I glance at her. Devon takes her hand. She intertwines her fingers with his and squeezes tight, keeping her eyes on the screen. I still find it surreal how alike they look, a blatant reminder they're twins. Even in the displayed picture of Sahara, her smile doesn't speak of the monster she truly is. She looks like a teenager who likes to go to movies and sneak out with friends on a school night.

"A former EON, as you know," Nelly states. Her tone is even, as it was with the previous monsters she officially introduced. "An adept fighter with a quick mind."

The GMP and Henchmen-S are listed as associates, as expected. Her name on the screen is written as Elena "Sahara" Alamy. I type that into my notes.

Nelly moves on from Sahara, introducing monsters that initially look human-like until I study their picture, and note their eyes. Black, dead, soulless. Faces deadpan, skin ashen. Something is off about their jawline; it's too long. I find their name and type it into my notes. Dorei, Japanese for the word slave. Hybrids. Named and classified by Eiko herself. They come in different shapes and sizes and genders of the human form, all of them reanimated dead.

Reanimated dead? Zombies?

I swallow hard and continue reading.

Adequate fighters, most effective in large groups. Typically found in Japan, though they've been sighted across Asia and Europe. No sightings in the USA. Thank God.

"You know," Vic leans over, whispering, "all these files are accessible through the computers or any device on the server. You don't really need to take notes."

I shrug a little, whispering back, "I know," not sure how to explain to him that I need to write this down for my own benefit.

The next image pops on the screen, and my eyes widen. A tall, humanoid beast with long, dangling arms. His arms are full of sinewy tissue, down to his thin taloned fingers. Its round, oblong head hangs at an awkward angle, on its muscled neck. Dark, hollowed-out holes where the eyes should be. The mouth hangs open with dark drool— nope, *blood*, blood dripping from its sharp, irregular spread of teeth.

The others stare at me, their gazes heavy as they gauge my reaction. I try to keep my own gaze steady, despite my thudding heart, and take my notes. The clacking of computer keys like small detonations in my own ears.

"Boogeymen," Nelly says. "Rare, but they exist all over North America, especially in forested areas. It's been speculated this is what people see when they claim to have seen Bigfoot. Generally easy to kill, and to scare off if you appear bigger."

I slow-blink, reading the monster's specs. They're recorded to be seven feet tall or more. How on earth could I appear bigger at my five feet, four inches?

"But just because they scare easy, don't underestimate them," Nelly adds. "They are extremely aggressive." She gives Jonah a pointed look, and I don't look at him to see why. "The AIO is still uncertain of how they came to be, but evidence shows they're of human origin with demon essence. It's been speculated they're the result of a freak experiment gone wrong. Earliest sighting comes from the late eighties."

I notice that the Boogeymen are under Hybrid, but with a note marked *Inconclusive*.

She shows a couple more monsters, each as gruesome as the Boogeymen, and all of them Earth Dwellers. Ghouls, imps, redcaps.

Nothing is shown on Monarchs. Either they have nothing on these netherworld demons or they're saving it for a different time.

Demons. Still not as ridiculous as ninjas somehow.

Next up on the screen: humans associated with studying and using these monsters for sinister agendas. These are scientists. They don't look evil in their headshots, unless you consider the college professor look evil. Most wear thick-rimmed glasses and simple dress shirts. Some have soft smiles; others do not. They look harmless.

"Their power is all in their minds," Nelly says, her voice serious. "Just because they don't have elongated arms or needles for teeth, doesn't mean they won't try to kill you. A gun is equally effective."

The profile currently displayed is one for a Dr. Clive Davis. Most of the scientists have degrees in genetic engineering, bioengineering, biochemistry. He has a PhD in all three. He has a handsome face with a stern jawline, blond hair combed back away from his face, and intense blue eyes that stare into your soul—even as his are soulless.

I type these scientists down in my notes, putting them in a category all their own. Monsters of the Worst Kind. As humans, they should know better.

The screen goes black. I blink, giving my head a small shake.

"That'll be enough for today," Nelly says. "Profiles get updated monthly, if not more often with the increase in sightings." Fatigue has crept into her voice, like she's just cleaned up the mess and now she's back to cleaning it up again. A mess that could be avoided.

"Thoughts, Mika? Questions?"

"Hm." I bite the inside of my lip. "Um, what is 'essence', exactly?"

"Essence of demon is bound into its very being. It makes them faithful to darkness, hate, fear, and aggression." Nelly speaks evenly and clearly. "No empathy, only apathy. They thrive off hurting others, relish the pain they cause."

"But," I say, scrunching my eyes, "how do they—the scientists—get it? The essence? Do they capture a...uh..." I wrack my brain for an Earth Dwelling demon name. "Capture a redcap and take its blood and separate the essence? Or is their blood considered essence?"

"That's the simplest way to put it. Their blood is essence." Nelly shifts the tablet in her hands. "Earth Dweller demons are the usual targets for the scientists, easier to find compared to their netherworld relatives."

"But the ones who come over from the netherworld are a lot more powerful," Elizabeth interjects. "A gold ticket item. Pretty sure it's what the GMPs are made from. A monarch."

"Hasn't been proven," Adam says, voice quiet even as it carries down from the back.

"Essence of a Monarch demon." I murmur. "Would that affect the blood color?"

Everyone turns to me.

"The, uh, the..." I glance at my notes for their name of the mountain lion beast. "The GMP has black blood."

Nelly frowns. "Are you sure of that?"

The others remain silent, waiting for me to continue.

"When—" I clear my throat and drop my hands to my lap. "When it caused the car accident, I saw it. Its nose was bleeding. I remember it because it wasn't normal. And the henchmen, they had darkish gray blood."

"The blood color does indicate to some degree what

they're made from," Nelly says. "Gray is typically what we see from Hybrids made of Earth Dwellers." She pauses, then fixes me with a hard look. I try not to shrink away. "Are you positive the blood of the GMP was black?"

I nod. I am. But with how intense she's being, I wonder if I haven't mistaken the color. It had been dark. I did have a concussion. But it's so vivid in my mind, I don't even have to close my eyes to picture it.

"So, she has access to a monarch demon," Nelly says with a heavy sigh, shoulders sagging a little. "Or at least is working with someone who does. All right, class dismissed. Boys, I expect you all to be in the gym and warmed up in twenty. Elizabeth, why don't you show Mika the room she'll soon call hers?"

CHAPTER TWENTY-TWO

MORE ON EIKO

Elizabeth turns on the light to the room that'll soon be mine. A warm yellow glow of LEDs set in the four corners of the ceiling, and one in the center, illuminate the whole room. She motions me inside with an encouraging smile. "My room is just across the hall from yours. Hogan doesn't anticipate any more students in this unit, so we can have our own bathrooms."

There's an empty bookcase along one wall, a desk with an office chair at the back of the room near the door that leads to the bathroom, and a twin bed—a plain white sheet, covering the mattress from solid oak headboard to solid oak footboard—set on a low-profile gray rug. A matte black lamp set stands atop an oak nightstand. The closet is set into the wall with French doors.

I step inside and cross the hardwood floor to the bookcase that reaches all the way to the ceiling. I run my fingers along a shelf, the oak smooth and clean of dust.

The three books I own will have plenty of space.

The closet has shelves on both sides within. A wooden rod along the top to hang items. Guess I'll invest in some hangers.

When I open the bathroom door, the light automatically turns on, starting at a soft dim and gradually glowing to fully lit. Empty shelves above and between the sink and the toilet. A shower stands on the other side, the plain gray curtain open to reveal the empty tub and chrome fixtures that match the chrome in the rest of the bathroom. I pull the door closed and approach the nightstand, where I turn on the lamp and note the power strip with one outlet and two USB ports on its base.

I take a seat at the desk and swivel in the chair.

"Overwhelming, huh?" Elizabeth perches on the edge of the bed.

I huff an exhale, puffing out my cheeks, and trace a finger along the desk. "I've never done anything like this. Ever. As cool as it is. Like, I've never been to summer camp, or spent the night away from my family for more than a day."

She chuckles. "That's not what I was talking about, but yeah, moving away from home is intimidating."

"Oh." I rub the bridge of my nose. "What were you talking about?"

She gives me a look, eyebrows raised. "The monsters and demons. That's usually what gets people."

"I think…" I pause, tap the desk, then clasp my hands

in my lap. "I'm still trying to process it all. Learning how to fight these things to keep others safe is what I want to do though. Even if the training is going to kick my butt."

It'll give me a purpose. A way to bring Aaron justice. A distraction.

"Spoken like a true EON. That's why Eiko founded the OSE."

I sit up. "What came first? The school or the organization?"

Elizabeth picks at her cast, frowning at it. "The school. It wasn't called the OSE when she was still alive though; they changed the name in her honor. The AIO didn't form until shortly after her death. They're the ones who took her dream of creating a network of schools all over the world and made it a reality. Here in Colorado, we have a research lab down in the Springs, but over in Europe, South America, and Asia, there's around two dozen schools and a handful of research labs throughout."

"I bet she'd have loved to see it. Eiko sounds pretty interesting." I lean forward with my elbows on my knees. "From the little I read about her from the brochures."

"Oh, only a fraction of the story is told on the brochures. The woman is a legend, dude." She sits up, face glowing with adoration. "She kept journals of all her experiences, documented the death of her adopted family, who were killed by these flesh-eating demons called ghouls. She ignored haters and found others like her. People who've faced monsters and lived to tell about it.

"While not the most adept fighter, she knew how to use various weapons from swords to throwing axes to crossbows, and she was very thorough in documenting any monster sightings or interactions and questioning people about them. Someone could give one or two traits of a monster, and she'd know which journal to reference if she'd heard of the monster before."

She pauses, lips pursed. "I think there are twelve journals in total. All of them can be found in the school's online library.

"Anyway, she started the first school with twelve pupils, and two martial arts teachers. A few of the pupils were exiled nuns."

"Exiled nuns?" I frown. "What'd they do?"

She shrugs. "They were cast out for actually believing that demons are real. Funny how some people are so against evil, but refuse to acknowledge it when it exists."

"Huh." I sit back up and run my hand along the desk again, liking the feel of the cool wood under my skin. Nuns not being believed by their own parish is a little sad. I mean, a lot sad. And they did what I'm doing now. Joining a school to learn to fight and protect against the monsters no one believes in.

But how useful can I be? I skip out on all the physical games at social gatherings. Even simple games like tag. Nothing special about me except that I was in the wrong place at the wrong time, due to my own idiocy. Imposter syndrome starts to nag at the back of my mind.

"And there's the whole training part," I say quietly.

"You shouldn't worry too much about the training." Elizabeth leans against the footboard, picking at her cast again. "You bike to work. What's that, like, twelve miles? That's pretty good. And, in the forest, when we were rescued, you ran a mile in about six minutes. Which is really good for not training and running through a forest."

I raise my eyebrows. "A mile? Really? Is six minutes fast?"

She laughs, bringing her braid over her shoulder. "It's faster than the average. You're stronger than you think."

"Adrenaline, I guess." I shift in my seat and inspect the desk. There's a blue ink stain on the honey-colored wood.

"Yeah, that's part of it." She stands. "Don't worry, we'll whip you into shape. It took me over a year to do one full, real pull-up." She plays with the end of her braid. "My sister could do them since birth."

"Well, you kicked her butt back there," I say, then cast her an embarrassed grimace. I'm sure she'd rather not have to fight her sister. It must be painful for her; her twin is actually *the* evil twin.

Elizabeth chuckles, not bitter or mean, but kind of sad. "It may have taken me longer to perform strength moves. Pull-ups, handstands, climbing to the top of the rope. But I have always had the better reflexes. Which is a bit more essential when it comes to combat."

I remember her taking down the henchman in less than two heartbeats and dodging her sister's attacks with the electrical rod and knife, all while injured. Reaction time at its finest.

We exit the room, and I hit the light switch as we leave.

I hope it doesn't take me a year to do a pull-up, but hey, I'll be happy when I can perform a real push-up. I look at my arms. Zero muscle definition. They're just long, flabby meat sticks. I resist the urge to shake them to confirm they are indeed flabby. My arms are quite adept at being arms, and that's all I've ever asked them to be. I haven't demanded much from them.

"You have sisters, right?"

I jerk my head up. "Yeah, two." I tell her about Carol, her love for animals and going to vet school, and about Anita and her knack for videogames.

Her eyes light up and her lips twitch up in half a grin. "What kind of games does she play?"

"A lot of fantasy, first-person shooter type games, I guess." I struggle to think of the titles of games. Elizabeth lists a few as we ascend the stairs and make our way to the game room/living room.

I nod at the names I recognize. "She loves the warrior princess one."

"Same! The artwork alone is breathtaking, but throw in some kickass characters and an amazing storyline." She lets out a sigh, grinning. She flops on the couch, and I sit in an armchair. "I'd love to compare notes with her."

I nod, smiling. "She'd love that, honestly. She plays online with others, but most of them are guys. There are some good ones, for sure, but a few of them are irritating to say the least.”

“Tell me about it,” Elizabeth groans, but she’s smiling. “Partly why I’m glad you’re part of the fam, because as much as I love the boys, they can be so dumb.” She presses her fingers to her eyes. “Like, you’ve met Jonah. Lovable, but also you wanna strangle him.”

I chuckle, remembering his antics from the tour. “He’s very extra.” I almost ask about Adam, but something stops me. Instead, I make teasing eyes at her. “What about Devon, huh? You two seem pretty cozy.” I waggle my eyebrows.

The blush spreads across her face and down her neck. “I figured you’d notice. We don’t hide it. I adore him. So much. He’s been amazing since day one.” She fixes me with a playful warning look. “But do *not* play any sort of board game with him. He’s like an evil mastermind and will make you miserable the whole time.”

She starts ranting about Devon: his inability to understand physics, his hatred for math, playing the same song on repeat for days on end.

The whole time she’s ragging on him, she’s smiling, and I can’t help but smile too. And laugh. We laugh a lot at Devon’s expense. Even when he walks into the room with Vic, we’re still laughing and making fun of him. Especially his chosen hairstyle in music videos. Oh, yes. We make great fun about him.

“I don’t like this.” Devon eyes us with mock wariness.

"I feel attacked."

Vic laughs, clapping the older boy's shoulder. "That's what you get for being in a boy band."

"Oh, the things I could tell you about my best friend here," I say to Elizabeth, jerking a thumb in Vic's direction.

"We have to compare stories." Elizabeth giggles.

"Does he ask any of you guys to squish or remove the spiders from the room when he discovers them?" I peek at Vic, an evil grin twisting on my lips.

"Oh, my gosh, yes!" She throws her head back with laughter. "He can take on fighters twice his size and not even blink. But a spider smaller than a dime has him cowering in the corner."

Vic looks at Devon. "You're right. I don't like this either."

CHAPTER TWENTY-THREE

THE JERK

Elizabeth, Vic, Devon, and Jonah are all in the game room, playing some sort of cartoon racing game. Their shouts and jabs fade to the background as I walk down the hall to the bathroom. I pause with my hand on the doorknob, not needing to use the facilities. It was an excuse to leave the room. The events over the past couple days are an overwhelming din, making me feel small and nauseous.

A stairway is to my right. I tap my fingers against the brushed silver doorknob, then head downstairs. I note the mark on the wall where Jonah wacked his elbow as a kid, then pass what I think is the schoolroom and push open the next door. I stare into the weapons room. Empty of people. I reach in to grab the door to pull it closed, then pause. I step into the room, gazing at the displays, lit with soft, warm LED lights.

The room is cold, yet somehow welcoming. I peek at

the sword I'd been admiring earlier, the curved Damascus steel blade complemented with the dark wood and black stone hilt. It truly is beautiful. I run a finger over the cool metal, then lean closer, examining what look like tiny symbols etched into the metal.

Is that how they "bless" blades?

A shiver runs down my spine, and I let my hand fall to my side. Chewing the inside of my bottom lip, I turn to exit the room, feeling like I shouldn't be in here unsupervised.

"Blessed blades," I murmur to myself, envisioning a priest dousing kitchen knives with holy water. I chuckle a little, then bump into something and take an immediate step back. I look up into Adam's scowling face.

"What are you doing in here?" His hard gaze leveled on me as he reaches around me to pull the door shut.

"Blessed blades," I say quickly, face heating and my heart feeling like it's causing a riot in my stomach. "How are they made?"

"You shouldn't be in here until you're officially a student."

I duck my head and grimace. "Um, okay. But blessed blades—"

"You'll learn about that when the time comes." He motions me down the hall.

I don't move, glancing at the weapons room closed door. "Do they use holy water or what?"

He stares at me with an expression that makes me feel

like I asked the stupidest question a person could ever ask. Like, holy water isn't real. Blessed blades, what? I shift my weight, turning to head down the hall. His footsteps almost inaudible as he follows me.

"Holy fire?" I look back at him.

His nostrils flare with a loud inhale.

"Come on, dude." I turn on him. "Cut me some slack. If I'm going to learn about it anyways, why does it matter *when* I learn about it?"

The set of his jaw makes me throw up my hands in defeat and continue down the hall. While I'm sure he'd like to herd me back to the others, I have other plans. Defiant plans. I push open the first door I come to. The schoolroom is before me, with all its desks, the projector screen dark, but the overhead lights are set to a dim glow.

The information I'd learned earlier rushes to the front of my mind like a flood as I step into the room. I run my hand along the back of a chair before taking a seat and slumping my head into my arms on the desk. Part of me— a big part of me—worries that I'm in over my head. Demons. Monarch demons. Acronyms.

I peek up to see Adam standing off to the side, glowering at me as is he's trying to drill holes into my skull. I clear my throat. "So, is there a ritual they perform to bless the blades? Do they bless the nunchucks too? I noticed the little…carved…symbols…"

He blinks slowly at me.

I shift in my seat, reaching my toes for the floor,

knowing I should leave but I remain seated. Being all awkward.

"Can't believe this is what Hogan and Nelly have resorted to," he mutters, shaking his head. His murderous glare leaving me. "They let anyone in the OSE these days."

I snap my mouth shut and match his annoyed expression. "You know what?" I scoot from the stool and somehow land on steady feet, even as the anger flares. "You're a jerk." I spin on my heel and head toward the door. Heat creeps up my neck and to my face. *The nerve of that guy! What is his problem?*

Hogan enters the room, halting my exit. He's followed by Elizabeth and Jonah.

"Oh, Mika. Perfect." The man looks at me. I lift a hand to scratch my forehead, attempting to hide my angry blush. "Good, you're here," he acknowledges Adam. "There's been a GMP sighting. I'm sending Devon and Vic out to make sure it stays out of populated areas."

~

Hogan sits at one of the front desks, tablet in hand and wearing a Bluetooth earpiece. I sit at a desk across the walkway from him with Elizabeth and Jonah. Adam stands next to Hogan. The others were distracted enough by the GMP's appearance, not noticing my red face or the friction between me and Adam.

In my angered state, it took me a moment to translate GMP to Genetically Modified Puma to "mountain lion beast." Freaking acronyms.

When any of the group is out on a mission, the schoolroom becomes the headquarters for communication and tracking. A map is projected on the screen at the front of the room. A red "OSE" marks the location of the school. Two small dots move slowly across the terrain mark where Devon and Vic are.

"They have eyes on it heading west," Hogan says, tone even and clear. "Don't intercept. Just see where it goes."

"There's nothing out there," Jonah says, propping his elbows on the desk as he peers at the map. "Just National Forest. Sahara's new hideout?"

Elizabeth murmurs a word of agreement under her breath.

"Where is her old one?" My pulse hammers in my neck.

"About twenty miles southeast of the school," Jonah says, leaning back as he riffles through the desk. He emerges with a thin, round, silver stick the size of a pinky finger. He points it at the screen, and a green laser-dot appears. "Here is Sahara's lair, and up here is the GMP."

"Okay." I'm chewing my bottom lip again. "Where's my house?"

My heart thuds in my chest as I stare at the laser beam, the green laser dot moving past Sahara's old lair and stopping far too close for comfort at where Jonah says my house is. I squint at the screen, confirming the nearby street name and the cross street.

"Don't worry," he says. "She's abandoned the old hideout. She's not close by anymore. I doubt she'd want to attract the attention of attacking a household, and we're certain she doesn't know where you live."

Hogan looks over at me. "From the conversation she had with Elizabeth when you were both captive. She thinks you're with the OSE. Your home, your family are safe."

I nod, wanting to believe them, but fear creeps in. Am I putting them in more danger by being with the OSE? If Sahara discovers my family, where we live—I shudder, not wanting to finish the thought, but I know without a doubt what she'd do. She stared into my eyes and drank in my pain when she burned me. She wouldn't hesitate to use my family against her enemies.

Ten minutes pass while I try not to shift in my seat. Unease sets into my bones. The want—the need—to check on my family is overpowering. Sure, they don't want anything to do with me, but I don't want anything to happen to them.

"They've lost it," Hogan informs us, his hand going to his ear. "If you don't pick up the trail in ten minutes, Circe will pick you up in the meadow, two miles east."

Circe? Adam mentioned that name when he'd rescued Elizabeth and me. Led us to a meadow where we were picked up in a helicopter. Circe is Nelly. Code names? I guess that makes sense; they are ninjas doing covert operations, relaying information over radios. What did

Elizabeth call Adam when we were rescued?

"Can I go with her?" Elizabeth gets to her feet.

Hogan nods his permission. She excuses herself from the room.

A muddle of emotions has me unfocused, staring into space. I'm relieved Vic and Devon didn't have to face down the beast, but disappointment and fear are pervasive; not knowing where the GMP is, or where it now calls home. Even with Hogan's reassurance that Sahara doesn't know who I am or where I live, I can't help the nagging trepidation.

"Mika?" A hand touches my shoulder.

I blink to attention, inhaling sharply.

Jonah's bushy eyebrows draw together. "You good, girl?"

"Yes. Yeah. Lost in my thoughts, that's all. So…" I rub my hands against my pants. "Do you all have code names, or is Nelly the only one because she can fly a helicopter?"

He laughs, leaning back in his chair. "Yeah, kinda. Vic is Jagerbomb. Or just Jager for short, using his middle name." He rolls his eyes and scoffs. "As if he's ever had the drink." He pauses and squints off to the side. "He's been to Europe several times, so maybe he has… Anyway, Jacqulyn is Crimson. I'm Jo. Devon's Dev. Lame, I know, but we legit don't respond to anything else. I've tried."

He gives me a forlorn look. "I've tried. I wanted to be called Maverick or Saber, but alas, nothing sticks."

He tosses a nod in Adam's direction, who stands next

to Hogan, looking down at the tablet as the man swipes at the screen. "He's Elvis."

Ah, right.

Adam's shoulders tense at the mention of his code name, but Jonah carries on, not noticing or maybe not caring about his little brother's reaction. "He likes to say 'Elvis is in the building.'"

Jonah chuckles. "Freaking genius. Anyway, Elizabeth is Savanna, and uh…Sahara, well…"

"Ah, gotcha." I nod, saving him from having to explain. "Sahara and Savanna. Both related to the desert. Well, one *is* the desert."

"Yeah, they had those nicknames since they were little, I think." He taps his fingers against the desk, looking away as his easy grin falters. He clears his throat. "Hogan is HQ. Well, he's HQ because he's the one who stays here at headquarters and does all—" He gestures to the room, the map on the projector. "—this."

"Okay." I nod, pursing my lips. "So, there's a code name for anonymity to the outside world, and it has to be a name one responds to. Will I get a code name?"

The grin is back, his face like a kid being given a giant ice cream cone with his favorite flavors. "Heck, yeah, girl! You can pick something cool, like, like, Atomic or Shuriken. Call you Shuri for short." He rattles on about what he thinks a good code name would be: nothing too mainstream.

From the corner of my eye, Hogan leans over to Adam

and says, "You should save her from your brother."

"If she's going to live here, she'll have to get used to it."

With that, he leaves the room. Hogan frowns after him. I pretend I didn't hear their exchange and smile at whatever subject Jonah is going on about passionately. Something to do with weapons.

CHAPTER TWENTY-FOUR

SPILL

I sit on a bench outside the boys' locker room, which is located through the medical room—the room with the unsettling, adjustable chairs—but instead of going straight back, you make a hard left and go through a door I didn't notice before. Elizabeth is sitting beside me, picking at her cast.

"Itchy?" I wore a cast for a month and a half. My humerus bone had been fractured in the accident. The worst part was when there'd be an itch and there was nothing I could do to relieve it.

"Yeah. Sucks."

Devon emerges, hair wet and dressed in sweats and a long-sleeve shirt. OSE is embroidered on the left breast. He offers me a smile, telling me that Vic will be out in a second; then Devon and Elizabeth leave together. "Knowledge. Courage. Integrity" is printed in bold letters on the back of his shirt.

I continue to wait, sitting on my hands, tracing a scuff mark on the floor with the toe of my shoe.

"Dude, I don't know how you're not curled up in a corner sobbing." Vic exits the locker room, hair slicked back with water, black towel draped around his neck. Like Devon, he's also in sweatpants and an OSE T-shirt. He slumps down beside me. "The GMP is unnerving to say the least. One of the most massive monsters I've encountered."

I almost tell him that I have sobbed in a corner, many times, but instead I say, "So, this is the first time you've seen it?"

"Mhm." He rubs the towel in his hair. "I've either been gone or otherwise occupied when one makes an appearance. I've dealt with some flesh-eating, child-like monsters." He shudders. "But something about that GMP, dude."

"Maybe because it's too big to kill," I say, leaning back and resting my head against the wall. "You think the brains will figure out a weakness? Like the right holy water to holy oil ratio for a blessed blade?"

He bursts out laughing, throwing his head back.

"What?" I give him a look. "No one is elaborating on the whole blessed blade stuff."

He runs his hand through his hair, slicking back what stuck up from the towel dry. "Our weapons for missions are all made at a forge in the Middle East. I can tell you there's an in-depth purifying process that, yes, involves holy people. Priests and priestesses. Blessed blades can penetrate the supernatural armor demon essence creates. Though, the stronger the monsters and monarchs are, the more difficult it is to dispel their power."

He grins and nudges me. "Nice use of the lingo, by the way."

"Right. Something's been eating at me about the GMP." I close my eyes as I try to arrange my thoughts.

"Spill."

"Well, you guys were alerted to the beast today like that." I snap my fingers, sit up and look at him.

"You're wondering if the OSE was alerted to its presence when you first saw it," he says, not a question but confirmation of my thought.

"Yeah, and I hit it with my car. It was bleeding. There was blood. I know there was blood. But…"

"Nothing was found at the scene," he says slowly.

"Or what if somebody… I don't know." It's crazy. Crazier than DeeDee87 from the *Strange and Unusual* forum claiming she's seen Bigfoot.

"You think someone cleaned up the evidence of the GMP." Again, not a question, but a confirmation.

"Yeah. I don't know. Maybe." I rub my arm, the one I broke. "The vehicle did roll several times; I had a concussion. I don't know." I shake my head. "Forget it."

He doesn't deny what I'm saying, doesn't say that I'm crazy. He just leans back against the wall, a faraway look in his eye. I examine his face. Trying to read what he's thinking. He catches my look and smiles. But it's forced, tight, not reaching his eyes.

"What is it?" I keep my eyes on his.

"It's just…" His gaze flickers away for a second. "It's just you never really talk about the accident."

"Oh." I slump back against the wall. "It was all over the news."

He leans forward. "Mika." A sad sigh, but also a plea.

I guess I don't tell him everything either. Like, I've told him about the beast, the trouble with my family, but I didn't tell him about how I felt during the accident. Or the fact that I obsess over forums, trying to find answers. And that if I could, I would switch places with Aaron in a heartbeat. He should be the one alive, playing video games with his twin.

He pushes to his feet. "I guess I deserve that."

"What?"

"The silence." He pulls the towel from his neck, and tosses it into a hamper just inside the locker room door. "I've kept a lot from you. There's still stuff I'm not sure how to put in words."

"Taking the words right out of my mouth, buddy." I get to my feet as well. I'm too exhausted from thinking, anxiety, and existing in general to pry any more today. "But we'll get there again. Like you say, we've got a lot to unpack."

"True, very true. And we'll have plenty of time because soon, you're going to be official, and living here at the

OSE." He grins, and I can't help it. Despite the uneasiness swirling in my gut, I grin back.

A low, melodic hum greets our ears. We both look toward the door leading into the house. Adam appears, tablet in hand. His hums stop abruptly when he sees me. He crosses the floor, shoves the tablet at Vic.

"Report." Then he exits the room quicker than he entered.

The loud, deep sigh groans from my nose before I can stop it. I head for the pedestrian door that leads to the courtyard.

"Where you going?"

"Home." I step outside, crossing the cobblestone to my bike. A light dusting of snow shimmers in sun.

"You okay?" Vic follows me out, flip-flops making the muted slaps that they do.

I shrug at the question. I ignore him regarding me with his pursed lips and thoughtful expression.

"I noticed Adam giving you the cold shoulder. Is that—"

"Please." I cut him off, adjusting my helmet. "I've got bigger concerns than him." And I do. Like giant mountain lions that shouldn't exist, an evil psycho who's working with a demon, dealing with the Karens at work. My best friend keeping secrets from me, and vice versa, though my secrets are much smaller. I've much more to be concerned about than some stuck-up, pretty boy.

"He's not usually this...aloof."

"Aloof," I say with a snort. "Like, what did I ever do to him? He seemed, whatever at first, but he acts like I'm—ugh! Sorry I was kidnapped by a psycho that y'all should have taken care of a long time ago. Because if y'all would have, he wouldn't have had to rescue me. Is he scared I'm going to blab that I met *One Times Three?* And that they're ninjas?"

I snort again, shaking my head. Crossing and uncrossing my arms. "No one would believe me."

I, myself, have a hard time believing this, and I am currently living it.

Vic's lips are pressed together as he tries to suppress laughter, but his eyes betray him. I narrow my eyes at him and grab my bike with short, jerking movements. I'm not in the mood to be teased about my old crush.

"Hey, I'm sorry. I wasn't expecting you to be that worked up." He sets his hand on my bike's handlebars. "Give him time. He's going through some stuff."

"Like what?" I give him a challenging look.

Unfortunately, knowing my best friend, he won't tell me what's going on in Adam's life. He considers that gossip, and gossiping is rude. As if it's not rude teasing your best friend when she's already feeling down.

"I'm *also* going through some stuff," I say, words clipped with bitterness. "It doesn't give him the right to act like a jerk when I haven't done anything to him."

And with that, I push off. Pedaling down the driveway, switching gears to propel myself to a speedy exit. Pretty sure I'll make it home in record time.

CHAPTER TWENTY-FIVE

Don't Make Him Beg

Of course, when I have the opening shift, I have the hardest time falling asleep. Trepidation about living close to Sahara's old hideout, irritation about Adam's attitude toward me, and frustration about my best friend taking his side. Not to mention the beast's scratch on my arm is itchy as it heals. The skin's tight and dry with scabbing. Same with the stupid burn on my neck.

Like *I* don't have a lot going on. My brother's dead, my family's alienating me, ninjas exist in Colorado, and giant, genetically modified mountain lions and demons and monsters are real.

Out on the front porch, I pause, glaring at the six inches of snow on the ground and the flakes falling from the sky. Great. Perfect. Wonderful. This is really going to suck riding to work all winter. I trudge around the side of the house to my bike.

The muffled rumble of a vehicle coming down the road

breaks the muted silence snow seems to create. Headlights flash over me as it rounds the bend. For a moment, I wish I would quit being scared and get my driver's license. But the very idea of driving makes my skin crawl.

I brush the snow off my bike seat and start to walk it down to the road, footsteps heavy—until I stop short at the sight of a dark SUV idling in front of my house. I stare at the driver's window. In the soft LED glow of the dashboard, I can make out the silhouette of a driver. I breathe deeply, trying to still my quickening pulse. No need to freak out. People stop in front of the house all the time. Usually, they're lost. Though not typically at four in the morning.

The SUV door opens. My heart thumps hard. Neck muscles tightening. I do not want to deal with this. Whoever this is, I cannot deal with them, even if all I have to do is tell them how to get back to the main road. The SUV's overhead lights illuminate the driver. My anxiety settles, only to be replaced by ire and a scowl.

Ugh. You've got to be kidding me.

Adam exits, closing the door behind him. He shoves his hands in his pockets, shoulders bunching against the cold. Might help if he wore a jacket. Boys really are allergic to jackets, aren't they? He strides up to me, snowflakes contrasting his dark hair.

I grip my bike's handlebars and straighten up. "What are you doing here?"

He pauses in front of me. "Do you not read your text

messages?"

"Uh. What?"

In my sleep-deprived hesitation, he manages to ease the bike from my grasp. He's halfway to the SUV with it before I can protest. Instead, I take a couple of seconds to pinch myself, making sure I'm not having a bizarre dream.

He gestures me toward the SUV, striding around to the passenger side and opening the door for me. "Heat's on," he says, as if he isn't holding my bike hostage.

I'm too tired to argue. The chill is starting to seep through my gloves and into my fingers. I jog over and climb in. The heat is, indeed, on. My hands and face relish the warmth.

"Again—do you not read your texts?" He pulls on his seatbelt.

"Huh? Oh. Not when I'm sleeping." God, what a stupid answer. "Notifications are on silent when I sleep."

I retrieve the phone from my jacket pocket, confirming that he did text me, saying he would take me to work. Suspicion builds: why is he bothering to do me this "favor"? Perhaps so I'll owe him something in return? First off, I didn't ask him to do this, and second—

—I'm getting ahead of myself. Doesn't mean I'm any less suspicious, though.

"You should at least have it on vibrate in case we need to contact you. Seatbelt."

"Huh?"

He gestures to his seat belt, then to me.

"Oh, right. Sorry." I wince and secure my seat belt.

The soundtrack for the next couple of minutes is the rumble of tires on the road. I watch the glistening white landscape stream by, relieved that I'm not viewing the scene from my bicycle. I should consider getting my driver's license. To have a warm, dry ride to and from work. Bliss. But I don't deserve bliss.

"I'd like to help you," Adam says. His voice makes me jump.

"And what do I need your help for?" I stare out the window and take a subtle deep breath to calm my racing heart.

"We could get a head start on your training. Not the fighting, but building your strength and endurance. Maybe some self-defense skills."

"Why?" I turn to him. "To help you with the next instructor exam?"

He glances at me, a quick flash of his eyes. He shifts in his seat. "Yeah, that's part of the reason."

"Yeah, right," I scoff. "You mean the *only* reason." My heart is pounding so hard. Part anxiety, part anger, but all because he has the audacity to even suggest an idea. He must think he's all that if he believes I'll do him this favor after how he's been acting with me.

He opens his mouth, only to snap it shut. He looks like he wants to argue. I hold my breath as I resume watching the world pass by. As awkward as the drive is, at least I'm warm and dry.

"You're right." His admission a soft word, none of the curtness I've associated with him. "You're fresh blood, and it'll look great on the recommendation for instructor training."

I face him again, eyebrow cocked. "Why would I agree to that? You haven't exactly been welcoming." Wow! Am I truly going to deny hanging out with the guy I used to have a crush on? The keywords here are "used to." Past tense. Kind of hard to have a crush on a guy who acts like a jerk, even if he is Adam Stehn.

"Again, you're right. I don't know how many times you want me to say so. I don't know how many times I'll need to apologize for being a jerk, but can you just give me a chance to make it right?" He gives me a long look while we wait at a stop sign. "I mean, you'll hate me during training because I'm going to push you to challenge yourself. It can get pretty intense sometimes."

"I don't know. Sounds like you're just looking for an excuse to be a jerk to me."

The whites of his eyes, and the gentle silhouette of his face against the dashboard lights, are all I can make out.

He drops his head. "Just…will you at least think about it before saying no?"

I don't want to think about it. I've got enough going on without him adding to the load.

"Vic would be more than willing to train me," I say. "I don't need your help."

"Eh." He goes quiet, keeping his eyes on the road as he takes a corner. We're on the main road. This early in the morning, and with the amount of snow, we have it to ourselves.

"This was Vic's idea," he says.

I blink. And blink again. Eyes narrowing to slits. "Oh."

Oh, that boy. Of course, Vic thought up this scheme. He probably thinks he's doing me a big favor playing matchmaker. He knows Adam is the one I had a crush on back in the day. Back in the day? What am I? An eighty-year-old woman? I'm going to have a talk with that punk, maybe plant a bunch of fake spiders in his room or something.

"So, will you think about it?" Adam asks. "Please?"

I pinch the bridge of my nose. "Fine. I'll think about it."

CHAPTER TWENTY-SIX

HAVE PITY ON THE BOY

Another girl missing. She's the fifth one since July. The disappearances are happening closer together. The last two girls went missing only days apart, instead of weeks.

This subject is a hot topic at work, especially with Brittney. The girl who just went missing lives in her neighborhood. Or maybe "lived" is the more appropriate tense. The thought leaves me queasy and despondent. Considering none of the other girls have been found— dead or alive—I don't think they're coming back

Not a happy or uplifting conversation in any way, but it keeps my mind off Adam's offer. I'd rather not think about it. Or the fact that Vic came up with the plot. The urge to strangle him is powerful.

But when Brittney says she's signed up for self-defense classes, something she's been putting off for a long time— the latest missing girl being the incentive she needed—my own decision is made before I realize it. I'm still going to strangle Vic, plant spiders in his room, shoes, wherever, but I will give Adam a chance to train me.

Speaking of that audacious jerk, he returns to pick me up ten minutes before my shift ends. I ignore the stares from Brittney and Shayla (the coworker who typically only works weekends) when Adam walks in to ask me for my bike's lock combination so he can load it.

I refuse to give him the code, however, insisting I unlock my bike myself.

"Do you like coffee or tea?" I ask him.

"Huh?"

"Coffee or tea?" I finish unlocking my bike and wrap the cord around my hand, glancing up at him. My face heats up as I ask the next question: "Or are you still a hot chocolate kind of guy?"

"Oh." He hesitates, gaze jumping from the bike to me. "I guess mochas aren't bad."

"But if you had to choose, hot chocolate or mocha?"

I swear his lips actually twitch with a hint of a smile.

"Hot cocoa. All the way."

"Sweet." I head back into the shop.

"Okay, even at the risk of sounding like Carter. I have to ask." Brittney looks at me before glancing at Adam, who is lifting my bike into the back of the SUV. Shayla shamelessly stares at him, brushing a lock of her silky, ash blonde hair behind her ear.

Brittany finally voices her question. "Is that your boyfriend?"

A Carter question, indeed.

"He doesn't even qualify as a friend," I say with a huff.

They don't have a chance to respond, as customers arrive. I do the few dishes that are in the sink, wipe down countertops, then clock out.

I make the hot chocolate for Adam, and a tea—with an ample amount of cardamom—for myself, finishing them both without interruption. I say my goodbyes and see-ya-laters, and trudge outside, bracing against the chill. It wasn't snowing when I'd given my bike to Adam, but it is now. Teeny, tiny flakes pelt me in the face as I walk.

"Here you go." I pass the hot chocolate over to him.

He takes a slow, tentative sip.

"It's safe," I say, ready to embarrass myself with more knowledge of Adam Stehn. He frowns at me, and I hide my face behind my own beverage. "I made it with almond milk."

There it is. The knowledge of his lactose intolerance. Not something he'd broadcast a lot in his *One Times Three* days, but I remember his brothers mentioning it in one of the behind-the-scenes of a music video.

I cringe inwardly at the flashback of the fridge they'd stocked with almond milk for their little brother. A sweet sentiment on their part, but I still hate that I know it.

"Oh." His face relaxes, and he takes a longer, deeper sip. "This is pretty good."

"Yes, well, when you make around twenty of them almost every day, you get good."

He responds with a "Mm." I honestly don't know if it's an acknowledgment of what I said, or an expression of contentment with how delicious the beverage is. Either way, the response is appropriate.

"So…" He drags out the "o," sparing a glance in my direction as he maneuvers the vehicle from the parking lot.

I remain silent.

"Have you thought about it? Me training you?"

As if I need clarification of what he's talking about. I continue my silence, and he starts to ramble.

"I guess you've been working, not a lot of time to think."

He has no idea how much I can think, does he? Poor soul. I sip my tea. It's good—could use more cinnamon though.

"I know I've been a bit of a jerk. I do feel bad. I do. I shouldn't have acted the way I did. It doesn't matter what I'm going through either. Everybody's going through something, right?" He mutters something about going off topic before continuing: "While this statement may not hold much weight, I promise you'll not regret it."

The spices mull on my tongue. There's plenty of cardamom. Definitely add a touch more cinnamon next time though.

"Okay," I say.

"You will?" He practically jumps out of his seat with excitement. Good thing we're at a red light.

"Uh, I just want you to stop talking." I press my lips together, surprised at my ability to appear impassive.

"Oh." He cringes, glancing out the side window and rubbing the back of his neck. "I do that sometimes. Babble."

He deserves this awkward torture, but I've got to stop being mean. Even so, I let the feeling between us simmer before saying, "But I did give it some thought. Mostly about how I want to plant spiders for Vic to find."

Adam nods. "He is scared of spiders. Kind of ironic in a way. Guy is like a spider himself, the way he can scale a wall."

A horn beeps behind us. We both look up at the now-green light, and Adam gets the car moving.

"I'll do it," I say, "under one condition."

"Of course. I expect nothing less."

I wait until we stop at the next red light. The wait is only a couple of minutes, but he's rapidly tapping the steering wheel with anticipation.

"If I feel like you're being a jerk in any way, and not just pushing me to challenge myself, we're done." I'd like to go as far to say I'd make sure he never gets a training position in his career, but realistically, I don't have that kind of pull. I don't have any pull. I'm not even an official student yet.

He reaches his hand over to me. "Deal."

I regard him, ignoring thoughts about how grown-up he looks, so handsome and strong. The baby fat in his face is replaced with sharp cheekbones and a strong jawline. Bringing to mind a phrase Carol always says, "the prettier, the meaner." I don't want to think like that, though.

"Deal," I say.

We shake hands. I hope I didn't just make the biggest mistake of my life.

CHAPTER TWENTY-SEVEN

LET THE TRAINING BEGIN

I am completely covered in sweat, my lungs begging for air, my heart threatening to slam out of my chest. And I ache. God, I ache in every muscle I have. How much time has passed since I agreed to Adam's offer? An hour.

One. Freaking. Hour.

I glance at the phone propped up against a bench, the stopwatch app ticking away. We're twenty minutes into the workout. Or technically, according to Adam, only ten minutes into the workout. The first ten were a warm-up; light stretching, light cardio—jumping jacks, jogging in place.

He's putting me through some "drills." Squat jumps. Twenty-second plank hold. Front kicks. Split squats. Push-ups, which I am doing on an incline with a picnic table since I am unable to do a single one from the ground. And the horror of all horrors: burpees.

The anatomy of a burpee is as follows: squat down,

jump legs back to a plank position, jump legs to return to squat position, then jump as high as I can from the squat position. And I thought the squat jumps alone were awful.

He has me do twenty repetitions of the lower body work, then ten reps of the upper body and core work. The burpees are as many as I can do within thirty seconds. With good form. He talks about good form a lot. I understand why, but when my pulse is hitting hard in my head, trying to beat out through my temples, proper form is the last thing on my mind.

We're at a park, abandoned because of the winter chill. We made a quick stop at a public bathroom so I could switch into the workout gear Adam brought for me. I hate that he assumed I didn't own any sweat-wicking clothing, even though he was right. But it is kind of exciting, wearing the smooth joggers and form-fitting long-sleeve shirt with the letters OSE printed on the front. It gives me a sense of belonging.

Or, at least it *was* exciting, until he had me doing my second round of drills.

As for why we're outside at a park, and not in the school? Working out in a dry, cool—as opposed to a freezing-cold and snow-covered—environment? What we're doing can't be done on school property due to liability issues, since I am not officially a student yet. While it makes sense, it also doesn't. The school literally trains people to fight monsters. How is that not a liability?

"You've got a lot of power in your legs," he says. He's

in front of me, facing me, moving with me on each drill so I can see how each move is meant to be performed, and so he can give me cues to correct my form. "Push through the heel of your front leg."

I grit my teeth against the burn in my quads as well as my glutes while we do split squats, an exercise where you start with one leg forward and one leg back. We lower down, knees bending to a ninety-degree angle. The back knee just barely touches the ground before you push back into the starting position.

To keep myself from cursing him out, I follow his breathing. Inhale as we go down, exhale on the way back up. Not an easy feat when all I want to do is punch him in the face. Which brings up a question.

"When...do we..." I exhale with a hiss. "Get to...the fighting?"

Isn't it supposed to be cold out? Why isn't it cold out? It must be around sixty degrees out here. I ignore the rational part of my brain, telling me that the temperature is at least thirty-two, considering the sprinkling of tiny frozen flakes from the sky.

"You said." Inhale and don't pass out. Lower down. How badly are my knees going to hurt after this? "I'd learn...self-defense."

"We'll get there. Switch legs."

I do as he commands, moving slowly to give my muscles a break. "When?"

"After burpees."

I stop mid-lunge, gaping at him. "What? I'm not." He's got to be joking, right? "I'm not going…to have the energy…for that!" As much as I want to have a head start on being able to defend myself and being useful in a fight, I don't think I'll be able to throw a punch when we're done, much less stand.

"I didn't say after today's burpees, did I? Breathe. You're doing great."

I scowl, and I could agree he didn't specify when, but that's beside the point. I breathe as deeply as my lungs will let me, lower into the dreadful position, and exhale my way back up. We move on to push-ups. I do two, my arms trembling with effort. When I go down for the third, I collapse. Frustration swells in my chest, making it harder to breathe.

Adam is saying something, but unless the words are "We're done for the day," I don't think I'll find the will to move.

"Hey, Mika." He taps my arm. "Switch to negative push-ups. Watch me."

Fine. One deep inhale and I peel my eyes open and observe. He lowers down on the table next to me, slowly to the count of three, then steps forward to take the weight from his arms so he can straighten them. He steps back into the plank position, then repeats the process.

I follow his lead, listening to his count and lowering as he does. My arms still tremble, threatening to drop my weight, but the break of not having to push myself back up is all I need to power through the rest.

Now, burpees: the final round of torture. He talks me through the low-impact modification. Omit the jumping and step back into the plank position. He encourages me to do the jumps, though. I skip them. My head is pounding. I'll probably vomit if I keep jarring my body with explosive movements.

"Ten seconds left, Mika. Do a couple of jumps," he says, while doing full-on jumping burpees.

I don't see perspiration on his forehead or sweat soaking the usual places on a shirt: chest, armpits, back. Unlike me, with sweat running down in my eyes and between my shoulder blades. Soaking my calves, of all things.

The ten seconds are up. I got three final burpees in. No jumping. He doesn't comment on the lack of jumps, which I'm thankful for. I don't think I can take criticism right now.

"You were excellent, Mika. You've got good strength in your lower body and endurance, which I figured you'd have from riding your bike to work." He shows me the first of the cooldown stretches. "Upper-body strength needs work. A lot of work."

If I wasn't so beat, I'd glare at him.

"But you'll see that build tremendously when we start the self-defense stuff. You'll be amazed at how shadow boxing works your muscles."

"I'll take your word for it," I mutter. My legs shake as

I stretch them, the sensation both aching and glorious.

We move on to a hamstring stretch. There's a sort of love-hate relationship forming between stretching my sore muscles and my mind. How can something so uncomfortable also be so soothing?

We go through some shoulder, chest, and triceps stretches before we're on the ground, doing a hip and low back stretch. The snow is refreshing as it melts against my neck. I could lie here forever.

"All right, let's get some protein." Adam appears above me, extending his hand.

I let him help me to my feet, doing my best to not hiss at all my soreness. I doubt I'll be able to move in the morning. Good thing I don't have work until later in the day tomorrow.

CHAPTER TWENTY-EIGHT

ARACHNID PAYBACK

I peek into the living room of the OSE, where Vic lounges on the couch, thumb swiping his phone, and I assess my plan. It's not really a plan, not a full-fledged one with steps and a backup strategy. I mostly just have an idea and an urge.

Elizabeth sidles up next to me. I do a double take, almost not recognizing her. Her hair is free of its usual braid, cascading over her shoulders in beautiful, dark brunette waves. Light mascara and eyeliner highlight her green eyes. A sheen of pink gloss coats her lips. She's wearing a long, flowing lavender dress with short, ruffled sleeves. I think of Carol. The only time my older sister ever puts on make-up is when she's going on a date—as rare as her dates are.

"Cute dress," I say. "You and Devon going out?"

"Thanks, it has pockets." She puts her hands in said pockets, smiling. Her eyes scrunch up at the corners.

"We're going to dinner and a movie. You know."

"Sure." I nod as if I do know, but I don't.

"What's up?" She looks between me and Vic, somehow understanding I'm trying to be sneaky. Props to her.

I hold up my hand, uncurling my fingers to reveal one of the dozen integral items of my agenda. Her eyes widen, a malicious grin curling her lips. She gives me a thumbs-up. We both walk into the room.

"How did training with Adam go?" Her tone's even and curious, not overdoing it. She's good.

Vic looks up at us. "Yeah, how'd it go?" He waggles his stupid eyebrows at me.

I clench my jaw and inhale deeply through my nose. "Burpees happened. How do you think it went?"

He laughs, setting his phone down and putting an arm behind his head to prop himself up as he watches me. I sit down at his feet. Elizabeth slumps down in the armchair, pulling out her phone.

"Oof," she says, giving me a sympathetic look. "Brutal."

"With the push-up?" Vic asks. I can hear the smile in his voice.

I turn my head slowly to look at him. "There's a push-up?" I think about how you jump back into the plank position, perfect setup for push-ups. Thank god Adam didn't add that, or I may have walked away. EON training is supposed to be intense, I get that, but so much that you can't move? I don't know about that.

He laughs again. "Don't worry, you'll get there. But otherwise, it went well, right?" He searches my face, and I try to channel Hogan and remain stoic.

"Sure. But I'm not going to be able to walk tomorrow." I place the object at his feet, then groan as I push to a stand.

"You'll get there, dude." Vic chuckles sympathetically.

I give him a dirty look and round the couch, hand going into my hoodie pocket. Preparing another object of terror. "How do you implement burpees against fighting monsters?"

"They increase your stamina and strength."

This comment from Elizabeth, who is clearly trying not to watch me for too long as I place an object on the back of the couch. The little black piece of plastic, with legs balanced just out of Vic's eyeline.

He's retrieved his phone. "Jumping and explosive movements build power in your legs. Stronger kicks."

My quads scream at me as I lower down at the side of the couch, resting my chin on the armrest. Vic's scrolling through an article.

"Oh, sure." I reach around and place another little eight-legged piece of plastic next to his arm. "What are you reading?"

"I have to write an essay for biology. I'm just looking for an idea."

"Hm." I place another spider next to his arm. "Going

to write something on bugs?"

Elizabeth chokes and coughs.

"You good, Sav," Vic asks, not even looking at her.

I place another, my last one. "Ooh, I know. Face your fears. Write one about spiders."

He frowns and scoffs. "Please—" He turns to face me, freezes, eyes going wide. The color drains from his face. He lets out a yelp, leaping from the couch, his phone clutched in his hand. He skitters away, shaking his arms and making strangled, panicked noises.

Elizabeth's face is red as she laughs, holding her stomach with her casted hand. Her other hand holds up her phone, probably recording the moment.

Vic stands in the middle of the room, gasping, looking between me and Elizabeth. My abs protest at me as I laugh, tears springing to my eyes. I collapse to the floor, picking up one of the spiders and holding it up. It only has seven legs.

"Come on," he moans. "That's not funny."

"You're right," Elizabeth wheezes, unable to catch her breath. She sees me with the spider, and the fit of laughter starts all over again.

"It's freaking," I pant around a laugh, "hilarious!"

Vic shudders, shoulders hunched. "Why?"

"Payback," I manage to say between heaved laughter that makes my whole body protest. He lets out a disgusted snort, then leaves the room, brushing at his body and muttering in German.

"That was," Elizabeth gets to her feet, wiping at her eyes as she walks over to me, "perfect." She holds her hand out to me.

I wave it away, wiping at my own eyes. "I think I'll stay down here a moment. It's less painful. Did you get that on video?"

"I did, indeed. Gotta have blackmail, girl. Useful when it comes to monthly chores." She slumps down on the couch, grabbing the spider I set on the back of the couch and observes it in her palm. "These are not anatomically correct. Vic should base his essay on how important it is for spiders to be properly represented, even as Halloween decorations."

"Honestly, yes." I look at the one in my hand. "This one is missing a leg."

CHAPTER TWENTY-NINE

LIGHT AS A FEATHER, CUT TO THE QUICK

I'm having the usual nightmare. The car accident that kills Aaron, no matter what I try to do to prevent it, always ends the same. He's dead, and I'm facing down a beast that shouldn't exist.

Only this time, during the nightmare, every bone and muscle in my body aches from the jarring crash. I can't move without my entire being ringing with pain.

My phone wakes me, vibrating under my pillow. It takes a bit for my sleep-fogged brain to realize what's going on. That I'm not trapped in a vehicle with a giant mountain lion ready to pounce. I'm in my bed at home. Body aching because of the workout Adam put me through yesterday.

Maneuvering my arms is a hassle, but I manage to retrieve the obnoxious device. On seeing who's calling, I almost don't answer, but what if Adam is calling about something important?

"What?" I grumble out the word.

"How you feeling this morning?"

"Like…I've been through another car accident."

"That bad, huh? Take a quick, cold shower to wake up and let's go for a run."

I must have misheard him. I pull the phone away from my ear and look at the time. "It's five in the morning. I have…stuff…today." Stuff being school and work. And I'm already drifting back to sleep.

"Which is why we should go now." His voice is chipper. Like how birds sound, being all proud of themselves for being up before the crack of dawn.

I let my heavy eyelids close. "No."

"It'll be a short run, I promise. You'll have time to nap after." The cheerfulness in his voice is grating.

But I'm already falling asleep. I hang up, not surprised when he instantly calls back. I ignore it, dropping the phone on a pile of clothes on the floor, and move to the other side of my bed. Abdomen and shoulders reject the movement but settle when I relax enough to fall into a restless sleep.

The dreams continue. But not of the car accident. A ninja named Elvis is waiting for me. His voice commanding, *We have to go! We have to go now!* No matter how hard I try to move, I can't. Either my body won't cooperate, or something unseen is holding me back.

The sun's rays that burst through the opening in my

curtains wake me. My attempt to roll out of bed reminds me why I didn't get up earlier.

I moan as I push myself up, arms and abs shaking. I swing my legs over the edge and slowly stand.

"Aah," I breathe. "And he wanted to drag me on a run this morning."

By some miracle, I make it to the bathroom. A warm shower does wonders, but as soon as the chill sets in after I exit, my muscles stiffen and continue their protests as I dress.

Back in my room, I reach for my phone, but stop mid-reach when I see my journal on the nightstand.

I flip the book open to the bookmarked pages and frown at the attempted sketch of the beast. I've been wanting to prove the beast is real for such a long time that I'm torn between keeping my mouth shut or showing my family the facts. Do they really need the truth?

Anita comes to mind first. The very idea of the beast would terrify her. Would she ever brave leaving the house?

Carol comes to mind next. She's made it clear she doesn't believe what I saw, and if a giant mountain lion did run into the road, the creature would not be at fault for crashing the vehicle that night. I am the one at fault. Even if Aaron didn't die, she would still take the animal's side over her own sister.

That settles the debate. No matter how badly I want to tell them, to clear my name, I was the one behind the wheel. My actions led to Aaron's death. Beast or no beast.

The dread in the pit of my stomach continues to swirl, making a permanent home.

I pitch the journal across the room, glaring at it as if I could set it aflame, in the process burning the real beast off the face of the earth. But alas, real life doesn't work like that.

Yeah, real life shouldn't have genetically modified pumas. Puma. Cougar. Mountain lion. Demon.

I amble from the room, giving my phone a once over. Not my phone, it's the phone Nelly is letting me use. I still need to go to my carrier's store and report my phone lost and purchase a new one and return this one to the OSE. I make a mental note to leave an hour and a half earlier than usual for work.

The sooner I can replace my phone, the better. Something about borrowing another person's property, I don't know, it's unsettling. Feels like I owe someone something.

I chuckle under my breath. They're taking me into their school of excellence, and I'm concerned about something as ridiculous as borrowing their phone for too long.

The doorbell resounds through the house. I pause my venture to the kitchen and peek into the living room where Anita is. She glances to me then at the door.

"I'll get it," I say halfheartedly.

I peer through the peephole. My heart jumps into my throat with a mixture of anxiety and irritation. I undo the deadbolt and pull the door open, just wide enough for my head to poke out. I press my lips together, running my eyes over Adam in his workout gear.

"What?" I was going for annoyed and curt, but the word just comes out drained and tired.

He gives me a quick onceover. I realize my hair is a damp mess and I'm wearing an oversized sweater and neon-green sweatpants. While they are my comfiest pants, they are super attention grabbing. Can't be as bad as me covered in sweat, blood, and my own vomit.

"Being visible is good for running along the road so cars are aware of you," he says. "But I don't think that's the best running attire."

My glower deepens. "I'm not going today. Have you been out here all morning?"

"Would you feel bad if I was?"

It's 9:00 a.m. now. If he'd been out here all morning, he'd have waited around four hours.

I snort a laugh. "Nope. It's your fault for standing out in the cold like a moron." He's at least wearing a long-sleeve shirt, unlike the T-shirt he wore yesterday.

"Mika!" Carol shouts from the kitchen. "The heat bill doesn't pay itself. Either invite your friend in or go out."

Got to love the oldest sibling. They're basically parent 3.0.

Adam's gaze shoots behind me. "So?"

"So, what?" I raise an eyebrow. "If you think I'm inviting you inside, you're sorely mistaken, buddy boy."

"Mika." The warning is a threat in Carol's annoyed

tone.

"Well, see you at school later," I say, then close the door in his face.

I wait a moment, listening. Anita is focused on her game. Carol is in the kitchen; the microwave door pops open. I peek through the peephole. Adam still stands on the porch, brooding. His lips move in a mutter, words too quiet for me to hear. Then he strides to the SUV.

With a sigh of relief, I slump against the door and look over to see Carol standing in the doorway to the kitchen, the scent of breakfast burrito wafting through the room as the microwave hums.

"Who was that?" Carol asks me.

I hesitate. If anyone in my family would recognize Adam, it would be Carol. Devon had been her *One Times Three* crush, but she spent a good amount of time watching their music videos too.

"Uh, he's a classmate," I say, pushing away from the door and heading to the kitchen, squeezing past her.

"Uh-huh. I see. Do all your classmates look like models for sports attire?"

"Just the annoying ones." I peek over at her, waiting to see if recognition dawns on her. Instead, her lips turn up at the sides. Her stern eyes gleaming with—dare I say— amusement at my comment. Be still my heart! Did I just make my older sister smile?

"Sounds about right," she says. The microwave beeps, and she collects her food.

"Unfortunately." I turn away from her, finding myself some breakfast, not wanting to test my luck. But also dying—*dying*—to continue this conversation of pretty boys being annoying jerks just so I can talk with her. Reconnect.

I can't risk it, though. Doesn't matter anyway. When I turn around, bowl in hand for cereal, I'm alone. But the usual emptiness after interacting with Carol isn't there.

My entire mood shifts. Despite my physical soreness, my emotional and mental state are lighter since the accident. A pep in my step, or at least it feels like it.

I eat, put on clothes appropriate for a bike ride, then put my school laptop and work clothes in my backpack. Though my legs and arms protest, I'm as light as a feather as I pedal to the OSE.

~

Adam's stiff, irritated expression doesn't faze me. He's outside, sitting on the steps leading to the mansion's side entrance near the garages. A book sits open in his lap. His attention snaps up to me when I arrive. I park my bike, take my time undoing my helmet, then walk over to him. He fixes me with a stern look.

"Do you want to be a ninja or not?"

I pause at his question, adjusting the shoulder strap on my backpack. "I don't think you have much say in the matter."

"Being an EON is about way more than just learning

to throw a punch and do fancy flips, Mika." He shuts the book with a slap. "This is about commitment and perseverance. Pushing through the uncomfortable to become better, to be stronger and faster and smarter than the monsters you'll face. There'll be times when you're exhausted and beat, but you're going to have to push past that. Unless you want to fail, which leads to not only your death, but the death of your teammates. They need to be able to rely on you."

His gaze intensifies as he stares up at me. Something in his eyes—I don't know. But I'm determined not to let him ruin my good mood.

"Doubt I'll be going on missions any time soon." I move to step past him. "Considering I'm new."

"Exactly my point." He stands, blocking me. He's not much taller than me, but I feel small under his criticism. "How will you ever expect to be ready with an attitude like that? This isn't a game. This is real. People can—people *will* die due to your lack of training and preparation."

I can name it now, the look in his eyes. I see the same thing when I look in the mirror. Fear. Regret. It reminds me of what Vic said, that Adam is going through a lot. This is something more than him not passing the instructor exam.

"Are you… Is there something you want to tell me?" The sympathy is heavy in my voice. I don't mean for it to be, but it is. Instinctively I reach out a hand to him. "What happened?"

Adam recoils from me, taking a step back. "Wh— Nothing. Nothing happened. Why would you think something happened?"

"Yep, denial. You're so tough and manly right now. Just gets me all…" I wave my hands, not sure where I'm going with this. "Very macho."

"You're going to make fun of me because I don't want to talk? What about you? Do you wanna talk about your situation?" His face darkens with a sneer. "Family still not talking to you? How's the guilt for killing Aaron, huh?"

I stare at him. Ears ringing. My hand lifts to my face as if he slapped me. He may as well have because it hurt.

No. I would have preferred a slap. It would have hurt less. Tears swell, and I blink them back, steeling myself by dropping my hand and curling them both into fists.

"You. Have no idea. What you're talking about." I speak around the lump in my throat and the quivering of my chin. My chest constricts, like my heart has been ripped open. The flood of tears escapes, and I spin on my heel, rushing over to my bike.

I'm speeding down the driveway. Adam calls after me, but with the wind, my pulse, and my sobs, his voice is drowned out.

CHAPTER THIRTY

GIVE CHASE

If anyone is waiting to drive me home after my shift ends, I'll spit in their face and ignore them. I toss the garbage in the dumpster, not bothering to glance around the parking lot for a familiar vehicle. I'm not accepting any rides. And if my bike is taken hostage, I guess I'm freaking walking home.

Back inside, the playful, flirtatious banter of my coworkers Carter and Shayla assails my ears. They've been at it the whole shift. She doesn't usually work with him, so she has no idea how obnoxious he is. Maybe she doesn't care.

I ignore them as I finish my cleaning tasks, the last of which is the bathroom. Tonight, that's fine by me. I close the door, muffling their cheery voices.

Wiping down the mirror, I'm forced to face my reflection. My cheeks are splotchy and flushed, my eyes are red and puffy. Annoying, but the customer service guy at the phone place didn't try to haggle with me to buy accessories when I went in to replace my lost cell. When you look like you're going to burst into tears, most people leave you alone.

Thankfully, my coworkers didn't—aren't—bothering to make small talk with me. Partly because the evening is busy, thank god, but mostly because they're flirting with each other.

As gross and explicit as their banter gets, I prefer it over the sting of Adam's words. I've cried all the tears I can cry for today, and I bristle at the memory. Hoping for the chance to spit in his face.

Jerk.

Deliberately and mechanically, I put the cleaning supplies away under the sink. My grip tight, knuckles white and red. I picture strangling the life out of—the GMP comes to mind first. I force it away, trying to picture Adam. But Sahara comes to mind next. I force her away, again trying to picture Adam, to no avail.

When I stand, I see my stupid reflection again, staring at me. Angry, sad, hurt.

My chin quivers.

Nope. Nada. No. Not doing that again. Nope.

Resolve restored, I exit the bathroom. I clock out, calling a halfhearted goodbye to my coworkers—who actually acknowledge me with a return farewell.

The frigid breeze nips at my cheeks and arms, cutting through the hoodie I'm wearing, but I welcome the refreshing air. I ignore the disappointment when I involuntarily search for a familiar SUV and don't see one. Instead, I let anger roil through me as I mount my bike without my helmet. It's somewhere on OSE grounds. Putting on my helmet hadn't been the first thing on my mind when I fled the scene.

As I ride down the street, making my way toward the bike path, my entire body complains. As it has been all day. A soreness that came from Adam's training. Yet another reason for me to want—

Ugh! I need him out of my head. Someone like him doesn't deserve any allocation of brainpower.

At the parking lot I use as a shortcut, I hesitate. Something isn't right.

Several cars are parked over on the far side of the lot for a twenty-four-hour supermarket, and two cars on the opposite side—where I am. One is a van, the other a small sedan. Nothing out of the ordinary. Except the towering security lights aren't on.

I peer around the dark space, biting the inside of my lip. My hair stands on the back on my neck.

Have those overhead lights always been broken on this side?

It's been a while since I've come this way. On a typical day, I follow the road rules and take the main road, but tonight I'm avoiding people and taking the bike path—the path I avoid at night because I have to go under a bridge. Not creepy in the daytime with the sunlight to ward off the shadows. At night, though, the shadows seem to come to life, and, with what I know now, maybe they do.

I shiver.

Remaining where I am, I stare at the light poles as if that'll turn them on.

A figure making their way across the lot catches my attention. I hold my breath, heart thumping. As they grow closer, I relax a little. A young ponytailed blonde woman, maybe around Carol's age—early twenties—beelines toward the sedan with a bag of groceries in each hand. I figure we can keep each other company—at a distance— in this creepy lot.

With an embarrassed chuckle, I make my way across and scold myself for being paranoid. Of course, my brain then makes the argument that, with all the stuff the OSE has taught me, I'd be crazy to *not* be at least a little paranoid.

An engine rumbles to life just as I make it to the other side. I glance back, silently wishing my blonde parking lot companion a farewell—

My thoughts halt. The van a few spaces over from her rolls forward, headlights off. I stare at it as it pulls up alongside her. The side door slides open. A scream of warning erupts from me. The woman looks up just as arms reach out and snatch her into the dark shadows of the van. Her grocery bags spill to the ground.

Do something, Mika! Do something!

I scream again, this one a war cry. I race toward the vehicle. But by the time I'm halfway across, the van is on the main road. My pulse escalates as I speed across the road, cutting through traffic. Horns blare. A truck blasts past me, the wind whipping my hair and shaking my core. I drive my legs hard, barely able to keep the van in sight as it turns down a road, toward a deserted warehouse district.

Can't be a proper bad guy without a warehouse.

"Concentrate," I gasp, trying to pull air into my lungs. My body's telling me to slow down, to stop. It's tired. But I fight it, not wanting to lose track of the kidnappers.

What's your plan?

The thought stalls my brain for a moment. I almost miss the van turning between two buildings up ahead.

Gravel crunches under my tires as the road narrows from two lanes to one. I swerve onto the uneven asphalt, bumpy with overgrown weeds and grass but quieter than rolling along the gravel shoulder. I keep my eyes glued to where the van has turned between two warehouses, slowing as I approach. My pulse is like a drum solo for a heavy metal band.

I'll call the cops.

Better to have a location of where they took the girl than a useless description of the van. I didn't have a chance to get—or to think about getting—the license plate number or the make and model. It's a van. A dark van with tinted windows. Not super helpful info.

Like I do with my keys when I'm locking up work late at night, I keep my movements slow and deliberate. I lean my bike against the rusting wall of a warehouse. Random articles of trash litter the ground: plastic bags, papers, fast-food bags, plastic cups. Dilapidated wood pallets are stacked along some walls. Graffiti overlapping graffiti covers chipped concrete barriers and metal garage doors.

Patches of snow that didn't melt in the afternoon sun glisten under the moonlight. Wind cuts through the air, freezing the sweat on my face. The litter rustles against the ground. I crouch down and move to peek out around the corner. Keeping my feet on the asphalt to avoid the noise of stepping on dried vegetation.

The van is a couple of rows down. Another vehicle idles next to it, a large SUV. Two figures, shrouded in darkness, lean against the van. Their voices carry down to me, but not loud enough for me to make out words. A dumpster sits askew against the wall, missing the plastic lid flaps, about halfway between me and the waiting vehicles. I stare at it for a moment, then back to the kidnappers.

Nothing's happening. Yet.

Just call the cops, my mind scolds me.

I pull back around the corner and slide off my backpack. Unzipping the bag, slowly, quietly, I fish out my brand-new phone and tap the screen to life. I jerk back, blinking hard against the screen's illumination. I turn the brightness all the way down and put the device on silent. I don't want to get caught because of some poorly timed notification.

The two figures haven't moved. Against the objections of my inner voice, I stay crouched and hug the wall as I make my way to the dumpster, scanning the ground as I try to avoid anything that'll crunch underfoot.

Three car doors open and slam closed. Footsteps, a boot scuffing against the asphalt and kicking a piece of gravel. Silence. Then a metallic click, like a lighter being used. Silence again.

"That was quick," a voice says. A familiar monotone, void of emotion.

I freeze, staring in the direction of the vehicles. I can't see them from the dumpster, but I know that voice. The foul, acrid scent of cigarette smoke turns my stomach ill. The wound on my neck pulses with pain at the memory.

Oh, my god.

"I'm nothing if not efficient," says a voice, deep and masculine. "Especially for my favorite, best-paying client."

I swallow hard and peek out from around the dumpster. One of the figures who'd been leaning against the van now stands straight, approaching the smaller, familiar figure. Two tall, broad-shouldered men stand on either side of her. Despite being unable to make out any distinguishable features in the dark, I know who it is.

"Let's see what you brought me," Sahara says, after taking a long drag on the cigarette. The tip glows a bright, fiery orange.

I clutch my phone tight, the realization dawning on me.

INDUCTION

Sahara is responsible for the missing girls.

CHAPTER THIRTY-ONE

ANIMAL PROWESS

I gotta get out of here!

My mind is screaming at me as I huddle next to the dumpster, staring wide-eyed at my exit. My heartbeat is so loud it drowns Sahara's and the kidnappers chatter as they presumably seem to examine the young woman.

Oh, god. I fear what they plan to do with her. Something I had a small taste of while in Sahara's grasp. The burn scar on my neck stings.

A tremor in my hands makes it difficult to unlock my phone. My eyes go in and out of focus, the image of Sahara jabbing the electrical prod into her sister playing over and over behind my eyes. Somehow, I get the messenger app open. Maybe I should call 911. That'd be the smart thing to do. But I don't. I open a chat with Vic, texting "SOS. Sahara," tap the send button, and share my location.

"She'll do," Sahara states, her tone empty and blasé.

With the message sent, I find the will to move. Legs shaky and aching as I shift forward. I move slowly along the wall, using it to keep me from falling, while keeping a death grip on my phone. The need to run to safety overwhelms my ability to breathe. Not wanting to be in the clutches of that psycho again—

CRUNCH!

I freeze. A heartbeat passes. I glance at my feet. A dirty plastic cup from a fast-food restaurant is crushed under my foot.

I'm dead.

"Did you hear that?"

"Someone's there."

"Go check it out," Sahara's apathetic voice commands. "You two, load up the girl."

I sprint for my bike. Shouts erupts behind me, joined by the thudding footsteps of rapid pursuit. Phone still clutched in my hand, I push my bike, racing alongside it before jumping on. A hand brushes the back of my arm and I let out a panicked whimper.

I pedal hard and fast, switching gears to pick up speed. Curses ring out behind me. Fear and adrenaline ward off the aches and chill as I navigate my escape route, locking on the streetlights and traffic sounds.

Something heavy strikes me between my shoulder blades. My body slams forward, and I hit the ground hard. The rough surface grinds against my cheek. Gravel rips through the knees of my pants, tearing my flesh. Some protruding metal on my bike stabs my calf. I groan, push myself up and stumble forward.

"You again?"

The voice brings me to a halt. My hands shake violently, fingers numb. Warm blood trickles down the side of my face, cooling as it reaches my neck.

"God, they really are desperate, aren't they?" Sahara punctuates her statement with a humorless laugh. The sound drains any remaining warmth from my body. I'm going to die. Or something worse.

Go! Run!

I try following the commands my brain shouts at me. My legs are heavy like lead, but I lift them. Limping forward like a zombie, but I'm moving.

"Are we really doing this? Look at yourself." Her footsteps follow me; they're slow and patient. "You can barely move."

She's right. My movements are stiff, slow. Whatever hit me in the back has me struggling for air. Running is more of a desperate shuffle.

"This is one of the most pathetic things I've ever seen." She sighs. "I do admire your tenacity, though." Her tone says otherwise.

If I can't run, maybe I can stall.

I turn to face her. Her dark clothing—combat boots, tactical pants, and jacket—make her almost invisible against the night as she bends down and picks up a long metal rod from the ground near my bike: the object that must have hit me in the back. Her henchmen and the kidnappers are nowhere to be seen, probably securing the girl they kidnapped. She must be alone, I realize, and this steels my resolve. I need to keep her occupied for a bit, just until Vic and the others arrive.

"So, it's you." I gasp, words tearing painfully from my throat. "You're the one. Taking the girls."

"Am I?"

She comes toward me, and I take a step back, an instinctual recoil.

"I saw you. You hired those men to kidnap someone."

"How do you know I wasn't stopping those men?"

I scoff, taking another step back. "Yeah, you seem the type to go out of your way to help people."

Her teeth flash white in a grin. The menacing grin of a predator. "Perhaps. That all depends on your definition of help."

"Mine differs from yours. One-hundred percent." Another step back, and I try to convince my body to find the strength to run. But whatever adrenaline I had is spent.

Please, please hurry, Vic! I clutch my hands, realizing they're empty.

The dim glow of my phone draws my attention. It's on the ground, a few feet from my bike. I wonder how much time has passed between now and when I sent the text. Has it been minutes? Mere seconds? I have to keep stalling, but I don't think I can stall for ten minutes, much less five. Sahara doesn't seem the type to carry on a monologue for that long.

She confirms this doubt as she lets out another sigh and lengthens her stride, continuing toward me casually holding the metal rod. I flash back to the electric rod she used while I was in her captivity. The sound of sizzling flesh, emphasized by the stench of burnt meat. The memory pumps a little more energy into my muscles.

I spin on my heel and take off running. The flash of adrenaline keeps the limp from my step. The main road is in sight, and I race toward the red glow of brake lights lining up on the busy street. I will not stumble. I refuse to be taken again. The others will show up, and they'll take her down. This nightmare will be over.

Thwack!

Metal connects with the back of my legs. I fall to the ground. Hands and knees catch me from face-planting. My jaw is forced shut by the jarring hit, and my teeth clamp down on my tongue. Blood fills my mouth. I scramble across the ground on all fours, knees wet with snow, unable to find my feet.

There's a chain link fence in front of me, nearly collapsed. I scurry under it to an empty field littered with plastic and paper. Blood drips from my mouth onto a torn napkin from a fast-food chain, Bo's Fried Chicken. I stare at the yellow chicken head logo for a discombobulated moment.

Clink, clink, clink, clink.

The sound of metal being dragged across the fence,

tapping the poles meant to keep it erect, propels me to get my butt in gear. I push to my feet only to collapse to my knees. Tears stream down my face, mixing with blood and spit and dripping off my chin. I crawl to a log. No. Not a log—a downed light pole.

The metal rattles, followed by a thump.

Mika, run!

But I can't. I can't even breathe my throat is so tight with fear. I'm going to die.

"Despite my animal-like prowess, I hate the chase," Sahara says, her voice too close for comfort. "I find it tedious and unnecessary."

I start to climb over the light pole. If I can just—

She kicks me between the shoulder blades. Not hard, but I collapse to my stomach. She grabs a handful of my hair and pulls my head back. I cry out. She slams her knee into my back, pinning me down. My flailing does nothing to stop her.

"I'm left with a decision," she whispers in my ear, her breath hot and rotten against my numb face. "Do I kill you? A quick snap of your neck. Or…" She yanks my head back harder.

I yelp, and more tears fall, stinging the abrasion on my face.

"Do I use you? The thorn in my side that you've been, it would almost be poetic."

"Just—" I swallow, trying to find my voice.

"What's that?" She lowers her head beside mine, her

hair a short, dark curtain framing her face. Her pupils fully dilated, making her eyes appear completely black.

"Do it. Get it over with. I thought you didn't like being tedious."

A displeased snarl of a grin splits her face. "As you wish."

My chin quivers, and I close my eyes. She lets go of my hair and lifts her knee from my back. I clench my jaw, bracing myself, then roll to the right. I grab her leg and yank hard. She comes off balance, a strangled growl of surprise breaking her menacing character as she falls to the ground.

Go, go, go!

I half crawl, half lumber like a hunchback. Wanting—*needing* to get as much distance between us as I can.

"You. Little. Bit—"

She doesn't finish her curse. I don't look to see why, until—

"Mika!"

CHAPTER THIRTY-TWO

Thorns

My heart swells, eyes flooding again, but with relief.

"Mika!" Vic pulls me to my feet. My best friend, clad in black from head to toe, wraps his arms around me in a death grip of a hug. I relish the safety of his warmth.

Our reunion is interrupted when Vic spins around, pulling me behind him in one easy, fluid movement. He lifts a sword to block a hit from Sahara. A sharp clang rings out as the weapons collide. She swings the rod again. He blocks, pivots, then kicks. His long legs knocking her back several feet.

A low chuckle rises from her, and she lifts her chin to him. "Method clean, but raw. Vicky, sweetie, what are they teaching you at the school?"

"Why don't you stick around and find out?" This comes from a figure standing behind her. Clad in the same black gear as Vic. The voice familiar, and not unwelcome at the moment. Adam shifts in his position, the blade of his sword almost invisible, the metal as black as his clothes.

"Ah, Elvis has joined the chat," she says, her words cut with bitterness as she glances at him. "You tried to blow me up."

"Sorry I missed," Adam says.

Sahara looks between the three of us. Her gaze finds me, and the look makes my skin crawl. That evil grin stretches her face, and she lunges toward me.

Vic spins me out of the way and blocks the blow. But Sahara anticipates and ducks around him. I panic, stumbling backward, the metal rod swinging inches from my face. I hit the ground hard. But I don't feel anything. Sahara's bloodthirsty eyes lock onto me as she moves in for a killing strike.

Clang!

My heart hammers. *I can't…I can't…* My eyes grow wide as I stare at the rod inches from my face, a black blade stopping it from smashing into my skull.

Adam pushes the rod away, then spins and kicks, catching her low on the leg. She's not fazed, raising the rod to block a hit from Vic. Adam tandems with him, launching his own strike against Sahara. She dances out of reach, growling. She sprints and does the most ninja thing out of all of them: somersaulting out of range.

An odd hush settles over the area. The boys pant, watching and waiting. I'm still on my butt, staring up at them, hands curled into the ground. Something is pricking my palms, but I don't dare look away.

Sahara shifts. The boys tense. She flings a disc on the ground at their feet, and they both jump back. One of them lets out a curse. Smoke vents from the object. She races toward them, swinging at Adam. He blocks, ducking and pivoting out of her reach. She dives and rolls, arching the rod in a low hit. It connects with his knee. He lets out a grunt, stumbling to the side.

That's all she needs. She springs to her feet and charges him. The smoke spreads, compromising my view of the fight. Vic shouts something, his blade flashing gold in the moonlight. I see him block a fatal blow to Adam's face before the dark cloud completely envelops them. There are clangs of metal, and grunts and hisses.

I don't know what to do. But I don't have to decide.

Vic bursts from the smoke, grabs my arm and pulls me up. We're running across the field, away from the fight.

"What…what about—" I gasp. I can't catch my breath to save my life, much less form a sentence. But I'm sure Vic has a game plan, right? They're trained for this.

Right?

We keep moving, skirting gopher holes, tumbleweeds, and patches of snow until we reach a dirt road where an SUV is parked. Vic reaches his hand to his ear, staring in the direction we've come, visibility impeded by the night. I think I can just make out the smoke cloud.

"Vic—" I start to say, but then the ninja speaks.

"Copy that," he says, hand to his ear. "We're at the

SUV."

He's alert, taking in his surroundings.

The rush from fleeing for my life is wearing off, and I realize the ninja in front of me, speaking through a communication device in his ear, isn't Vic. For one, that was not his voice. For two, he's too short, his eyes nearly level with mine.

"Copy that." The masked figure pulls off his mask.

Adam.

Panting, he gives me a relieved look. I think it's the first time I've ever seen him gasping for air. He didn't gasp for breath like this when we ran through the forest, away from Sahara.

"She's retreating," he says.

The statement should provide relief, but apprehension prevails. She's still out there. A shiver works its way through me, pulling my body tense. And I'm standing here with the guy I hate.

"You're freezing." He moves his gloved grip from my arm down to my hand. Pain pricks into my palm and I yelp, jerking away from him. I lift my hands. The glow of the moon revealing little round thorns stuck in my flesh. Goathead thorns, my parents always called them. Famous for popping bike tires with their horn-like spikes.

"Let me," he says softly. In a quick, unreal movement, he sheaths the sword on his back. He takes my hand in both of his and I tense, wanting to pull away.

He just saved your life. You almost died.

I grit my teeth, but allow him to pull three thorns from my right hand and one from my other hand. The flesh stings, and little dots of blood well up. When he's done, I pull away, grinding my teeth so hard my jaw aches.

"Come on." He reaches toward me, and I recoil. The fear from Sahara fading, the anger at Adam reigniting.

His eyes flash and his lips part, but he doesn't say anything. He moves to the SUV and opens the passenger door. "Should get your face looked at too. It's bleeding."

A dozen snarky comments come to mind—Thanks, Captain Obvious. No shit, Sherlock. You think, dumbass? But do I say them? No. My jaw is locked tight. If I try to talk, in all likelihood, I'll start crying.

He is right about one thing, though. I am freezing and injured. Keeping as safe a distance from him that I can, I situate myself in the passenger seat. I ignore the hurt blatant on his face, but can't ignore his slight limp as he rounds the SUV to the driver's side.

He brings the vehicle to life with a turn of a key. He turns the heat on full blast, then reaches over and adjusts the vents to blow directly at me. The warmth is calming and soothing, and much appreciated.

I still hate the guy though.

CHAPTER THIRTY-THREE

IMPS

An awkward—but thankfully short—car ride with Adam, a warm shower, a recounting of how I wound up in Sahara's sights again, and three butterfly bandages to my face later, Elizabeth and I enter my house through the back entrance. The kitchen is dark, save for the dim glow coming from the living room.

Elizabeth volunteered to stay at my house for the night, just in case. No one argued, despite her hand still being in a cast. We had to use the spare key at the back of the house to get in, since I'd lost my backpack at the warehouse district. There were some homeless folks about. It's possible one of them snatched it, which would be the best-case scenario. I try not to think about what Sahara could learn from the contents of my backpack.

A soft ruff comes from the living room.

"It's okay, Lick," I call in a hushed whisper. Her paws click on the hardwood floor as her dark form lumbers into the kitchen, tail wagging low in greeting. I crouch down, crooning, "Hey, who's the best girl?"

Elizabeth joins me in the crouched position and holds her hand out to the black lab. "She's so cute." The dog sniffs her hand and decides she's good by licking her knuckles, then shoving her head into the girl's hand to receive pets. Elizabeth gratefully obliges, cooing compliments to the old dog.

With the creak of a floorboard, a figure appears from the living room. My dad's voice whispers across the kitchen, "You're home awful late, boo."

"I know. I'm sorry," I whisper back as I move forward to greet him. Elizabeth follows me. We're illuminated by soft light cast by the TV. My mouth bobs as I try to come up with an explanation for why I've brought a friend over.

"Who—Oh, god, Mika! What happened to your face?" Dad's eyes widen, and he reaches out, as if to touch my face, then lets his hand fall to the side. The wrinkles of concern, and his sunken eyes, make him look as if he's aged well over fifty, though he turned forty-eight just last month.

"I fell. Off by bike." My pulse hammers in my ears at the lie, but it's not a complete lie. Not really.

"You've got to wear your helmet," he says as he shakes his head at me, reaching down to pet Licorice as the dog ambles past before curling up in her bed. Dad's attention turns to the dark-haired girl standing beside me.

"This is Elizabeth. She's a classmate at the new

school." I gesture between the two. "This is my dad."

"It's nice to meet you, Mr. Finley." Elizabeth smiles and offers her hand.

"Nice to meet you as well." They shake, then he looks at me again, his lips pinched. "Be careful, okay?" He then returns to the couch to watch late night shows.

Something in his voice makes me think he knows exactly what kind of school—and risks—I'm getting myself into.

Thankfully, Elizabeth doesn't comment, and ten minutes later I'm inflating a twin-size air mattress in my bedroom for her. She brought a velvet pack of throwing knives with her, as well as a long knife with a curved, garnet red blade and an equally red wooden hilt. She lays it on the floor next to her backpack.

"You didn't have to do this," I say, putting on the fitted sheet.

"I know. I'm sure Vic could have stayed over—your family knows him—but…" She falls silent, pulling down the corners of the sheet on her side.

I halt my bed-making a moment to regard her sitting on her knees on the other side of the mattress. A sad, regretful expression crosses her face.

"But what?" I prod gently, reaching for the flat sheet.

"You should know what happened," she says, her voice so quiet I almost don't hear her.

The sheet in my hands is a light blue with pink roses on it. My family's had these since I was a kid. Maybe longer. I run my fingers along it, tracing the flowers, waiting for her to tell her and her evil twin's story.

"I told you when Elena…" She rubs a hand over her face. "When *Sahara* and I were kids, we were attacked by imps."

"What are imps?" *God, Mika, let the girl tell her story.*

She's not bothered by my interruption though. "They're a type of ghoul, but what classifies them as imps is that they're small, about the size of a five-year-old kid. So, like, three feet tall, give or take a few inches. They're flesh-eaters, with rows of needles for teeth and grimy, eight-fingered hands."

"They live under bridges that people pass under. So, if the bridge is over water, but has a path that leads under it, they live there. But if there isn't some path for humans, they don't care about the bridge."

I nod. "Makes sense. They're flesh-eaters. No use hanging out where the food won't walk by."

"Anyway." She lets out a long breath. "We wanted to go to the corner store to get some snacks, our parents told us no, not by ourselves, but we went anyway. Snuck out. Our parents knew to come look for us because the house was too quiet without us home bickering.

"They saved our stupid little behinds just in time. And our world was never the same. We had nightmares for months, and then our parents knew they couldn't keep us out of the ninja world." She looks up at me with a sad smile. "Mom always said being in the organization was a black hole. Anyone close enough will get pulled in and lost in the abyss."

I keep quiet, holding the flat sheet.

"They enrolled us in the OSE, but they—'they' being my mom—were very hesitant. I'm not sure why. Maybe she didn't think we were ready for it, as we were only eight years old. But we knew monsters existed and that our parents knew how to fight them. We either needed to be trained, or we'd die doing something stupid." She chuckles a little, but it's strained with sadness.

"Looking back, I remember Dad being all about it. Mom wasn't so happy, but she also pushed us the hardest, until we turned fourteen and were assigned our first mission. She almost didn't let us out the door but didn't have a choice. Sahara and I were excited. We were like trusted adults. And we did really good. We were so in sync, reading each other's minds, knowing when to cut the crap and get serious."

She's quiet again. I set the sheet on the bed, my hands clammy from holding it. I'm not sure I want to hear what she's building up the strength to say, but I know I need to hear it. I was at the mercy—or lack thereof—of her sister twice in less than a week. Like her mother said, the AIO is a black hole, and I've been pulled in. Whether I like it or not.

"Mom was not the same after that," she continues. "She grew quiet, withdrawn, her actions bordering on paranoia. Not using the tablets or laptops or cell phones assigned by the organization. Sahara had pointed these things out to me, and I just chalked it up to Mom being scared of losing her kids. It made sense." She swallows hard. "Last spring, Mom and Dad went out for the night. It was their anniversary. Mom was happy again. But something happened.

"The report says they went to save a homeless man from some imps, but it was a trap. The homeless man wasn't that at all, but something worse. Like an imp on steroids. The SOS sent from my dad's phone was not received in time. Their bodies were found torn. Ripped..." She struggles to continue, but I get enough of the picture that she doesn't have to explain.

Her parents are dead, a failed SOS leaving them without backup. Her sister takes that as a betrayal of the AIO, the OSE, and leaves them. Joining up with whoever decided it's a good idea to mix together a mountain lion and a demon.

"I get it. We all get it," she says, wiping the tears from her cheeks. "We get why Sahara is so hurt."

I scoff. A quiet one, but it's a scoff all the same. "That's not the word I'd use."

Immediately feeling like a jerk, I start to apologize when she waves me off.

"No. You're right. She's hurting, but she's also pissed off, enraged, and using that to justify her actions of hurting others: you, those girls she's taking. Who even knows." She sighs, picking at her cast, face pinched in thought. Possibly wondering about all the evil, sadistic things her sister could be up to.

"Well..." I have no words though. No encouragement or reassurance. Her own sister is the villain in this story. What is anybody supposed to do about that?

"Thanks," she says, reaching for the sheet and pulling it open.

"What for?" I help her situate the sheet.

"For listening. And not, I don't know, hating me, I guess."

I grab two pillows and place them at the head of the mattress. "I mean, I'm not happy about it. Your sister. I feel...I don't know. The situation with Sahara could have been dealt with sooner, but you told me the truth from the start. And you saved my life." I shrug, offering a little smile. "Play some video games with my sister in the morning, and we can be friends."

She reaches her hand over to me. "Deal."

We both yawn big, our eyes watering after. A silent agreement that it's time for sleep. She gets settled in the bed, tucking the throwing knives and garnet knife under the pillows before she pulls the comforter up to her chin.

I turn off the lights and get into my bed. The heaviness of the day settles in. My heart took a beating, aching as much as the muscles overworked from Adam's session the day before.

God, that feels like such a long time ago. I don't want to think about it, and yet, I'm sure as I fall asleep, that's what I'll dream about. Visions of metal rods, malicious grins from an Elizabeth lookalike, and a monster version of Aaron with rows of needle-like teeth.

CHAPTER THIRTY-FOUR

WHAT BEST FRIENDS ARE FOR

I wake to animated, upbeat music, along with overdone slashing of *sshings* and grunts. I lie in my bed, blinking hard at the ceiling, then glance down at the floor to see the air mattress empty of Elizabeth. I frown. No way she just gets up and goes to play videogames in a strange house.

I force myself to sit up, mildly surprised my body doesn't ache as much as I thought it would. My palms feel bruised, and the abrasion on my face is kind of itchy, along with the cut on my calf and scratched knees, but yesterday's tormenting soreness is faint.

Out in the living room, I first spot Elizabeth on the end of the couch, focused on the TV in front of her. Her long, dark braid hangs over her shoulder. Anita sits next to her with a smirk of confidence, controller in hand and clad in her warrior princess pajamas. A gold headband restrains her wavy auburn hair.

I hear his voice before I see him, and I'm grinning. The

girls are giggling as Vic struggles to maneuver his avatar. His hair pulled back in a ponytail, short free-flies framing his face. Him being here explains why Elizabeth is up and about.

While I know he's a decent gamer, it fills my heart to see him "struggling" for Anita's benefit, making comments about how he can take down people twice his size in real life but not a tiny digital fairy character. He mock-growls in defeat as Anita's avatar does a victory dance on his character's downed body.

"Best two out of three," he prompts.

"That's not how math works. What were the first four matches?" Anita makes a face at him.

"Practice," he says.

Anita shrugs, swiftly maneuvering through the game menu to set up another match. "Sucks to suck. What map do you want?"

He catches me watching from the hall and smiles a little, then turns back to the game. He passes the remote to Elizabeth. "You know what? I bow to the queen, but do not mistake my retreat as surrender. See if you can beat this champ. Pretty sure she passed the Elven Tower of Darkness on the highest difficulty."

"Really?" Anita looks up at Elizabeth, face full of disbelief and admiration. "I'm working on tier seven."

"Oof, the Bard of Jayda is rough. Took me two months to get past him."

Anita starts to reply but her gaze jumps to me, her

brown eyes growing with horror. "Mika, your face, what happened?"

Both Vic and Elizabeth look between us. Vic's mouth opens.

"This is what happens when you don't wear your helmet," I say, beating my friend to the punch, raising a hand to my cheek.

"Yikes. Wear a helmet next time." Anita shakes her head and clicks her tongue at me. "Anyway." She turns to Elizabeth. "For defeating the Bard, did you focus more on upgrading your magic or your weapons?"

The two start to compare stories. Vic and I head into the kitchen.

"Thanks for entertaining her," I say. "I mean that."

"No problem. She's actually gotten better since we last played." He pours some coffee in a mug, then glances at me with a smile. His smile doesn't reach his eyes though. Probably as unsettled and pissed off about Sahara as I am.

"So, what did Adam do to you?" He keeps his voice low with a glance toward the living room, where the game sounds as lively as ever, along with the sustained chatter of two game nerds.

I puff out a breath. So maybe he isn't thinking about Sahara and her evil plans. My spat with Adam feels so long ago. Gotta say, I'm irked at Vic for bringing it up. I slump down at the dining table and pick at a crack in the wood.

"He was freaking out yesterday, wouldn't elaborate why. Kept saying that he messed up," Vic continues, leaning against the counter, cradling his coffee. He almost looks relaxed, except his gaze bores into me, a seriousness in his eyes. Reminding me of how his mother interrogates him and his younger brother when they're trying to hide something from her. "How badly do I need to kick his ass?"

As much as I would love to see that, I don't want to relive the interaction with Adam. I lean back and look out the window to the backyard, where Licorice lies in a patch of sunlight. Content. Happy. I wish I could be her. My worst problem would be finding a proper place to lie in the sun.

"You said he was going through something," I say, changing the subject. I fix Vic with my own no-nonsense look. "He gave me a whole speech about needing to train even when I feel like I got hit by a car, or else people will die. Did someone close to him die?"

With a muttering of words in another language, he sits down across the table from me. He stares into his coffee. He's always been sensitive when talking about other people's troubles and backgrounds. He says it's weird and wrong.

"While it's not my story to tell—"

I let out an exhale through clenched teeth, but he holds up his hand to keep me from interrupting.

"But Adam isn't on my nice list right now." He takes a small sip, then sets the mug down, curling his fingers into fists. His knuckles turn white and red. He's angrier than I thought. At least he's back on my side now, which is where the best friend is supposed to be.

"I'm not privy to all the details. The reports don't have the full story. They never do." He releases his fists and traces his fingers along the coffee mug.

"It happened in January. Adam was on a mission with his mentor in New York. It went really, really bad. He was in the hospital for a couple of months. You'd never guess he just learned how to walk again six months ago." He pushes the mug away from himself. "And Celine, his mentor, has been in a vegetative state since."

Oh. While I thought it was something along those lines, I didn't expect to feel like a jerk for my earlier actions, trying to drag this out of Adam.

Nope. He was a jerk to you first. It's not your fault.

Nevertheless, the guilt weighs me down. Why couldn't I have been more understanding? I knew he was going through something. Even if I didn't have details, the shame was etched on his face. The same grief and guilt also live in the very depths of my soul.

"I have a feeling he's the one who messed up, and Celine paid the price." He clears his throat. "He's waiting for the inevitable phone call from her partner—we all are—whenever she decides it's time to pull the plug." The last words come out in a whisper.

Oh, god. Poor Adam.

Even the music from Anita's game in the living room has turned somber. A solo piano piece.

"Anyway." Vic takes the mug in one hand and raises an eyebrow. "How badly do I need to destroy him? Broken bones in sparring are rare, but they do happen."

I blink at the sudden segue, and take a hot second to process what he said.

"What? No. That's—Really? You would break his leg or something?"

He chuckles, a sinister sound emphasized by a perfect-toothed grin. "Dislocated shoulders, dislocated knees, broken noses, broken fingers, broken foot, broken ribs, and a chipped tooth. All injuries I've been responsible for when sparring got a little rowdy. Oh, and I've knocked a couple people out."

"Oh." I frown at the table. Am I willing to accept the hazards of ninja training? Currently, I'm beaten and bruised. Might as well give the injuries a purpose. Right?

"So, you going to tell me, or not?"

"Not." I rub the bridge of my nose, thinking about bartering with him, quid pro quo. He has stuff he's not telling me, but does that matter? He'll tell me when he's ready. He always has. The confrontation with Adam is begging to be acknowledged.

"I just…" I tell him what Adam said about my guilt over Aaron's death.

"That wasn't your fault," he hisses, trying to keep his voice down. He moves the coffee mug away from him, the dark liquid sloshing. "He's dead." His following string of words come out in mixed English and German, maybe some French.

"He should know—he *does* know better!" Vic is on his feet, pacing the length of the floor between the table and the kitchen island.

"I, uh." I swallow the lump in my throat, low-key hating myself for saying this, but I do. "His reactions weren't completely unwarranted. I may have…" I wince. "Goaded him."

He stops pacing as I explain what I said to Adam. With a slump of his shoulders, his anger dissipates. "This is a mess. I should have told you what his deal was sooner. I hate talking about people like that though." A conflicted expression twists his face. "Lame excuse in this case."

I shrug, wanting this conversation to end. "Who knows, dude. I could have still said the same stupid thing."

He purses his lips, eyes narrowing. "I'm still going to break something on his person. As the best friend, I have a responsibility to do so."

I chuckle, but it's halfhearted. I won't object to that. Adam's words hurt. If Vic wants to break his ankles or nose in a "mishap" while sparring, I won't argue.

CHAPTER THIRTY-FIVE

ANOTHER STICKY SITUATION

Vic and I are hanging out in the schoolroom, after a debrief and follow-up from last night's events.

"So, if demons are real, that implies angels are too," I say, gazing up at the projector screen. He sits next to me, filling out a report that he was meant to do last night.

"Uh, yeah, I guess," he says, preoccupied. "I mean, I don't know. Just because things are implied doesn't mean that they are."

"Hm." I mull that over but wind up getting distracted when I look over at him filling out his report about fighting Sahara at the warehouse district.

On arriving at the school this morning, Hogan informed us that the AIO liaison with local law enforcement was told of Sahara's possible connection to the missing girls. They'd have teams on the lookout for her and the men she'd hired.

"Do you think the police liaison was told about me

seeing the beast? From the car accident?" I'm watching Vic type but not reading the words. At my question, his fingers pause, hovering over the tablet.

"Uh, maybe." He shifts in his seat, pulling his legs up to sit on them cross-legged. "I don't know. Correspondence with the liaison go through Hogan or Nelly, and sometimes Jacqulyn."

"Hm."

Jacqulyn and Devon did a more in-depth recon mission of the abandoned warehouse district, noting squatters and vagrants sleeping in the buildings' deepest recesses. The area was only used by Sahara as a meeting place, a place to exchange a human life for money.

"What do you think Sahara wants with those girls?" They had all been around Sahara's own age. Was that a clue? I frown at the projector screen, as if it's the one failing to present the answer.

Vic continues tapping away. "Do you really want to know what she's doing to them?"

I grimace at that question. He has a point. We're dealing with a psycho who not only tampers with DNA but is also in league with a demon. Thinking of her old hideout's empty, bloodstained cells, I pull my knees up and hug them close.

"Why didn't you guys take down Sahara sooner?" It's a big question, but I've been attacked by her twice, and I think I deserve an answer.

Vic sighs and sets the tablet down, looking haggard.

Despite his usual stupid grin and upbeat demeanor, this whole situation, and whatever secrets he holds, seem to be wearing on him. "We didn't know where her hideout was. About two months ago the AIO approved GPS tracking chips for all EONs who go on missions. Elizabeth was one of the first of us to get one, which is what led us to finding you both in the first place."

I recall the story of how Elizabeth lost her parents. Sahara's comment "They've approved the trackers too late" makes sense now. If their parents would have had the trackers, maybe they'd still be alive. But with how paranoid their mom had started to become about the AIO, would she have gotten one? I guess their dad would have.

More questions come to mind that Vic may not have the answers to, but I ask the one he might.

"Why didn't you all take her down when you rescued me and Elizabeth?"

"We didn't have the manpower to operate a full assault." The voice comes from behind us, and we both turn to see Adam. He stands at a desk across the walkway. His hands are shoved in his pants pockets, shoulders hunched to better portray his misery.

"Vic was in Peru, Elizabeth was held captive," he continues, not looking at us, "and we didn't know what kind of shape she was in. There wasn't time to get outside backup, and we knew we needed to initiate a rescue mission. Hogan has been working through the AIO channels for some backup for a future elimination mission, but until we know where to strike, there's nothing we can do."

His eyes lift briefly to mine. "Can I talk with you?"

"After I break your jaw, no, you won't be able to," Vic says, his tone convivial but his expression hard.

Adam ducks his head. "It's a little late for that remedy."

"Maybe, but it'd still hurt. I'd feel better, Mika would feel better, and you would be in pain." Vic shrugs, nonchalant despite the topic. "Our goal: achieved."

An uncomfortable silence fills the room. The two lock gazes. My best friend, somehow both relaxed and angry. Adam has a miserable frown pulling at his lips. I shift in my seat, wanting to break the silence. While I'd like to have Adam knocked down a peg, I'd rather Vic not get in trouble for that.

"Oh, there you are." Nelly's southern twang carries from the entrance of the schoolroom. "Hogan found a loophole, honey. I have some papers for you to sign."

I don't realize she's talking to me until she hands me a tablet. She doesn't seem to notice the tension, but being a teacher, maybe she's immune to the fluctuating, hormonally-charged atmosphere that teenagers create.

Adam turns away, fidgeting with the laptop on the desk he's leaning against. Vic's locked on him, like a predator watching prey.

"We'll be able to train you on property." Nelly shows me where to sign on the tablet, and hands me the stylus.

I'm beginning to realize that when they say paper, they mean "virtual" paper. Which is good for the trees, I guess.

Does that matter? You're starting your training! You're going to learn how to fight!

Vic snaps his attention away from his kill stare at Adam. He turns to Nelly, grinning big. "Oh, sick! It's about freaking time!"

The older woman chuckles, crow's feet deepening with her smile. "Yeah, I know." She props her tattooed hand on her hip and drags the other through her short black hair. "Politics."

I'd squeal like a fangirl if I was the type. Instead, I just grin and sign my name, not bothering to read the paper first.

"Oh, Mika, since you and Adam have been working together," she says, "we'll continue that. Give him a chance to work toward the instructor position."

My hand freezes while scrawling my last name, the length of the L in "Finley" cut short. Horror seizes me. The excitement that was building collapses harshly to the ground. *What? No!*

The guy who savagely ripped open my old wound, with no regard for the consequences, says, "Um, I don't know."

"You want the teaching experience, hon." Nelly turns to him. "This is the best opportunity you'll have. Take advantage of it for the next, what, two months, until she's officially part of the OSE."

Somehow, I manage to finish my signature, unable to

find the words to object to Nelly's decision.

"We'll assess how you're feeling in a couple of days," the older woman continues, placing her tattooed hand on my shoulder. "And Adam will get you started. Welcome to the family, honey." She squeezes my shoulder with a wink, then leaves the room with the tablet. Completely oblivious to the revulsion she just caused.

The three of us stare at each other, Adam's face blanched and sick. Can't say I'm not wearing the same expression, though, as my stomach ties into knots. Vic looks confused and annoyed, huffing unintelligible words under his breath.

"Maybe I can talk her out of it," Adam says, sending an apologetic glance my way.

"Good luck," Vic murmurs, his tone instilling more dread than Nelly's words. "No one talks her out of anything. Plus, it would be uncharacteristic of you to deny the opportunity to teach."

"But—"

"I can't—"

Adam and I both speak at the same time. I avoid looking at him.

Vic dismisses our objections with a wave and stands, saying, "I don't like it either, but the woman has spoken. Plus, if you told her what was going on, she'd turn it into another learning opportunity.

"Remember Pierce and Reno?" he continues. He gives Adam a serious look. "She had them take all their classes and training together? Even made them sit next to each other at the dinner table." He glances at me. "Those two are real pieces of work. They still hate each other."

"Not helpful," I mutter, sinking in my chair. I hide my face in my hands. The sting from the abrasion is a welcome disruption from this ludicrous outcome.

Adam sighs with defeat. "He's right."

Am I really supposed to accept this? I'd rather face Sahara again. What happens if I "offend" Adam again?

I have to deal with the guilt and shame every single time I return home, any time I reconsider getting my driver's license, or when I wake up from a nightmare. I can't have someone who doesn't know me shoving it in my face.

"Don't worry." Vic returns to his seat next to me. "I'll be around as much as I'm able to." He ducks his head, trying to get my attention.

When I do peek at him from behind my hands, he says, "He so much as steps out of line, I break one of his bones."

It's a nice promise and sentiment, but does nothing to ease the tension and dread.

CHAPTER THIRTY-SIX

LET THE REAL WORK BEGIN

Four days later, Jacqulyn picks me up on her way home from work and examines the abrasion on my cheek. A thin, red, healing scar is all that remains from my latest run-in with Sahara. The beast's scratches on my arm are turning pink with scar tissue, as is the cigarette burn on my neck.

Jacqulyn clears me for self-defense training. Part of me wishes she didn't. I take my sweet time getting my butt to the gym on the top floor of the school, where I'm sure Adam waits. Hopefully Vic is already there, as promised by his text five minutes ago.

I glance into the dining room as I pass. Elizabeth sits at the table, earbuds in, head bobbing as she writes in a notebook next to an open textbook.

Devon emerges from the door leading to the kitchen behind her, carrying a plate of apple slices. He catches me looking in and says, "Physics," complete with a derisive gesture at the textbook.

I give him a sympathetic look before continuing on my way. Trying to wrap my head around physics sounds way more appealing than dealing with Adam.

Jonah's in the game room, with a piano keyboard set up facing the window. He plays a short melody before stopping and leaning forward to write on the papers arrayed on the music rack. I wonder if he's writing a new song or something. He's not in a band anymore, but that doesn't mean he'd stop composing music, right?

How does a boy band become a band of ninjas? Or vice versa, I think, as I remember Elizabeth saying they're second—third?—generation OSE. They were born into the ninja game.

I cross the floor, staying light on my feet so as to not disturb him. Once I'm close enough, I read the notes he's writing... Recipes. Unless the amount of butter used on a Thanksgiving turkey is code for what keys he needs to play on the piano, it's unlikely he's composing music.

I tiptoe out of the room and continue my slow trod, pulling my arms around myself. Attempting to ward off the nausea. *Deep breaths, Mika. Deep breaths.* I repeat the mantra as I climb the staircase.

"Is today the day?" Hogan's coming down the stairs ahead of me, tablet in hand. He's not smiling, but there's a gentler expression on his face than his usual stoic one.

I nod. Words aren't something I'm capable of forming.

He stops next to me. "Nervous?"

Another nod and an attempt at a smile.

"Understandable. Adam doesn't have a lot of experience teaching, but he's always had a lot of patience. You've met his brothers." He pauses. "Well, when I say brothers, I mean Jonah."

"I guess so."

"You'll do fine." He pats my back and resumes his descent.

"You really think so?" I ask. The older man stops, now several stairs below me, and looks up at me. I continue before he can speak. "I mean, you guys typically recruit people with backgrounds in martial arts or an above average GPA. I…I don't have any of that."

He regards me for a moment before saying, "We don't just look for physical and academic aptitude, Mika. There's more to being an EON than that. What good is a fighter with no morals or integrity? Loyalty and trust? Willpower and initiative?"

He winks at me. He truly is Nelly's husband with just that mannerism.

"You'll do fine," he repeats and continues on his way.

I know his words were meant to be encouraging, but my shoulders sag, along with my mouth. He made being a ninja sound so noble. Like being a knight of the round table or one of the truth scholars in Anita's videogames.

Can I do this?

Upbeat music carries down the hall at the top of the stairs, pulling me from my thoughts. The singer's smooth, resolute voice insists that she's unstoppable.

"Can't relate," I mutter.

I'm at the entrance of the training room, standing out of view from anyone inside. Taking deep breaths to still my racing heart. The song ends and silence rings in my ears.

The next song starts up, quiet at first before the drums intro the singer. The guitar and bass complement his raw, aggressive voice, telling the listener to "Get up!" I lift my head.

The lyrics lead into the first verse, and I straighten my posture as the singer tells me to get out of my head, to not let them control me. I inhale deeply, my exhale slow and controlled, and I step into the room just as the chorus starts. The singer asks, "Are you ready?" The next line of the lyrics states, "They aren't ready for me."

If three pep talks isn't motivational, I don't know what is.

At first glance, the room appears empty. The mat is empty of sparring partners, the weight machines void of someone trying to gain muscle mass. No one swings across the monkey bars or leaps from wall to wall with the parkour setup. The equipment is intimidating because of my ignorance of how to use it, and the height of the jungle gym is imposing. I was hoping Vic would be here already. He said he would be.

Movement catches my eye. At the back of the room, behind all the equipment, Adam climbs up one of the ropes. His legs are straight, toes pointed as he holds his body in a V-shape. Looking like a professional gymnast. He's halfway to the top, arm and back muscles bulked with strength as he reaches hand over hand. Movements fluid and fast. Effortless.

Even though I hate the guy, I can't stop staring, mouth agape with wonder and—dare I admit it—admiration. How long will it take for me to be that strong? And make it look easy?

He taps the ceiling then drops to the floor. I gasp, eyes going wide. He lands in a sort of crouched position, rolling forward over his shoulder and up onto his feet. A move so casual, I'm not sure it even happened. He walks through the maze of equipment, head lowered as he looks at his watch. A small smile spreads across his lips. He comes to a stop at a bench along the wall, picks up a small notebook, and writes in it.

I hate how absolutely impossible it is to peel my gaze from him. Is it because he's not wearing a shirt? No. I've seen shirtless guys before. I've been to the lake and the swimming pool.

Sure, but were they as well muscled as this guy?

Oh, geez.

Or am I staring because of the several pale, long scars marring his back. Similar to the scar I have from the beast on my arm. Did those happen from his botched mission? The one that left him hospitalized for months and his mentor in a vegetative state?

This is the first I've seen him since Nelly decided he'd continue my training, both of us avoiding each other as much as possible until this inevitable day. He catches me looking at him. Surprise flashes across his face before he corrects himself and acknowledges me with a nod, before turning back to his notebook.

I shift from one foot to the other. Relieved when I get my stupid eyeballs to stop ogling him. I glance at the entrance for Vic. He did say he'd be here, right? Because I'm here. Alone. With Adam. The animosity between us is straining our already fragile relationship.

The music drops several decibels to a conversation level.

"So, I guess we start with some warm-ups like last time." He sounds about as enthusiastic as I feel, which is to say, not at all. At least the feeling is mutual. "We'll take it easier this time."

"Okay," I say, turning to face him. "Sounds good."

He pulls on a T-shirt—thank god—then picks up his notebook, eyes closing for a short moment, chest rising and lowering in a controlled breath. "Um, do you have something you can track your workouts in? Like, a notebook or your phone?"

"Um, yeah. I can find something." I nod, though he's not looking at me. This is dumb. Where is Vic?

Adam continues, "Good. Keeping notes of how you feel after each workout can tell you if you need to change anything." He studies me. "Also, it's a good way to show

how much you've improved."

I gesture to the ropes at the back of the room. "Was that an improvement today?"

"You saw?"

Is he blushing right now? I swear his moderately suntanned face is flushed with red.

"Yeah. It was neat." Try freaking awesome, but I won't speak those words aloud. Not to him. Ever.

He rubs the back of his neck, a sheepish expression on his face. "Thanks. Um. Broke my record, actually."

"Cool." I nod. *Don't ask what his record is. You don't care. You're here for training.*

"Anyway. We should start. I…uhm…" He clears his throat. "I wanted to say something."

"Oh?" By the look on his face, I have a pretty good idea what he wants to say. My heart decides to start warming up now for cardio by racing.

He takes a tentative step toward me. "About what I said to you, I—"

"This doesn't look like training. How are we going to kick ass standing around like this?" Vic's voice carries across the room in a rather merry tone, hardly befitting of the current mood, but my only thought is *Oh, thank god!* My shoulders relax a little.

Adam's eyes narrow a fraction of a centimeter, a barely audible sigh escaping him. "Dude. I'm trying to apologize here."

"Then do it." Vic sidles up to me. "You're good with

words. You've written how many songs? Shouldn't be too hard."

Yeah. If I'm not mistaken—and, embarrassingly, I'm not—*One Times Three* have a song titled "Sorry." Original, I know. Twelve-year-old me rocked out to that one. Hard. I'm glad I'm past all that nonsense.

Adam looks between us then focuses on me. "I'm sorry," he says in a quiet voice.

I'm not sure what I feel. The muddle of emotions canceling one another out is better than bursting into tears. I'll take the confusion over sobbing.

"Okay," I say, wanting to move on.

He and Vic both give me an incredulous look. An expression I expect from Vic, but Adam should at least be, I don't know, mad I didn't say "I forgive you" afterward. I don't think I'll ever be able to say that to him. Ever.

"Just okay?" Vic asks, stepping into my view and whispering, "Do I need to beat him up?"

"Jager," Adam huffs, voice heavy with exhaustion and irritation. "Let's get this over with. Come over here and punch me in the face, already. So we can move on."

An evil glint sparkles in my best friend's eye. He cocks an eyebrow, turning to face his fellow classmate. I grab his arm. The surprise on his face matches my own. Wouldn't it be nice to cause Adam some pain, for the pain he caused me? I don't know.

"Can we just train, please?" I look between the two,

the tension between them tighter than between Adam and me. I've never seen this protective side of Vic before. Granted, he never needed to be this protective of me before. But it feels…off.

"If that's what you want," Vic says.

"Please," I confirm.

I only have to train with Adam for two months. Once I'm official, Nelly takes over. I can last two months, and it'll be better for everyone if the boys get along.

With a final nod, Vic turns away and crosses the room to the stereo, switching Adam's music out for his own. Selecting some upbeat, electronic tunes. No music intro needed for this male vocalist, who starts singing as soon as the song blares from the speakers. The lyrics are in a different language.

It takes me a second, but when the singer says the one word in English, I recognize it. It's been a while since I listened to them, this K-pop group Vic introduced me to in his attempt to help me learn Korean. Which may have been beneficial if they offered Korean in my school. But alas, I can say "why" in Vic's dad's native language. That's it.

Adam and I share a look. While he is sad and apologetic, I'm defiant and determined—or at least I hope as such—as I raise my chin, steeling myself with a breath. That one English phrase in the song illustrates how I see Adam, the devil.

CHAPTER THIRTY-SEVEN

WRAITHS

Jonah makes homemade pizza for dinner, making both the dough and the sauce from scratch. He takes requests, calling today a special occasion, and makes everyone their own personal, twelve-inch pizza with custom toppings.

While I do sear the top of my mouth, it's probably the best pizza sauce I've ever had in my life. I have my pizza made with three different cheeses, along with ham and pineapple, which makes Vic mock gag. I punch him in the arm. Jonah obliges, though, saying something about the acidity in pineapples. I don't know. He's the cooking whiz.

I've eaten half my pizza before I remember that pineapple on pizza is also Adam's favorite. Or was, in his *One Times Three* days. Despite my failed attempts to ignore him, I notice he chose a salad, reminding me of his lactose intolerance. And the day I made hot chocolate for him. I seethe at the memory, unable to finish the rest of my dinner.

Afterward, we're all hanging out in the game room. Even Adam is there, standing behind the couch as he watches Elizabeth play through a level of the game she and Anita had been playing when she stayed the night at my house. I'm sitting with Vic as he plays a card game with Devon and Jonah. I opted out, feeling overwhelmed.

Training had gone well. Vic didn't beat up Adam. I learned about chokeholds and how to throw a punch. Adam took it easier on me, as promised, but I can already feel the soreness settling into my back muscles. I just hope I'll be able to move tomorrow, maybe my muscles are getting used to being put to work.

Jonah hums a bar of a song under his breath, and Devon harmonizes with him. Which, of course, brings me to my next big question.

"So, guys, what came first, the boy band or the ninja gig?"

"Fourteen." Devon glances up at me, then lays down the tally of cards he'd matched. The other two boys groan in defeat. "The boy band was kind of an accident."

"The fame was an accident," Jonah states, collecting the cards and shuffling them. "Mom and Dad wanted us to have a normal life. To us, normal was uploading our covers of hit songs for others to enjoy."

"Yeah, and normal exploded." Devon grabs his mug of tea and takes a sip.

"That happens when you're good," Vic says. He leans back in against the couch, typing away on his phone.

"The one video of us doing a cover of—"

"*The Sound of Silence*," I interrupt. "I know *that* origin story." They took the classic song and turned it into a gorgeous, breathtaking a cappella. The first of their videos that went viral, catching the eye—or really, the ear—of record label companies.

"Okay." Jonah deals out the cards, while giving me a look that borders on serious, even as his lips are slightly upturned. That might just be how his face is naturally shaped. "You're right. Everybody knows that part of the story, but the biggest reason Mom and Dad even agreed to let us sign on with a record label was because of a wraith attacking people along the West Coast. It was connected to the music scene."

"Wraith," I parrot.

The three of them nod, all very serious. I almost feel like they're joking.

"What are wraiths?" The obvious question, I think.

"Wraiths are," Jonah pauses, both in his speech and dealing of cards.

"Wispy demons," Devon and Vic say at the same time.

"Wispy demons," Elizabeth echoes from the couch where she continues her game. Adam is no longer standing behind the couch watching her. A quick glance around the area shows he's no longer in the room.

"Well, despite the term *wispy*," Jonah continues. "They are a solid form, and our blades can hurt them—if we can get close enough, and avoid being bitten. They're fast and feed off spinal fluid, taking it into their system by biting into the spine via the neck. Their bite can paralyze, cause brain damage, cause schizophrenic and dementia-like episodes, and also lead to death."

"What do they look like?"

Vic drops his cards and pulls out his phone. Devon shuffles his own cards, moving them around in whatever order he wants them in his hand. Jonah does the same. Elizabeth's game is muted, but her button-tapping fills the silence. Vic hands his phone to me.

The file on the wraith is formatted much like that of the other files of monsters I have been shown, with the details and specs of how the monster works and operates. But my eyes are drawn to the picture of the thing.

A dark shadowy form looms in a hallway of a building. Doors line the hall, the carpet a retro swirl of orange and green, reminding me of hotels. The LED lights do nothing to help the picture seem less photoshopped. I zoom in on the figure, making out the little wisps of how it got its nickname. Black tendrils seem to waft away from its body. There are no eyes, nose, mouth, or face that I can make out.

"Creepy." I pass the phone back to Vic.

"You guys dropped off the map after the tour though," I say, following the timeline in my head. The situation is serious enough that I don't feel embarrassed knowing these details of *One Times Three*. "Was the deal to get on the music scene, kill the wraith, and leave the music scene?"

"Jasmine Steele," Devon says quietly.

Jasmine Steele: singer, songwriter, dancer, and queen of the tween scene. She had luscious black hair and dark bronze skin, and a vocal range that put most popular singers to shame, until she allegedly committed suicide, crashing through the ten-story window of her hotel room. I rocked out pretty good to some of her music, too.

"This one," Jonah says, face pale and looking the most serious I've ever seen him. "I took that picture Vic showed you after it killed Jasmine Steele. It bit her, fed off her. She had a psychotic break, and I'm sure you know the rest."

My chest tightens. "Oh, I'm so sorry. That's why you guys left the music scene?"

"Yep," Devon says quickly.

They'd been on a West Coast tour with Jasmine Steele, who'd always seemed like a down-to-earth human being, and they'd probably all been friends. Talking about her death isn't fun, but they're sharing it with me.

"We'd only signed a contract for one album, two music videos, and a tour," Jonah says. "Reality hits hard sometimes." He sighs, then glances at me with a sympathetic look. "As you know." Then his goofball grin returns, his attention moving to Vic. "You got any queens?"

"Go Fish."

CHAPTER THIRTY-EIGHT

RECONCILIATION

The next two weeks go by without incident. Adam and I—and Adam and Vic—are civil during training sessions. There are no signs of Sahara. No more girls go missing. Which only leaves me more unsettled. It's a deafening silence and I'm straining to hear where the threat is coming from.

Today is the day before Thanksgiving, our first without Aaron. None of us are looking forward to it. Carol's crankier than usual, snapping at me about my chores. Anita's more absorbed in her games, barely acknowledging my questions about her day. And my parents, well, Mom is working extra shifts at the hospital, and Dad was called in for some electrical emergency in the dorms of the college. Not sure what the emergency could possibly be, since everyone is likely gone on holiday break.

But I don't blame either one of them for not being home.

So, on this clear blue morning, I am thankful for Adam's distraction of uphill sprints.

The sunshine has melted the past week's snow. The roads are dry and ice free. A gentle breeze is the cherry atop the delicious forty degrees—the perfect temperature for an upbeat workout. Colorado and it's bipolar weather at its finest. There'll probably be a blizzard tomorrow, who knows? It's weather roulette in this part of the country.

Adam finds us a forest clearing to do our warm-ups and stretches. And by us, I mean only Adam and me. Vic is at home with family for the holiday. He's never missed a Thanksgiving with his family. I wasn't going to let him miss a family gathering on account of the rocky relationship between my trainer and me.

We're on the final uphill sprint. Five sets of a four-hundred-meter climb on the road. I push, my quads screaming for a reprieve as I try to keep up with Adam, whose forehead actually glistens with sweat. The dude rarely sweats. Him and Vic both. And they never seem to struggle for breath. As opposed to me, covered in sweat, clothes pasted to my body, my lungs and heart not understanding the torture I bestow on them.

"Breathe. You've got this," Adam calls as he crests the hill.

If I'm focusing on my form—keeping my arms driving at my sides and not swinging across my body, keeping a slight lean forward, feet pushing off from the toes—I'm forgetting to breathe. And when I'm focusing on breathing, I'm forgetting my form.

Good thing I have a trainer to remind me.

At the top of the hill, fighting the urge to collapse, I follow Adam to the clearing where we started. I force myself upright and breathe, preparing for what'll happen next.

The last couple of training sessions, after the main workout, Adam's started to throw self-defense drills at me. It'll help build resilience, he says. Being attacked when I'm tired. I don't mind the surprise attacks. There's something about getting out of a hold that's satisfying, even when I'm out of breath. And I'm ready for it today.

I haven't worked on doing any of the holds yet, just getting out of them, but I want to try. Today I have my chance.

Adam tells me my times for the sprints. My second time is faster than my first, and the three after that slower than my first, but only by a couple of seconds. I angle my body so my back is almost fully to him, and I listen past the pounding of my pulse in my ears.

He's taking a drink of water. I swear I feel his gaze on me, and I fight the tension, switching to breathing through my mouth and bending forward slightly. Making a show of struggling for air. Waiting.

From the corner of my eye, I see his hand shoot out. He grabs my shoulder. I grab his hand with my opposite hand. Bring my elbow up, step back and twist around. His body is forced into a bent-over position, and I push him down and kick the back of his knees, sending him to the ground.

Now for the part I haven't been trained for. I leap onto his back, wrapping my arm around his neck in a chokehold.

"Oh!" He gives a surprised laugh, maybe even sounding a little impressed with my initiative. "Not bad execution."

"Yeah, it wasn't bad at all if I do say—"

I yelp as Adam rolls over, grabbing my foot and twisting it while shoving his elbow into the soft tissue of my calf. Another yelp, and I loosen my hold. I'm flipped around onto my stomach, and he has me in the same chokehold I had him in.

"Think you can figure it out?" he asks.

He just showed me. More than anything, I'm now more fueled by annoyance at him getting out of my hold so effortlessly. I grab his arms and heave, rolling my body hard, getting him on his back. He wraps his legs around my waist. I know what to do next, but with his arm pressing into my neck, panic starts to build, and I can't release my grip. I pull at his arm.

If this were a serious situation, you'd be dead, says a voice. A reminder Adam often gives me, which garners a glare from Vic. But I know Adam has a point. He's right, though I'll never tell him that.

Focus.

I release my grip from his arms. Stifling the panic. I faced down a giant freaking mountain lion. I can do this. I grab his foot, twisting, and jab my elbow into his leg. He grunts, grip loosening. I wriggle out and scramble to my feet. I bounce on my toes, fists raised and ready.

He gazes up at me from the ground, rubbing his leg where I jabbed my elbow. A soft grin on his face, clearly amused, as he says, "You know, in a real situation after escaping, you need to tuck tail and run."

"What? You scared you can't take me?" I throw a couple of punches. Jab, jab, cross. Making sure to put my weight into each punch, arms returning to protect my face. This he drilled into me. Even if I'm shadow boxing, always make sure to protect the face. Getting KO'd isn't fun.

While I haven't had my lights punched out, so to speak, I have been knocked out in other ways. The car accident, for one. Or Sahara's ear-piercing sound.

Yeah. Being KO'd isn't fun.

Adam cocks an eyebrow. He slowly pushes to his feet, body relaxed. He saunters toward me, raising his hands, keeping his hands open. I watch him and wonder if I should hit first. Generally, I'm the one on the defensive.

With that thought, I take action. I keep my left hand high, close to my face, and let my right fly toward his face in a quick jab. He blocks easily. Too easily, but he doesn't counter. I punch a couple more times, and each time he dodges or deflects. I focus, squinting my eyes, bracing as if I'm getting ready to hit him again. He's relaxed, watching me with an amused smirk.

I spring forward, going low with my arms wide, and tackle him. He utters a surprised "oomph" as we fall to the ground. When we hit the dirt, I roll off him and jump to my feet. A laugh rises in my throat, but before it can escape, a hand clamps my ankle and—

"Oof!" I hit the ground hard on my butt.

Adam straddles me, pinning my arms down at my sides. A grin of total amusement stretches across his face. "Honestly, that wasn't half bad, but you need to work on the running away part."

"I think I have that part down," I say, breathless. "But I don't need to run from you."

He blinks, head tilting, grin dissipating. I become ridiculously aware of his body on mine, his grip firm yet gentle around my wrists. His face inches from my own; I can make out the darker flecks of brown in his eyes. My stomach flips, butterflies doing a crazy dance. Heat rushes to my face.

He clears his throat and stands, then reaches his hand down to me. "You have a point. But maybe you should practice."

I take his hand and allow him help me to my feet. A soft reminder of the brutal words he spat at me sobers the butterflies' dancing flutter.

"And where should I run? I could probably make it home from here." I look down the road, the direction my house would be. The SUV is parked off to the side of the road. No cars have passed in the hour and a half we've been out here. The beauty of living in rural areas.

"But I wouldn't want to lead anyone home," I say, more to myself than him. "Do I run to—"

"I want to tell you something," he interrupts, speaking quickly. "With Vic around, he doesn't give me a chance to talk."

"Oh." This sudden change of subject sends my mind reeling. I'd rather not go through an awkward apology again. I'm not forgiving him. Ever. "You don't need to do this."

"I'm going to. I need to explain myself. It won't excuse my actions, but I owe you that much, okay?"

"Vic told me about your mentor," I whisper. I can't look him in the eye as I say it.

"That's okay. I know what happened to you."

No kidding! Everybody knows what happened to me. It was in the news, everywhere: online, physical paper, television. My tragedy wasn't a secret mission that could be hidden from the world.

"Just, listen. Please?"

I resign, hugging my arms. Somehow finding the nerve to look up at him. His gaze is far away as he speaks, face etched with pain.

"I've been trained my whole life to be an EON," he says. "I was born into it. Naturally, I was a little cocky about it. I excelled where most students hit a plateau. The right people noticed, and I was fast-tracked into a special program. Celine was my mentor and my friend. We were on a recon mission, a simple training exercise, and I became complacent."

His hands clench and unclench. "The mission went bad. I stumbled upon a nest of vipermorphs. They're venomous, shapeshifting monsters. I almost didn't make it out alive. Celine had to save me." He swallows hard before continuing. "She may as well be dead, and that's on me."

"So," I interrupt, "you were mad at me because you thought I was full of myself?"

He shakes his head. "No. Not that. I was mad at myself. And I was taking it out on you because…" A deep breath as he collects his thoughts. "The OSE doesn't recruit people without any sort of combat experience or some sort of incredible academic mind. It's rare. Vic is the most ideal candidate, being he's an adept fighter and fluent in several languages, and you, well…"

I nod, thinking I understand where he's going with this. "You thought I was a waste of the OSE's time?"

His ducks his head to hide his embarrassment. "Yeah. Pretty much. And when you refused to train after our first training day, I was mad. Furious. Annoyed. I thought you were weak and useless."

Ouch. My shoulders tense, imposter syndrome like a lead vest. A panicked look crosses his face, and I realize I'm stepping away from him, as if creating physical space will dull the pain or the emotion.

"But that's not that I think anymore." He speaks fast. "Mika, you proved me wrong. That night when you followed the kidnappers, you showed me just how crazy and brave you truly are."

Crazy, yes. Brave? Idiotic would be a more appropriate word. I could have died, or worse. If anything, my actions forced Sahara underground. Who knows when we'll see her again?

"You showed that you have the true heart of an EON. You were tired and beat from me working you out. And after what I said, oh my god, you must have been so hurt. But you went after those guys who took that girl. And I… You…" He gestures to me, taking a moment to catch his breath. "You proved me wrong. You didn't grow up knowing these monsters exist, and you didn't—you aren't backing down. And that's what being an Eiko Okada Ninja is all about."

He takes a couple of steps toward me, and to my surprise, I don't recoil. I stay where I am, an odd feeling swelling in my chest.

"I am so sorry for taking my pain out on you," he continues. "I deserve all your hate, and more. Especially the broken jaw Vic's promised me. And I'm not just saying that to lighten the mood."

I have to close my eyes for a moment, to fight back tears. Why am I crying? When I'm certain my voice isn't going to crack with a sob, I look up at him. He dips his head, as if he's waiting for me to bestow punishment.

"While that was the longest apology I've ever heard," I say, "I'm not sure I deserve it."

He frowns. "What? Mika, what I said was not okay—"

"Please, don't start up again." I hold up a hand, and he snaps his mouth shut. "Now, I accept your apology."

I feel I mean the words when I say them. They taste proper in my mouth. Not like a bitter lie.

"But I owe you an apology too," I add.

His mouth opens, and I give him a pleading, warning look. He closes his mouth, dark eyes solemn as he watches me.

"I said some things to you that I shouldn't have." *Deep breath. You can do this, Mika.* "I recognized the hurt and I wanted to help you, and when you rejected that—I shouldn't have said what I said just because you didn't want to open up to me. I'm a complete stranger. I wouldn't confide in me either."

Oh, geez. I'm starting to carry on like him. *Keep it clear and concise.*

"I got mad because of that. I had no reason to. And I'm so sorry for that." A little of the weight that's been hanging on me lifts. I can see it in his eyes, too. While we both have a long way to go with healing, at least we took the first steps.

He gives a slow nod, shoulders hunched. For someone so serious about proper form, his posture isn't always the greatest.

"So…" He peeks up at me, his eyes hidden in the

shadow of his brow. "Where are we?"

I press my lips together to smother a smile. "Outside. About ten miles from the OSE." I keep my expression as deadpan as possible.

He squints at me. "Very funny."

"I won't try to be your therapist," I say, "and you treat me like a human being. I'll keep Vic from breaking your jaw."

"Yeah, that'd be nice." He rubs his temple, then his jaw. He's not looking at me anymore; his eyes scan the forest, brow furrowed. I follow his gaze. Even though the aspens are naked, their leaves long since fallen, the pines are dense. Their shadows are dark, concealing whatever might be lurking within them. No wind, no birds chirping. Eerily quiet. Goosebumps spread across my arms, and I step closer to him.

"Let's go," he says, voice hushed. He waves his hand toward the SUV, but he doesn't take his attention off the forest. When I hesitate, he gives me a gentle push. "Go. I'm right behind—"

Crack! Crack!

Branches snap, reverberating like gunshots. All of my muscles go rigid. The beast from reality and my nightmares bursts from the forest, racing for us. My blood goes cold.

Adam grabs my arm and shoves me toward the vehicle. "Run! I'll hold it off!"

"But—"

"Run!"

CHAPTER THIRTY-NINE

HIT AND RUN

My arms windmill, and I stumble to a run, panic driving my legs and arms. I don't slow as I approach the SUV and slam into it. My hands won't stop shaking as I paw for the doorhandle.

Don't look back! Don't look—

I look. My already frozen heart jumps into my throat. Adam is engaging the beast. I scream for him, but he doesn't look at me. He continues to dodge and roll out of the way of sharp claws. Keeping the monster occupied so I can escape.

Think, Mika. Do something!

I force my attention to the SUV and climb inside. I search for a weapon. Anything. The sunlight reflects from the key chain. An idea sparks in my mind. Scrambling to the driver's seat, I twist the keys in the ignition.

The vehicle rumbles to life. I throw it into gear and rip the steering wheel to the side as I slam my foot down on the accelerator. Directing the vehicle to where Adam—stupid, foolish, moronic Adam—distracts the beast.

The uneven terrain bounces and jerks me around in the seat. I lay on the horn for a quick second to warn Adam. The wheel jerks hard to the left. I return my hand—grip tight, keeping the vehicle aimed at the threat.

Adam's attention snaps to me. A savior and a distraction. The beast swipes at him. He dodges too late. The hit flings him like ragdoll across the clearing. I scream. Half fear, half war cry. I brace myself. The vehicle crashes into the monster. The impact whips me forward out of the seat. The beast sails limply through the air. I slam on the brakes and am jerked back. My arms ache at the joints, trembling.

The vehicle skids to a stop. A sizzling sound over the idling engine, like something wet dripping onto something hot. My vision flashes back to the car accident: shattered glass, a hungry beast's gaze. My brother dead in the back seat.

I press my hands to my temples, trying to focus on what's happening now. The windshield is still intact. The beast lies several feet away. Lifeless. And I'm the only one in the SUV.

Adam!

I remember to shove the gear shift into park before I force the door open. Ankle rolling as I step down, I ignore the sharp pain and limp to a run, toward where I saw his body fly.

"Don't be dead, don't be dead. Please, don't be—"

My voice breaks, on the verge of hysteria when I approach him, dropping to my knees next to his still form.

"Adam?"

I touch his neck, trying to find a pulse. A bruise already starts to bloom down the side of his face.

He lets out a moan, eyelids fluttering. Relief is like a warm blanket, and I can breathe again. He's alive.

"Adam, wake up!" I give him a gentle shake, only to yank one of my hands back. Crimson coats my fingers and palm. I stare at my hand for a long second, fighting the nausea, then look down at the source of the blood. Deep, dark scratches are gouged into his arm. The relief evaporates, and leaves me cold.

"Oh, god. What do I do?" My voice cracks, hands hovering over him. Do I help him up? Do I move him at all? Do I apply pressure to the wound?

"Wh-where's the—" Adam gasps and hisses, grimacing. "Where's the GMP?"

Confusion sweeps over me. What on earth does that have to do with first aid? So much blood. The sticky, metallic scent almost makes me retch. But I can get sick about it later. I need to help Adam. But how?

"Mika, GMP. Status?" He blinks open his eyes, gaze unfocused.

Then it clicks. GMP. Genetically Modified Puma. They should just call it Abomination, but whatever. The OSE with their ABC names.

I glance over to where the monster lies. It remains still, no subtle movement of breath lifting its side. "Uh, dead." Does he really think I'd be sitting here fussing over him if the monster was up and about?

He continues to blink, squinting up at me. He's starting to look a little pale. His hand clamps around the wound on his arm, and the blood seeps through his fingers. I can't remember if there are arteries in the upper bicep of the arm, but I do know the vehicle is still running and I know how to drive. That is something I can do.

I take his uninjured arm and help him sit up. He bites down, jaw working hard. Blood runs down his neck from the back of his head. With a tentative touch, I move his hair and wipe away warm, dark blood to find the wound. It's about the size of a dime but doesn't appear to be deep.

From science class, about human anatomy, I remember that the back of the brain contains the vision part: the occipital lobe. No wonder he's having difficulty focusing his gaze. I ignore the intruding thoughts of blindness, and I help him the rest of the way to his feet.

He squints in the direction of the beast. "Is it dead?"

"Uh." I look again to where the beast lies motionless. Adam's vision must not be bad if he can see it from this far away. Or maybe he's guessing. "I don't know. We need to get out of here. Let the others worry about it."

He doesn't respond, swaying a little. I take his good arm, my other hand on his back, and I coax him forward.

As I get him buckled in, my hands do so without the

slightest tremor, but when I sit in the driver's seat and pull the belt over my shoulder, my bloodied fingers fumble like they're covered in butter, requiring extra focus just to secure myself.

"Hold on, this is going to be a little bumpy." I put the vehicle in reverse, white knuckles on the steering wheel, jaw clenched, mumbling apologies each time Adam lets out a moan or gasp.

"Should call—" Adam inhales sharply as the vehicle bounces onto the road. He continues after I start driving on the smooth asphalt, driving as fast as I dare toward the school. "Gotta call Nelly. Let her know."

I nod in agreement, and slow the vehicle to a stop, too terrified to take my eyes off the road while moving. It takes me a moment to find a phone—everything went flying from the impact—but I find one in the footwell on Adam's side. My fingers are wrapped so tightly around the steering wheel that it physically hurts when I release my death grip to retrieve the device.

I prompt the phone to life, blood smearing the screen while I find Nelly's contact and hit call, then the speaker button. I set the phone in the cup holder and get the vehicle moving again, hoping no one passes us. I'm not sure what the condition of the front of the vehicle is, but if it's as bloody as Adam is, it's sure to attract attention.

"Hey, Adam. You guys heading back? Jonah made—"

"Adam's hurt." I cut her off. "It was the GMP."

"Where are you? We'll take that monster down—"

"I already did."

"What?" Her tone sounds even more incredulous with the southern twang.

I relay what happened, where we are, where the GMP is—hopefully dead—about the deep scratches on Adam's arm and the wound on the back of his head. Not taking my eyes from the road, scanning the streets ahead for traffic coming to the crossroads. I slow down at an upcoming stop sign, but blow past it when I see I'm alone. If the road stays empty, we'll be back to the school in no time.

"That's damn impressive, Mika. The boys and I will come out to collect the GMP carcass. Maybe we can learn something. Dr. Castillo is on her way here." A pause. "How is Adam right now?"

"He's really pale, but responsive." I keep all my fearful thoughts to myself. I risk a glance at him. Even with the grimace and hazy eyes, he gives me a tortured wince and a weak thumbs-up.

"And you?"

"Freaked out, but okay."

I slow the vehicle, turning onto the road leading up to the school. We're almost to safety. And I can get out of the dreaded driver's seat.

CHAPTER FORTY

THE BEAST IS DEAD

The routine of filling out a report helps ease the panic and adrenaline. Hogan kindly told me to take my time with the report, saying that reports are something I will become accustomed to, as they're protocol after each mission or incident.

Nelly, Devon, and Jonah went to retrieve the GMP's dead body, after the brothers confirmed Adam wasn't in critical condition.

Sitting on the couch in the living room, I consider how they plan on getting such a large beast in the vehicle. I guess they can cut it up. My gorge rises a little. After all the blood from Adam's arm, the metallic odor still tainting my nose, the idea of more blood—ugh. I shove the thought aside.

"Are you sure you're okay?" Vic asks again for the hundredth time, his voice tinny through the small speakers of my cell phone. Shouts and laughter erupt on the other line, his family's Thanksgiving festivities in full effect.

"Yes," I say, putting force into the word.

I'm not okay. But the situation is taken care of and done. There's no need for him to leave home and piss off his family. His mom would probably hunt me down and kill me if I dragged him away. Thanksgiving is one of the few times he's home for more than a day or two.

My hand hovers over the tablet screen as I read over what I wrote, unimpressed with the dry, bland words. I guess with it being a report, flourish isn't needed. My current English teacher might disagree, but do I care? Nope.

Vic is talking about something. I sit up and arch my spine. A pinch in my upper back is setting in. The morning light makes its way across the floor from the window. My dog would love that patch of sunlight. I massage my shoulders. Sore, but at least I'm not a literal bloody mess.

Jaqueline and Hogan whisked Adam to the medical room as soon as I pulled to a stop. Dr. Castillo cleared me within five minutes of arriving at the school, asking straightforward Yes-No questions. I have mild whiplash, and I'm going to feel my joints in the morning, but other than that, I'm a healthy specimen.

Adam, on the other hand. Last I saw of him, before Hogan dragged me away, he was fighting to stay conscious, a sheen of sweat across his ghastly pale face, Jacqulyn prying his fingers from where he clutched his bleeding arm.

"And now the Jung family is in the house," Vic sighs, with defeat. "It's not my fault I got my mom's side of the family's height. I didn't ask to be a giraffe."

If I remember correctly, the Jungs are his dad's sister's family. As none of the members are over five-foot-four, they often verbally remind Vic of his height.

"Yeah, whatever, guy who can reach the top shelf," I mutter, picking at the seam of a couch cushion.

"Ha, ha, ha. Anyway, I gotta go—" He's cut off by someone yelling at him in Korean. He yells something back, then returns to me. "Hey, if you need me, I'm there in a heartbeat. I'd rather suffer my mom's wrath than—"

"Vicky!" someone in the background shouts in a giddy, teasing voice.

"I don't have the energy." He groans. "For cousins."

We say our goodbyes. At least someone is going to be having a good Thanksgiving. I reread my report. I'm unhappy with it, but I've detailed everything from when the GMP appeared to Adam and I pulling up in the driveway. I hope it'll suffice, and I push the tablet aside. I bring my knees up to my chest and press my face against them.

We could have died. I should be dead.

"Hey." Elizabeth sits down on the other end of the couch.

"Are they back?" I peek at her.

She shakes her head. "No. They arrived on scene about twenty minutes ago."

I rest my chin on my knees. "How's Adam?"

"Eh, Hogan kicked me out a while ago." She gives me a bashful wince. "I was being too expressive. How are you? Doing okay?"

"Yeah." The word quiet, not much belief behind it. "Maybe I should just call in sick."

"You have work today? On the eve of Thanksgiving?" She clicks her tongue and shakes her head. "I'd call in sick regardless."

"We close early, and we're closed tomorrow. It's not so bad." I let out a sigh, shifting my position and rolling my shoulders, trying to relieve the pinch that just won't give.

"Call in sick." She flexes her injured hand and rotates her wrist, free of the cast. The skin is scabbed and pink with scarring.

"How's your arm? That was legit one of the most hardcore things I've ever seen."

"It's pretty sore yet." She grins at me. "Hitting the GMP with the car was pretty hardcore! Talk about justice."

"Yeah, I don't know about that. I was terrified. I think I just back-tracked getting my driver's license forever." I shudder, remembering the feel of the wheel under my hands, the impact, the flashbacks.

"Hey, you did amazing! You drove Adam home too." She offers me an encouraging look. "You do realize that when the other EONs hear about this, you're going to become stuff of legends, right? Taking out a monster with a car."

Her expression turns tight and solemn. "I guess Sahara is still in the neighborhood. That or she unleashed the GMPs before she took off."

Another uncomfortable thought that I would really rather not think about. Sahara seems to have disappeared, dropping off the radar. I don't want to ask why, but the question plagues me daily with no resolution.

Elizabeth pushes to her feet and starts to pace. "You want anything? Water? Orange juice?"

She gives me such an eager, helpless expression that I nod, saying, "Either one is good."

"Be right back." She leaves the room.

The silence and creaks of the house ring in my ears. Sitting alone again, I wish Vic were here. I study my phone, sitting next to the tablet on the coffee table. Should I ask him to come over for just a few hours? A hug would do wonders for the melancholy atmosphere.

"Hey." Elizabeth pokes her head into the room. "They're back."

I leap to my feet, snatch up the tablet, and we head to the garage.

They didn't cut up the mountain lion to fit it in the back of the vehicle. I'm not sure how they lifted it in, but they did. With its massive, spittle-soaked jowls and bloodied nose, the beast takes up the entire back of the vehicle. One of the large paws, with menacing, talon-like claws, is stained red with Adam's blood.

We all stand in the garage, staring at the carcass, unease like a skin too tight on my body. The stench of urine, blood, and death lingers in the air.

"It's dead, Mika," Nelly says. I didn't realize how badly I needed to hear those words. My shoulders relax. And I notice that everyone is watching me.

"Good job," Jonah says. There's genuine respect in his eyes.

Everyone else joins in with the compliments and nods. I get a few gentle claps on the back, and I accept them with all the grace of a stunned deer.

"Thanks," I say, ducking my head, and wishing the blush away from my face. "But it was a team effort. Couldn't have done it without Adam."

Even if distracting the beast alone was the stupidest, most idiotic, brave thing he's ever done, our survival outweighs his asinine decision.

"Speaking of." Nelly gestures to the back of the garage.

We all turn to see Adam in the doorway leading to the medical/locker room, staring past us at the GMP. Both Jacqulyn and Dr. Castillo pause their clean-up to look out at the commotion, gazes settling on the dead beast.

"Adam!" Elizabeth crosses the floor, arms outstretched, but stops herself before throwing her arms around him.

Adam lifts his good arm, allowing her to give him a gentle side hug. His eyes are glued to the beast with a wary expression. Some color has returned to his complexion, but there is a blatant contrast between his usually tan skin and the darkness of his eyelashes—and the angry dark blue-and-purple bruise down the side of his face. His eye is swollen shut.

His injured arm is bandaged and resting in a sling. He wears sweatpants and a short-sleeve button-down shirt. The combination is odd, but I understand it's functional, and I realize my life would have been a little easier with my own beast-wounds if I'd worn button-downs too.

"What's the diagnosis?" Elizabeth steps back from him and peeks at his bandaged arm.

"Mild concussion. Bruised everything. And twenty-two stitches."

Devon laughs. Elizabeth joins in. Both Nelly and Jacqulyn smirk. Hogan and Dr. Castillo shake their heads. Adam manages some semblance of a smile. Jonah groans. And I don't get the joke.

"Jonah held the record for three years with twenty stitches," Elizabeth explains to me.

"Ah, gotcha." Of course, Jonah prides himself on the number of stitches he's had.

"Yes, well, we're glad you're both all right," Hogan says, placing a tentative hand on Adam's shoulder. His attention turns to the dead monster. "The science division is sending someone to retrieve the carcass, but they won't be here until morning." He points at Devon and Jonah. "Let's make some room in the cellar."

As everyone starts to disperse, I pass the tablet to Nelly, almost forgetting I'd brought it. She thanks me, telling me "good job" before she heads into the house. I wrap my arms around myself and take another step toward the beast.

"How does it feel?" Adam says.

I glance over at him. He leans his head against the doorframe. Jacqulyn and Dr. Castillo chat in Spanish in the medical room behind him.

"Like a really weird dream," I murmur, "I'm not sure how long it'll take to sink in."

I did just kill one of the beasts, or possibly *the* beast, that ran into the road and caused the accident. It could also be the one that attacked me in the forest. Though, I am the idiot in the latter story. The point is, I should feel, I don't know, vindicated. Mostly, I just feel relief, like I could nap until next November.

We both return our attention to the GMP, where Elizabeth is using a screwdriver to lift the lip of the beast's jowls. With a curious-yet-appalled expression, she examines the rows of pointed teeth, ideal for tearing flesh.

"You might just be one of the best," Adam says quietly.

I glance at him. He's regarding me with an almost reverent expression, and I realize his words are meant for me. I let out a short laugh and try to mentally rip the wings off all the happy butterflies in my stomach. I try to remind them: I don't like the guy.

"Yeah, that's the blood loss and concussion talking." I

turn back to the beast to hide my blush.

"Elizabeth," Nelly sighs, giving the girl a disapproving "tsk" as she emerges from the house. Elizabeth gives her a doe-eyed look, hiding the screwdriver behind her back as if the older woman didn't see it. "Help Adam inside, please."

She doesn't argue and sets the screwdriver down with one last glower at the beast. I join her in leading Adam across the garage into the house. Mostly because I don't want to be roped into moving the beast to the cellar. The very thought of touching it—I swallow back the urge to vomit.

"You want your room or the living room?" Elizabeth asks, pausing in the hall.

"Don't think I should deal with stairs." Adam squints with his one good eye. "Honestly, I'm not sure where we're at right now."

My heart stills for a moment, then I recall that short-term memory loss is one of the effects of concussions. I had one myself. First day in the hospital was very confusing, heart wrenching. I shove that memory away as we reach the living room.

Adam slowly takes a seat on the couch, resting the uninjured side of his face on the back couch cushion. His face is scrunched up for a long moment until he settles, and his good eye closes.

"You want anything to eat or drink?" Elizabeth produces a blanket from under the coffee table and drapes it over him.

"Meh."

She watches him, holding her healing wrist and flexing her fingers. She takes a seat on the other side of the couch, her expression one of remorse. Probably beating herself up over her sister's beasts' attacks, like how I beat myself up over my brother's death.

I step back and rub at the scars on my arm, chewing the inside of my bottom lip. The tightness in my chest is almost suffocating. A swirl of strange and conflicting emotions. I do not like Adam, at all, especially after he completely nailed the coffin closed to any possible friendship by snapping at me about my guilt.

Sure, he apologized—twice—and explained himself, and he'd been nothing but civil and motivational while training me, but his accusations, the sneer that came with them, continue to sting.

A part of me wanted to hurt him, whether I figured a way to do it myself, or if Vic did the honors, but not like this. Even with that thought, I swear a piece of me feels he deserves this. Maybe because he's okay and going to live, and it'd be different if he was on his deathbed. I don't know.

What I do know, though, is that I'd like to go home. I'll be living in this school soon enough, so I'll go home and hang out with my sisters until I have work. If they'll have me. If not, I'll take a nap. Everyone here is safe.

CHAPTER FORTY-ONE

VENOMOUS SNAKE

A nap is not a good idea. I toss and turn, and wake up drenched in sweat. The haze from restless sleep hangs over me.

Maybe I should call in sick.

I check the time, doing the math in my head about how late I will be if I ride my bike. Ten minutes late. I hover my finger over the assistant manager's number, Brittney. Little thoughts start tapping their way into my head, trying to remind me of earlier conversations and heartfelt apologies, brutal words that cut to the quick.

Ugh. I'd rather arrive late and force myself to stand for a few hours than deal with that nonsense running through my mind.

On autopilot, I dress for work. I put on deodorant but don't bother to run a brush through my hair, dragging my fingers through it instead as I leave my room. Carol's voice carries down the hall from the kitchen, along with the bopping music of Anita's videogame. My older sister sounds almost cheerful. Maybe she'll drive me to work, then I won't be late.

I rub Licorice's belly as I pass her in the hall. The black lab is sprawled out in a ray of sunshine spilling through the open door of my parents' room. The sweet old pup gives me a tail wag, and I continue on my way.

"Hey, Carol? Would you be able to give me a ride to work—"

I stop short in the kitchen doorway. A young woman dressed in jeans and riding boots stands with Carol. Her short dark hair is pulled up in a haphazard ponytail, her back to me as she listens to my sister talk.

"Oh, s-sorry. I didn't realize." I fumble my words, not expecting to have a random person in the house.

The unknown person turns around. Menacing eyes look me over, hidden behind sleek framed glasses and sparkling with sadistic amusement. For the second time today, my heart freezes.

Sahara.

"Mika. This is Elena, a new volunteer at the shelter." Carol grins. An actual, sincere grin. She hasn't smiled like that since before Aaron died. Apparently the person who can bring her out of the slump is a total psycho.

"Elena, this is my not-so-eloquent-or-graceful sister Mika." She says my name with a sigh and a lazy hand gesture in my direction.

"A pleasure to meet you." Sahara crosses the floor,

stretching her hand out to me. She raises an eyebrow, her sweet smile drawing a malicious turn with her lips, daring me. "I've heard so much about you."

I step back, glancing at her hand as if it's an angry rattlesnake.

"Wh—what?" My mind reels. This has to be a nightmare. This monster in human disguise is *not* in my house. She is *not* friends with my sister. This isn't real. For the sake of my sanity, it can't be. How did she even find my sister?

"Add rude to that list," Carol says, oblivious to the fear I'm sure is broadcasted across my face. Like I'm staring at the devil itself.

Sahara's expression softens as she turns back to Carol. "No, I get it. I can be awkward sometimes. Remember when we first met?" She laughs, and Carol joins in. I stare in dumbstruck horror. How does my sister not see that her new best friend is evil?

"Horse manure," my sister manages to say between breaths, holding her stomach as she laughs. "Everywhere."

"I still have manure in places I shouldn't!"

That comment sends Carol into a harder fit of giggles. Her eyes squeeze shut, and she's laughing so hard no sound comes out.

"Carol, can we—" I start to speak, watching Sahara.

"Oh, right." My older sister wipes at her eyes, as if she's laughed herself to tears. "You want a ride to work? I don't think I have time—"

"I can take her," Sahara suggests, smiling a little, helpful and innocent. "She works at the coffee shop near the Phoenix Gym, right? I'm heading that way."

Alone in a car with the psycho? Yeah, that's going to be a hard no. "Uh, I don't—"

"That would be great." Carol crosses over to me, drapes her arm around my shoulders and gives me a stern look while smiling. She hisses, "Be nice. She's my friend."

Well, this is just great. My sister is friends with a psycho—and not just any psycho—the one who kidnapped and tortured me. The one who's kidnapping girls and torturing them. The one who controls the monsters that caused the accident.

I open my mouth to object, to tell her that her new best friend is a sadistic monster whose only intention is to kill me, not drive me to work. But I catch the look Sahara gives me, a chilling, predatory narrowing of her eyes. Daring me to do something. Images of my sisters chained up in the same cell I was kept in, being tortured with burns and electricity, flash in my mind. The sickening scent of burnt meat lurks at the edges of the horrid thought.

I'd rather chew off my own hand than leave with Sahara, but the best thing I can do for my sisters is to go with her. Get her out of the house. I clench my fists behind my back and agree to let her take me.

This isn't going to end well. There's got to be something I can do.

Carol and Sahara hug, my sister thanking her for being so kind. I take that moment to bring up Nelly's contact info and call her number. I turn the sound off and hide the phone in the sleeve of my hoodie. They'll know something's wrong. They'll be able to track my phone. They'll come after me, and we'll have Sahara.

At least I *hope* they're able to track my phone.

I follow Carol and the psycho out to her car, a compact SUV. Smaller than the vehicle she used to meet with the kidnappers. The two talk longer, chatting about their schedules as I stand by the passenger door, nerves on edge. Skin tingling and tight. Hair on end. Hands clammy and cold. Instinct tells me to run, but I can't. I need to get her away from my family.

Once I'm inside the car, I let the phone slide from my sleeve, using minimal movements to hide it between the seat and the doorframe, careful not to end the call. I won't have another chance to call anyone.

From the corner of my eye, I see how she found us. Found Carol. My backpack sits in the back seat. She'd obviously taken it during her escape that night when I'd discovered her with the kidnappers. I have an emergency contact card with my parents' numbers, their work numbers, Carol's number, and her work numbers. Something meant to help me in a time of trouble has assisted my demise.

Irony at its finest.

Carol stands on the porch, watching us leave with a

stupid smile on her face. *Oh, man, if you only knew, Carol.* She wouldn't give this monster a second look. She'd cross the road to avoid her.

"Do you have any idea how easy it was to befriend your sister?" Sahara asks through her innocent smile. "All I had to do was diss the human male species and sing the praises of the animals. Wrapped. Around. My. Finger."

She singsongs the last words. A sound more eerie than her usual monotone voice.

"I could see her as a brain," she continues. "Very science savvy. Especially with biology. A different time, a different place, I could use her." She gives me an evil smirk. "Maybe I still can."

I grit my teeth and try to focus, needing to find a way to escape. "So, Elena, you're going by that name again?"

I don't have any clue how to talk to a psycho. I don't know what she wants. Even if I did, I wouldn't be able to give it to her. What if I am what she wants? What are her plans for me?

"Elena died a long time ago." Her tone evens out to her familiar monotone. "The EONs failed her, as they fail everyone. Let today be proof of that."

"I see."

She slows to a stop at the crossroads. "No. No, you don't."

I contemplate my options. Grab the steering wheel to cause a crash? I've been in one too many vehicle collisions already, do I really want to be in another one? To get away from this monster? Yeah. I'd risk it.

"Whatever you're thinking of doing, don't." Her voice is heavy with unspoken threat, but the command nudges something in me.

She gets the vehicle moving up to speed. My heart hammers with such anticipation I feel it in my teeth. I grab the steering wheel, yanking hard. The vehicle swerves toward the ditch.

Sahara curses. Her elbow connects with my nose. Pain explodes behind my eyes. Her hand slaps down on my shoulder, the initial hit masking the prick of something. My shoulder starts to burn, searing up my neck and down my arm and into my torso. She shoves me back into my seat, the vehicle already righted on the road.

I grab desperately at the door handle. I should have run sooner. My arms, let alone my fingers, lag with numbness. My vision swims, not only with tears of defeat and the unknown, but with fading vision. Thick tendrils of nausea twist my belly, working their way up. The bitter taste of bile in the back of my throat.

No, please no… Even my thoughts have little energy to form.

Sahara sighs and says something, but I can't hear for the ringing panic in my ears. The whole world is tilting. Maybe we did crash. But we're moving, driving. A steady rumble of moving tires reverberates underfoot. My vision darkens by the second. The forest passes like a smeared watercolor, and I succumb to the sedative.

CHAPTER FORTY-TWO

ANOTHER MONOLOGUE

The smell wakes me. The antiseptic, hand-sanitizer, brand-new bandage scent of a hospital.

Did we crash? I passed out on impact, and my panicked mind filled in the blanks with the worst outcome, right?

The beeps of a heart monitor jump up a notch from their even and steady staccato.

The act of opening my eyes is a hassle, like my eyelashes are woven together, but I manage to pry them open. I blink hard against a blinding white light overhead. I flinch, and moan against a sore, burning pain in my face, centered around my nose.

Oh, no…

I try moving my hand to shield my eyes, to examine my nose, but my hand moves a fraction of an inch before stopping. I'm held down at the wrists. I try my other arm—same thing. I try moving my legs to no avail; they're strapped down at the ankles and thighs. I try lifting my head, but I'm restrained from head to toe.

This isn't happening!

The monitor beeps faster, along with my pulse racing in my ears. The realization is taking hold. We *didn't* crash. And now I'm—I don't know where I am, but it can't be good. Being strapped down and attached to a heart monitor is never a good thing.

"Oh, lovely," says a nasally, masculine voice. A face bobs into view—an oblong, skinny face with the lower half hidden behind a white mask. His thinning hair is gelled back. "I was just getting ready to wake you. We retrieve more accurate data when the subject is awake." His pale eyes scrunch up, crow's feet deepening, as if he's smiling under his mask.

"Wh—whe—" I wince against the pain in my face and in the back of my throat. Swallowing several times, I try to wet my parched mouth and manage to croak out, "Where am I?"

"Oh, you don't need to worry about that." His face disappears off to the side.

A machine whirs, and my body tilts, legs down and head up, revealing the surrounding room. Drab gray walls. Concrete floor, complete with a drain a couple of feet ahead of me. I strain my eyes, trying to look side to side. A door to my left. The ceiling is tall, lined with long LED lights. Dark windows stretch from wall to wall in front of me.

I peer at the windows, trying to see outside. Maybe I

can find a landmark and—

—And what? There's literally nothing you can do with that information.

The door on the side of the room opens, and in walks Sahara, clad in a dark purple button-down shirt, black tactical pants, and combat boots. The door clangs shut behind her, and she saunters over, stopping directly in front of me. She's silent as she eyes me with scrutiny.

"Pictures last longer," I say, words scraping against my throat. My nose is clogged, like I have the common cold.

"The other girls begged for their lives, you know, not bothering to fight back." She raises her chin and tilts her head.

"Ah, so you admit you took them," I say, as if telling a joke will get me out of this.

"But you…you didn't beg. As pathetic and feeble your attempts were, you fought." She steps closer and leans in. "And I think your resilience is what we need, the final key, to make this work."

"Um. No, thanks." As if not giving my consent will make her send me back home. If only.

She turns, clasping her hands behind her back. "You see, we're close to figuring out the merging of a certain demon's essence with humans. Humans are frail things, and his power is a lot. You've seen the—what does the OSE call them? GMPs?" She faces me and proudly raises her chin. "I know you've seen them. Hell, you ran into one. Twice you've literally run into one with a car. Very courageous thing you did, saving Elvis."

I stare at her, trying to figure out how she knows all this. The first two incidents she'd for sure know about. The first one she'd have learned from the news and talking with Carol; the second time, she was there in the forest and her hideout. The third, though, that just happened. How would she know they're called GMPs? Does this mean she's been watching me this whole time?

"You've been spying on me," I say. "Creep."

She chuckles, dry and humorless. "I have my sources." Her smile turns chilling. I try not to squirm. "But your will to fight is not the only reason I chose you. That night, our last interaction, I made the connection of who. You. Are. Leaving your backpack behind." She tsks and shakes her head. "A confirmation that you aren't an EON or a brain. Useless and dumb."

I clench my jaw, hating the truth of her words.

"Victor Jager Choi's best friend. He doesn't shut up about you. He wanted to tell you about the whole ninja thing and introduce you to *One Times Three*. I'm just glad I got out of there before your brother died because then he really wouldn't shut up." She lets out a breath. "Taking you from him will be the equivalent of ripping out his heart." Her lips form a triumphant smirk.

"What did he ever do to you?"

"What everyone else in that sorry excuse for a family did." Her voice rises and her face darkens with a snarl as she leans forward, breath hot and foul against my face.

"They let my parents die. A preventable incident, and yet, here we are."

"Preventable?" Her parents were EONs who thought they were saving someone, and that someone turned out to be an even bigger monster. Not a lot the OSE or AIO could have done about that.

"Yes. Their SOS was ignored." She pulls back and smooths her shirt. I don't have a chance to think before she continues.

"You know, he said he believed me? Jager. He said he believed me that there was something off about the AIO, some things not adding up with reports submitted through OSEs around the world. But when I asked him to leave with me, he wouldn't. He said…"

She reaches her hand out, placing her fingers on my face, spreading them toward my broken nose. I swallow hard, waiting for her to inflict torture. Try as I may, I can't pull away. The restraints offer no leeway.

"Just like everyone else, he said I was crazy." She lets her hand drop. "I'll take everyone from them, and maybe then they'll learn. The OSE is a joke." Proclamation finished, she pulls away, hand dropping to her side, composure restored.

"Anyway, you should be proud, Mika. You're going to be part of something so much bigger than the OSE, the AIO, more powerful than any EON." She clasps her hands behind her back and raises her chin. "Too bad you won't live long enough to revel in it."

The room is quiet, except for the monitor. Her comments about Vic ring in my head. I worry there may be truth to her words. I may not live long enough to find out. My stomach drops and I fidget against the restraints.

"Though, I do suspect…"

At the sound of Sahara's voice, I freeze and glance at her.

"Maybe you want to die." She smirks. "With you being responsible for your brother's death. What was his name again?"

My jaw works as I fight that stupid lump building in my throat. I am not going to cry for her pleasure. I will not concede to that.

"Aaron. Poor, little Aaron," she croons, a sympathetic little frown that doesn't reach the sadistic gleam in her eye.

My chin quivers. She has no right letting his name pass her lips.

"Just get this stupid thing over with, would you?" I look away from her, hating the expression on her face. The contempt and the pleasure.

"Ooh," she says. "Did I touch a sore spot? You can thank me now. For doing you this favor. For doing your family this favor." She appears in my view and grabs my chin. Her nails dig in with sharp pricks of pain, faint compared to the wounds in my heart. "I know you agree with me. They're better off without you. You're welcome."

I clench my eyes shut, wanting to pull my face from

her grip. But I can't. The stupid tremble of my chin is uncontrollable. Hot tears slide down my cheeks. I can't find the words—or the will—to argue with her. That makes me angrier. The heart rate monitor beeps hasten, instilling even more helplessness than being strapped to a table.

Opening my eyes, I try to bring as much of that anger as I can into my expression. Sahara smiles, pleased. Satisfied. Enjoying the moment. I swirl saliva in my mouth, collecting it. Then I spit, hitting Sahara smack in the face. The viscous glob sticks and oozes down her chin.

She blinks, dumbfounded. Then fury and rage contort her features as she lifts her fist.

"Sahara," comes a cool, deep masculine voice over a loudspeaker.

Her face twitches with rage. She lowers her fist and stomps away.

CHAPTER FORTY-THREE

Induction

Lights illuminate the windows before me, revealing not the outside world, but another room. Like an observation room.

Chairs line the window, facing me. Several adults are chatting in there. Except one: a tall, white man with ash blond hair. His blue eyes are vibrant, even from a distance. He watches me with a cold, hard expression. He's familiar—I know I've seen him—but I can't place him.

"Dr. Travis," he says, over the intercom.

The doctor guy from before appears in my peripheral. "Yes, sir?"

"Proceed with Phase One."

The others in the observation room quiet their idle chatter and turn to face the room. A Black woman, hair buzzed short, peers down with hawklike eyes, a tablet in her hand.

A heavyset white man leans forward. He has a receding

hairline and a scar across his pudgy face. His elbows are propped on his knees. Bored.

An Indian couple—man and woman—sitting next to each other, both slight in stature and wearing glasses, watch with keen interest. Their eyes follow Dr. Travis as he moves about the room, setting up a tray next to me on a rolling table. They lean to each other and whisper every so often.

Remaining at the front is the blond man in charge. He's relaxed, hands behind his back. Cold eyes scan and dissect everything in the room. When his eyes fall on me, I swear my skin starts to itch, as if he's peeling away my flesh, skin cell after skin cell.

Dr. Travis takes my arm in his clammy, cold hands and ties a band around my bicep. I flinch as a cold wetness slides over my arm, right in the inner elbow. Goosebumps break over my flesh. I strain my eyes over and down, trying to see what's happening.

The doctor turns his back to me and says, "November twenty-third, Wednesday, twenty-three fifty-two."

I have to count on my fingers, tapping them against the metal to calculate the time. It's 11:52 p.m. I've been missing for nine—no, ten—hours. Dread weighs me down, and my breathing hitches. Any hope that the others are on their way to rescue me is gone. I don't know why I thought they'd be able to trace my phone. I should have done something—anything—besides get in the vehicle with Sahara.

Dr. Travis turns, lifting a syringe, inspecting the needle before lifting a vial with a clear yellow liquid. "Phase One. Injecting induction serum into Subject Number Seven."

Oh, god. I look away. The monitor beeps in time with my rapid pulse, my heart trying to make a break for it. A sharp prick in my arm. My hands tremble. Chest tightening, tears threatening to well up again.

He removes the band from my arm as a deep burn begins at the injection site.

Don't look, do NOT look! It's bad enough as is. But I look. Not that it matters, I can't see my arm. The burn spreads into my fingers and up to my shoulder.

When it hits my chest, I whimper in a hurried panic. The pain makes it hard to breathe. It spreads faster. My whimpers rise to screams. The heat twisting and roasting me from the inside out. My eyes threaten to burst from the searing heat. I pull hard against the restraints to no avail. The straps cut into my skin, adding to the torture.

"Phase Two, Dr. Travis," the blond man says.

"Yes, sir." The doctor recites the time. Five agonizing minutes have passed. "Phase Two. Injecting two-part serum: binding agent and MDV essence."

No. No, no. Tell him no and let me go! Please!

I hardly feel the Phase Two poke, but seconds later, pain stabs with a million pinpricks, spreading through my body and up into my head. A soft laugh flits through my mind. It isn't a kind, soft laugh, but one heavy with malice, pricking at my subconscious.

"Hello," purrs a sleek, feminine voice within my head. *"Nice of you to join me. Or perhaps, it's I who is joining you."*

I need to get away. I need to get away.

"Too late," the voice whispers, followed by a low, sinister cackle.

Inside my mind, a hand reaches for me with thin, curved fingers, nails long and sharp. I scream as I'm yanked into a dark, oily void.

CHAPTER FORTY-FOUR

HERE THERE BE DEMONS

I'm running through an endless abyss. Water splashes with each step, but my feet are dry. Something's behind me, snaking toward me. Whispers carry around me, words unintelligible. My skin is being ripped from me. My insides burn. I want to stop. I want to breathe. But I can't. Something is chasing me.

"Ring around your rosies." A low laugh follows the distorted singsong voice, running up my spine and tapping my head, making me stumble.

I push myself up. My hands drip red with blood. My body shakes, a violent tremor. Pain explodes behind my eyes as my face shifts, bones cracking. Everything flashes red.

"Ashes. Ashes." Another laugh, this one closer.

Get away! I need to get away! I start to run. Pain hammers in my skull. Another tremor racks my body. I fall to my knees, gripping my head. A scream tears from my throat as the pain digs deeper into my being. Needle-like stabs trying to find me. Kill me.

"You're... Gonna..." Hands clamp down on my shoulders,

forcing my body still. The breath from the unseen threat is frigid against my face, leaving a chill that seeps into my skin. A coolness that doesn't relieve the heat but adds to the pain. "Fall... Down..."

She shoves me hard. I hit the ground in an explosion of fiery pain. Needles stab and dig. Exposing my fears. Scattering them. The unseen threat cackles. She watches me stumble and crawl as I try frantically to gather my fears, hide them.

I can't let her see, but her hand creeps over my shoulder. Taloned fingers uncurling.

"Get out!" This voice is new, adding a heavy weight to my mind.

I wince and grab my head with one hand, guarding my fears with the other. The skeletal hand of the unseen threat pauses.

"You heard me! Get out! You don't belong here," demands a clear, masculine voice. It's a heavy weight in my mind, but it doesn't hurt. The voice is just too heavy. Too heavy with the unseen threat already digging into me.

My fears. I need to hide my fears. I'm exposed. Vulnerable. Weak. Oh, god. Aaron. It was all my fault!

"Get! Out!" the male voice demands again, shaking the walls of my mind.

"No. No!" She places a taloned hand on my shoulder, nails digging. "I like it here."

"Leave!"

She snorts, defiant, and hides behind me, keeping her grip on my shoulder. "She's mine. She's miiiine!"

"Mika? That's your name, right?" The voice is soothing and gentle despite its heaviness. "I can get you out of here, but I need your help."

I look for the owner of the voice.

"There you go. Easy now."

"NOOO! She's MINE!"

I gasp, grabbing my head. Something leaks from my nose and face. I'm dying. This is—Oh, this is Hell. I killed Aaron, and this is my punishment.

"Mika, don't let it control you." A warmth touches my shoulder with a heat somehow different from the fire that rages in my body, contorting my being.

I peek up. A soft white glow hovers before me.

"You didn't kill your brother. You didn't kill him."

"But…I did," I sob.

"Mine, mine." A maniacal cackle. Dead fingers slither along my back. "Get away. She's mine. Killed. You kill—"

"Shut! Up! Get out!" The light flashes brighter. The unseen threat wails, her icy grip leaving me. But I can feel her close by, watching, muttering curses under her breath in between insane laughs.

"We need you, Mika. Stand up."

I clench my jaw, but the warm glow coaxes me, and soon I'm on my feet. Legs shaking, but I'm standing. Fears in my hands. I clutch them close to my heart.

"You said you could get me out." I sniff, feeling drained but somehow renewed.

The glow smiles. I don't know how, but he is smiling. I can feel it.

"Yeah, and you've already done the hard part."

I don't see how I did the hard part. I could barely talk until a moment ago. My fears are still exposed, their pulses cold against my flesh, and everything hurts. He's the one who spooked the spook.

"I'm still heerree," shrieks the unseen threat.

"Yeah, yeah. Beat it." The glow takes my hand, warding off the stabbing touch, and walks me forward. "I got you. Let's go."

~

The pain is still here, but it's fading. My body is ragged. Each breath feels like its own separate battle, even as my mind clears. The ringing in my ears quiets. I can hear the monitor slowing to a steady, screaming beep. Hushed whispers in front of me. Not close by, but ahead of me. I blink my eyes open, vision dark and blurry, fighting to focus.

"She's stabilizing. Her vitals look amazing. Oh. My. God. We've done it, sir! We've done it!"

His nasally voice grates in my ears.

A growl gurgles in my throat. No one seems to notice. The scientists, doctors—or whatever they are—up in their safe little watch box are chatting with quick, excitement-clipped words.

"Imagine the applications for—"

"The binding of human and Monarch—"

"Impossible!"

They can't believe this experiment was a success.

Hey, neither can I. I went to a dark place for a minute there, a very dark place that left a bad taste in my mind. I swear I can still hear and feel—

"Oh, I'm still here." Her low, manic laugh punctuates her existence. *"I've just been benched. For now."*

Great. As if I don't have enough to deal with right now. What happened to the glow guy? I much prefer him.

I look at the blond doctor. He studies me, glacial eyes evaluating—then it clicks. I know where I've seen him. Those eyes. How could I forget? Oh, maybe because I was panicking about being strapped down to a table in an unfamiliar and terrifying place.

Dr. Clive Davis. I learned about him the day I had my introduction to monsters at the OSE. He's the one who has PhDs in genetic engineering, bioengineering, and biochemistry. His picture from the OSE profile doesn't do his apathetic and soulless eyes justice. In my personal notes, I had him categorized under Monsters of the Worst Kind.

He lifts his chin, his gaze never leaving me. His voice booms like thunder over the intercom: "Kill her."

CHAPTER FORTY-FIVE

OH, HUMANITY

Kill me? Oh, that's sweet.

Maybe they should have thought of that sooner. I'm pretty sure there are countless movies about why someone shouldn't mess around with DNA. Whether it's dinosaurs, aliens, or human, something bad always happens. In this story, I am that something bad.

The strength. I can feel it, waiting in my scrawny arms, ready. Begging to be used. I flex and yank hard. A ripping sound greets my ears, and I grin. My arms are free. I rip the restraint that holds my head, turning to where Dr. Travis stands wide-eyed and holding a syringe full of what likely contains my death.

Fool. He should be running.

I rip the binding that holds my waist and swing my legs forward, one at a time, destroying the last of the restraints. I hop to the floor and take two steps to cover the space separating me from the dumbstruck doctor. While he's bigger than me, taller and with broader shoulders, his expression shows reverence as he gapes at me, as if I'm the one looking down on him. The syringe clatters to the ground. A sharp, tingling sound bounces around my skull.

A single heartbeat. Then I slam him against the wall, holding him by his throat. His eyes bulge with raw fear, the expression I'm looking for. I inhale, relishing the joy it gives me, only to recoil. With a disgusted onceover, I see he's pissed himself. My eyelids flutter in annoyance and my grip tightens around his sorry excuse for a neck.

"Mika, no!" The warm glow voice is back, startling me.

Oh, crap. I'm strangling a person. I release my grip, and he falls limp to the floor. My hands tremble as I stare at him. Sure, he doesn't deserve to live, considering what he did to me. What he did to those other girls. But how do I qualify as his executioner?

"Ugh, really? You're going to let him call the shots? You were just starting to have fun." The unseen threat pouts, tickling the edges of my mind with an oily, demonic touch.

"You're the one in control, Mika. You. Not the demon. Don't forget that." His voice is strained, like he's reaching farther than he's capable of.

I try to reach out to him and send thoughts his way. Which way is that? I don't know.

But he rejects it, voice muffled as he says, *"No, Mika. Don't. Focus on getting out. They're on their way."*

Who's they? I try to relay this question with no results. He's gone. Not even a faint hint of his glow.

"Heads up," warns my bored, sadistic mind demon.

I spin around and catch the fist of one of the bald, buff henchmen—Henchmen-S. I nearly miss another fist coming at my head as I marvel at my own supernatural strength and speed. I duck, yanking the first henchman down with me, breaking his arm in the process. He doesn't give any indication that he's in pain. I grab his head and smash it into the ground. Dark gray blood oozes from his broken face.

A kick to my chest sends me rolling across the floor. I grab at the ground, digging my nails into the concrete to stop myself. A heavy booted foot kicks toward my face, and I grab it and twist hard. The henchman falls. I pounce on his body and snap his neck. An odd shiver rolls through me, like cool water on a hot day.

"Ooooh, see how nice that feels," the demon coos in my head, sultry and sweet.

They're not human, I repeat to myself, shutting down the excited voice.. They're not human. They're soulless drones sent to kill me.

A savage, pain-filled scream cuts my thought short. I grimace, covering my ears. Flashing back to the darkness and the wail of the unseen threat, but the scream isn't in my mind. It's *real*, and it came from outside this room.

Two more henchmen appear at the front door, but there's another door at the back of the room, where the screams continue to lament.

Both henchmen rush me. I leap up and barrel toward

the nearest one, tackling him. I grip his head and slam it into the ground, splattering him on the concrete. Another shiver courses under my flesh, sweet and refreshing.

The other henchman grabs my arms, yanking them hard. Pain shoots through my shoulders. I growl, vision jolting red. I jerk my elbows back, connecting with flesh, then smash my head back. The *crack* of broken bone resounds in my ears. I twist out of his grip and spin around to face him. I kick him in the stomach. Jab, jab, cross to his face. Bone shatters under my hands. He falls limp with a satisfying *thump*.

I turn to the door. In the seconds it took me to handle the henchmen, the scream has receded to strangled gasps. The slick, seeping aroma of fear is heavy, but I trace it to the observation window still lit from within. It's now empty of excited, chattering scientists.

"Delicious, isn't it?" the demon purrs. One of her long, sharp claws taps on the edge of my brain. *"How about you let me out and I'll show you just how enjoyable this power can truly be. Hmm?"*

"Shut up," I mutter, wiping the back of my hand under my nose. Snot, sweat, and blood wet my face. Time to find out what all the noise was about. I stride toward the door, ignoring the demon's voice.

The door pushes open easily and silently, revealing a laboratory—I assume it's a lab, since I've only ever seen them on TV, and I haven't taken chemistry yet. Computers blinking with screen savers, microscopes, beakers and test tubes, and other objects whose names elude me litter the countertops. Machines of various sizes, but all box shaped, hum with power.

A sharp inhale, followed by an agonized moan, drags my attention from the countertops and science equipment to the floor. Lying in a convulsing, fetal form is Sahara. Her skin wet with a sheen of sweat, face scrunched in torment. Two vials and a large syringe lie next to her.

I stare at her, a sickening part of me enthralled by her pain, savoring it. She put me, her sister, those girls she kidnapped and their families through so much agony. She deserves to wallow in her own medicine.

Did she inject both vials at the same time? Phase One and Phase Two? My skin and mind tingle uncomfortably at the reminder of the stabbing and burning. If she injected both serums simultaneously, is she going to die?

"You could speed up the process." The demon's voice tickles my ears, like a gentle breeze slipping past. *"All the horrid acts she's done. You deserve a little revenge, a little… justice."*

My fingers twitch. It would be so easy. She's vulnerable and weak. All our problems would be solved. One less psycho walking the earth. With all she's done, she would be considered a monster.

"Yeesss, that's iiit."

I hold back. The nice, glow voice said I'm the one in control. I need to keep it that way. Not let some malignant, demonic being guide me.

"Oh, but don't you see?" The icy tendrils of her voice slide

down my spine, seeping into my skin. *"I am you."* Her laugh sends me to my knees, clutching at my chest and fighting for air.

"I'm in control. I'm in control." The mantra hisses past my lips, but I'm losing the fight. Like when you're sick to your stomach, and the urge to throw up is heavy in your chest, and you know there's nothing you can do as saliva floods your mouth. The chill seeps deeper, spreading up the base of my skull. A black patina clouds my vision.

"Ring around your rosies."

The manic laugh bubbles from my own throat.

CHAPTER FORTY-SIX

THE WEAKLING IS GONE

I stumble back, tripping around the edge of a counter and falling to my knees. A small, glass-fronted fridge reflects my image, a distorted version of myself with ghastly pale skin and black voids where my eyes should be. That can't be me. I try move, but my body won't respond. Instead, the reflection responds with a toothy grin.

"Let me show you how to have a good time." My lips move with the words, my voice distorted with a sultry, menacing tone.

As my body with the grace and mindset of a predator stands, all I can do is hold on. I turn to Sahara. My body and thoughts of murder stop short. I stare at the empty floor. An exasperated sigh leaves me. The demonic thing mutters—with my mouth—about where Sahara could have gone.

I try to run for the door, or at least look around the room, but my commands fall short, not leaving *my* brain to apply them to *my* limbs.

The demon has full control.

I've got to get out of here, I say. But the words just bounce around in my skull, unspoken. If Sahara survived the transformation, she's even more dangerous than she was before. Combine the supernatural strength and speed with the years of fighting skills she's learned, and it's no contest.

"Oh, please—" The demon doesn't finish her retort before I'm flying across the room. Pain shoots through my gut. I slam into the wall next to the door, my spine protesting. I look up from my slumped position. Sahara stands across from me. Her eyes—blacked out like mine—stare in haunting amazement at her arms.

"Can I kill her now?" the demon asks inside my head, annoyance outweighing the anger.

Running is what I should be doing.

Sahara bares her teeth at me. "Now *this* is power."

Oh, god. Please, no.

"Oh, yes!"

My body surges forward, and a war cry rips from me, all momentum aimed at Sahara. But in movements that seem slow, yet so fast, she spins out of the way and kicks out. I crash into the countertop with a sickening *crack*.

The demon growls, shoving my body up to my feet, and lunges for Sahara again. Again, she evades, countering with her own attack. I tumble across the floor, coming to a brutal halt when I slam against the fridge. The door shatters upon impact, glass spilling around me in a hazardous puddle.

A sweet, metallic taste fills my mouth. I spit out the blood and push myself to my feet. Glass crunches underfoot. Sahara chuckles, again admiring her arms. The door is to my right. My exit, an escape from a losing fight, but the dark entity in charge is too pissed off to listen. She's going to get my body beaten to a pulp. Self-preservation isn't something she has, apparently.

"You keep forgetting," her voice whispers through my mind's ear, *"I am you."*

Right. The glow guy said I was the one in control, and look how that's working out.

So, I demand of myself, *take control and save your sorry excuse—*

The door bursts open. A ninja enters with a sword, the dark garnet blade stained with Henchmen-S's gray blood. The expression in her eyes morphs from steady seriousness to confusion and horror, as her gaze finds me before resting on her sister.

"Elle, is that you?" She pulls off her mask, keeping her sword at the ready.

A low, guttural laugh from Sahara. "No. The weakling is gone, sister."

She strides toward Elizabeth, who steps to the side, toward me. Holding her sword up, prepared to fight.

"I'd say join me, but we both know you couldn't handle the transformation. It was..." Sahara looks to the ground, head tilting, distracted. Like she's hearing something we can't. She might just be, her own mind demon perhaps offering advice.

"Mika," Elizabeth whispers, taking another slow, tentative step toward me. "You good?"

"I...I don't know." To my surprise, the words are spoken aloud, not just echoing in my head. I'm back in control. Maybe the freaking demon finally left the building that is my mind.

"I'll get you out of here. Come on."

Sahara's head shoots up, locking us both in a death glare. "No one is leaving. Not alive." Her lips curl into a sadistic grin.

Elizabeth puts herself between us and hisses, "Run!"

I do. Thankfully. I spin on my heel and race out the door. Sahara lets out a vicious howl, joined by a clang of metal and a curse of pain. In the room where I'd been altered, Dr. Travis is still slumped lifeless on the floor, but I swear I can hear his heartbeat as I run past him. A slow, quiet *thump*, compared to the crazed hammering staccato of mine.

I can't leave Elizabeth. Sahara has the same strength I do—she'll tear her sister apart. That thought stops me, and the bored demon in my head sighs, annoyed that I'm bothering to try saving someone. Shouldn't it be happy I've decided to go fight something? Isn't that what it wants?

A scream cuts into my eardrums, and my heart stops

briefly. Fearing the worst, I start back toward the lab when Elizabeth appears, swordless and holding her arm at an awkward angle. Her face is blanched, scrunched in pain.

I run to her, hand on her back, and move with her as we amble toward what is hopefully the exit. The scream sounds again, but we don't hesitate. We push through the door and enter a hall. A couple of henchmen bodies lie in pools of their weird gray blood. An odd, pungent scent hangs in the air. Footsteps come from behind, steady and determined, but not running.

"Go, hurry," I say, applying a little more pressure to Elizabeth's back. "She's coming!"

"Savanna!" Sahara screeches. "Sister!"

The scream turns my world red, and my eardrums ache like they're going to bleed.

"Keep going, just keep going," I say, even as I risk a glance over my shoulder.

Sahara follows in long, quick strides, holding Elizabeth's sword. The blade drips with dark red and viscous black fluid.

"You could take her. Easy. She's injured," the voice coos, sending chills throughout my body again.

I steel myself against the feeling, but the demon may have a point. Sahara only cements it as a sword comes flying past like a spear. The garnet blade misses my arm by a mere inch, clattering to the ground a few feet away, but the point is: she missed. She's off her game. I can take her.

The demonic energy within me howls with pleasure, tapping claws against my mind. Loving this change in me. I glance back again. Sahara is gripping her shoulder and panting like an enraged beast. Her blackened eyes lock with mine. She drops her hand and sprints toward us.

Oh, crap!

I shove Elizabeth to the side, spinning out of the way myself just as Sahara catches up. Her hand clamps down on my shoulder, nails digging in. I yelp in pain, but Adam's training kicks in. I grab her hand, twist around, my elbow up, forcing her into a bent-over position. I use all my strength to kick the back of her knee. Her scream is pain and rage as she crumples to the ground. I pounce on her, gripping her in a headlock.

Whatever she does, no matter what, do NOT let go.

"Get the sword," I gasp at Elizabeth, who's stumbling to her feet. Clutching her broken arm, face glistening with sweat, she shuffles across the hall. She steps over a dead henchman, edges around his gray blood, and reaches for the sword.

Sahara wriggles in my grip, unleashing outraged, choked screams. The urge to snap her neck is powerful. It'd be easy at this point in this position. So easy.

"Then do it. Do it now," the demon encourages with her purrs. Her chill wraps around my arms, prods my muscles to squeeze a little harder. Just a little bit more.

The psycho goes still, her body limp. Did I choke her out? But only a few seconds have passed since I took her down. Her pulse beats hard and steady against my arm. My hesitation is all she needs. She flexes, yanking my arms up, and squirms from my grip. Then she's up and pouncing.

"Eliza—" My scream of warning is too late, my reaction pitifully slow.

Sahara yanks the sword from her sister's hand, spins around, and slams the blade directly through her sister's heart.

CHAPTER FORTY-SEVEN

TORN IN TWO

The black patina envelops my vision. I leap across the hall. My hands wrap around Sahara's neck, with every intention set on killing her. Broadcasting my rage in a visceral growl.

We hit the ground in a scrambling, bone-cracking, and claws-out brawl. No elegance, just pure ferocity and wanting the other one dead. She has more skill, but with her injured shoulder from the blessed blade, I have the upper hand. She stops punching and hitting, and starts pushing and shoving.

I pin her against the wall, her injured arm twisted behind her back. Both of us pant. Her squirms are weak, but I don't relent. She tricked me once. I twist her arm harder. Her bone pops. Her cry of pain is music.

"You see? Do you see how much better this is? Isn't it beautiful?" the demon purrs, her pleasure pulsing through me. An intoxicating drug making my skin prickle, my muscles twitch with the desire to inflict torment. Not death, not

yet. A slow and painful death. Dragging out pain-filled screams until the psycho begs for death.

"They're going…to kill you…you know," Sahara says between gasps of pain, her head turned to the side. "You're a monster…now. You're the thing…they're trained to hunt…and kill. Poor, poor, Mika. Getting killed…by her best friend."

She chokes out a laugh, then spits a mouthful of black blood.

I stare at the liquid trailing down her chin, my horrified understanding now sinking in. Her blood is black. Black blood means Monarch demon. She injected herself with the same stuff that was forced upon me. Which means my blood—

"Oh, the look on your face, Jager. Better than I ever could have imagined."

Jager? Vic? What? All thoughts of my tainted blood dissipate.

I glance in the direction she's facing, seeing a figure from the corner of my eye. Then I fully turn my head to face him.

The blade of his sword glints gold as he holds it at the ready. His mask hides his full expression, but the story in his eyes cuts into my soul. The dismay and disgust stun me like a slap. That's all Sahara needs to escape my grasp. She shoves me against the opposite wall.

"You should have let me kill her," the demon hisses, annoyed.

I growl in frustration and race after my prey. I hear my name called from behind me. Something pings in my mind that I should stop, that I need to face this person. but I don't stop. Sahara is getting away. I can't let her get away. Not when I have the power to stop her.

I leap over decapitated henchmen and skirt around puddles of their gray blood, keeping Sahara within my sights. She disappears around a corner just as I round one. A rapid patter of feet follows me. Panic shoots through me. To be chased is to be prey, and I don't want to be prey.

I tell myself to focus on the objective: Stop Sahara.

"Then rip out the throats of those pursuing you," the demon adds with a sultry laugh.

As I round another corner, there's an ear-shattering blast. A *zing* of metal rips past me. A bullet? I drop to the ground and scramble back around the corner. Two more gunshots sound. I grip my head, gritting my teeth. My vision pounds with darkness. A growl gurgles in my throat. I wait for the disorientation of my hearing to subside, then stay low as I peek around the edge.

Down the hall, I see a glowing red EXIT sign. The Indian couple from the observation box—along with the blond, tall doctor, Dr. Clive Davis—are at the end of the hall. The men restrain Sahara, injecting her with quick, fluid movements. The woman holds a handgun as she watches the hallway for me. Her eyes lower to where my head is poking out. She aims the small weapon and pulls the trigger.

I jerk back, pressing my hands to my ears, the gunshots like explosives shattering my eardrums.

"Let's go!"

"We need to dispose of the other—"

"Let the EONs worry about her."

"She'll kill some of them while they try to save her."

When I pull my hands from my ears, I notice they're coated in dried gray blood, reminding me of my own blood. The demon taps against my brain, making me grit my teeth. She jabs a claw into me and forces my focus back on the task at hand: killing Sahara.

I peer around the edge. Slow and careful. The door at the end of the hall settles closed with a quiet thump, my target and her cohorts gone. The red glow of the EXIT sign illuminates my failure. My face twitches with irritation.

They won't get away that easily—

"Mika?"

The demon groans at the voice behind me, only to follow it with a laugh of anticipation. *Since our original prey has fled, might as well have some fun with this one.*

Right. I was being chased.

I turn around, lowering into a fighting/pouncing stance, and stop short. The demon's laugh is pushed to the back of my mind.

No longer wearing his mask, Vic stares at me, unable to look away from my blackened gaze. The demon gives me a gentle nudge, turning my attention to the gold sword he holds at the ready. Encouraging me to defend myself. Rip the guy's throat out. The feeling would be—

"Mika?" The panic and concern in my best friend's expression speak volumes. There's none of the horror and fear from before. He's not here to hurt me.

Oh, god. What have I done? I let the demon take over and I—What have I done?

My hands tremble as the patina fades from my tear-blurred vision. I slump to the floor, defeat and shame overwhelming whatever emotions the demon is throwing at me.

"Mika?" Vic approaches, slowly and carefully, his voice breaking as he says, "Mika, a-are you all right?"

He touches my shoulder, and I flinch, keeping my face turned away. He says my name again, arms going around me and pulling me toward him in a hug in which I find no consolation. His body shakes. It takes a second, but I realize he's crying.

"I thought you were dead," he says, voice straining around the sob. "I thought I lost you."

"I'm not me," I say, the words timid but heavy in warning. "I'm not me. I'm dangerous."

"No, no." He holds me tighter. "No."

"You don't understand!" I push away from him, chin quivering. "I wanted to kill you just then!"

"But you didn't." He holds my shoulders as he stares into my eyes. Cheeks streaked with tears. "You didn't."

He pulls me into another tight, cutting-off-air hug. God, I wish I felt peace from this.

"You're all going to kill me. That what you're all trained to do," I whisper, stomach full of dread. The demon whispers that I could take them. I could kill them all before they kill me. I'm stronger and faster than all of them.

Vic shakes his head. "No. They won't kill you. I don't know what they'll do. But I won't let them kill you."

"But how?"

He lets go of me, removes the communicator piece from his ear, and tucks it away in a pocket.

"Lie. We're going to lie," he says, words quick and low. He cups my face, holding it in both hands, the fear in his eyes making me shiver. "You hear me? I don't know what they'll do with you. What they'll do to you. We have to lie. We have to hide it."

What they'll do *with* me? What they'll do *to* me? Is the "they" the OSE or the AIO? Or both. Or their science division. I try to ask him what he's talking about, but the demon's voice slithers in my mind's ear.

"Do yourself a favor and snap his neck."

"Mika, do you hear me?" Vic's grip tightens on my shoulders. "If they ask, nothing happened to you. We arrived before they could do anything to you."

I shove the demon's voice to the back of my mind. "I don't—Vic, I think they recorded it."

Dr. Travis had recited the date and time. That had to

be for a recording. Any self-respecting scientist keeps detailed notes of their experiments. What's more detailed than a recording?

"I'll take care of that." His voice is a harsh whisper. "We don't have a lot of time. Come on." He takes my hand and helps me to my feet. "We need to find the recording. The emergency medical response team is going to be here any minute now, and the whole place is going to be crawling with investigators."

We head back toward the lab in silence. Vic opens doors and gives the rooms a quick onceover before we move on. Most of the rooms are empty offices, some full of desks and boxes. We're looking for something with computers. Monitors that show us the layout of the lab. Somewhere, they'd keep visual and audio recordings.

The scuff of our shoes. Liquid drips somewhere. The pounding of our hearts: mine a rapid drum, and Vic's a steady, even rhythm. His training keeping him calm. These sounds all create a din that I almost don't hear Vic tell me to wait behind him as we approach a door; one that differs from the other off-white doors. This one is stainless steel, taller and wider than normal doors. It could accommodate a small car.

He pushes open the door. Ice-cold air wafts out, along with a rancid, rotting fruit smell. We press our hands to our noses and mouths. The lights in the room flicker on with a soft buzzing hum as they illuminate the scene before us. Vic coughs, choking. He stumbles back from the door and turns to the side, heaving violently.

Oh, my god—

Inside the room, lying on gleaming stainless-steel tables, are six human bodies, cut open from the throat and down to the pelvis. Skin bereft of color, save for the dark, dried blood trailing from their open, glazed eyes and mouths.

My own gorge rises, burning my throat as saliva fills my mouth. Eyes stinging, I fall on all fours, heaving. The image of the girl closest to the entrance is stuck in my mind. Her blonde hair is dull and knotted with blood, but I recognize her. She's the girl I failed to save. The girl kidnapped from the parking lot.

The demon laughs, low and insane.

CHAPTER FORTY-EIGHT

LIES

If I hadn't freaked out and ran when I discovered Sahara, I would have stopped this. I would have saved her. If I hadn't been so concerned about myself, but instead followed Sahara here, I could have saved that poor girl before they did anything to her. I could have prevented this.

"Mika." Vic's hands pull at me, getting me away from the gruesome sight. I'm aware of his movements, trying to prod me along, but I can't seem to get my body to function. "We need to go."

I can't get the girl's dead eyes out of my head. I vaguely hear Vic apologize. Pain stings my cheek, and I jerk back, gaping up at my friend who just slapped me across the face. The discomfort is faint compared to the shock of him hitting me, but it brings me out of my stupor.

He gives me a somber look, lips pinched tight. "I know what you're thinking. This is not your fault. This is all on

Sahara."

He mumbles something after, something about the board of directors followed by a colorful curse, and I give him a quizzical look. He's already turned away and reaching toward the door.

I join him, and we both manage to pull the door closed. The stench of death remains heavy in the air, mixed with the fresh odor of vomit. As we walk away from the death scene, Vic, with trembling hands, puts the communication earbud back in his ear. He informs the team that he's found the missing girls, DOA.

Dead on arrival.

We reach the bodies of dead henchmen, a sign we're close to the lab.

A tormented cry issues from around the corner ahead. I cringe. Vic asks me if I'm all right, face creased with concern. I nod, trying to block out all the noise ravaging my ears: the cry, the drips, the hearts beating, footsteps, buzzing, humming, hissing. He keeps a hand on my arm as he brings me with him to the corner.

The lament sounds again. We peek around the corner. Down the hall, Devon yanks his mask off as he approaches Elizabeth's slumped form against the wall, his face contorted with shock. His steps are hesitant, as if what he's seeing isn't real. A smear of blood trails down to where she lies. Her eyes stuck open in a state of fear and surprise. Skin washed-out with death.

Devon falls to his knees in front of her, and tugs her

into his arms.

~

My chest tightens and I collapse. I could have stopped this death too. Vic is wrapping his arms around me again, his body shaking as his sobs join mine. Even the demon is silent.

How long do we sit in the hall and cry? Like there aren't dead henchmen around us, with their gray blood seeping onto our pant legs? I don't know.

Vic stands, pulling me up with him, revealing another side of my best friend I've never seen. It reminds me of his mother. Serious and resolved. His mission-oriented side. A showcase of his ability to compartmentalize.

He glances over his shoulder at Devon. Jacqulyn and Jonah try vainly to pull him from Elizabeth's corpse. They are too brokenhearted and shocked themselves to put energy behind it. Jonah's hands shake with each movement. Jacqulyn's face is streaked with tears, glistening under the harsh LED lights. She's clad in the same black attire as the rest of the group, her braids wrapped in a bun at the nape of her neck.

Vic gestures toward them, or really, toward the door down the hall from them. "The lab's down there?"

I nod. "Just past..." I can't even say it, but I don't have to. Vic gets the idea. He doesn't need more affirmation than a nod.

His eyes lifts to Jonah, who has managed to remove

Devon from Elizabeth's body. Blood is smeared across the older boy's face. Jonah hugs him close, keeping his gaze averted as Jacqulyn lays the girl's body out, checking her over. It's too late to do anything for her. Far too late. The woman's chin quivers, but her hand is steady as she closes Elizabeth's eyes.

I should have been faster. Should have snapped Sahara's neck the first chance I had.

"Duh," the demon retorts, scraping her claws against my mind. Sending a burst of pain behind my eyes. I grip my head, letting out a whimper. Maybe I should just let them kill me. Who knows what I'm capable of now?

"Not neck snapping, apparently." The demon sighs, tapping a single sharp claw in the soft tissue of my brain.

"She's fine." Vic's voice pulls me from the torment inside my head.

I pry my eyes open. Jacqulyn stands in front of me, eyes sad and lips pressed tight. She ignores Vic as he attempts to keep her from lowering me to the ground, to sit with my back against the wall. She slings a bag from around her shoulder, retrieves a penlight, and shines it into my eyes.

"Did they do anything to you?" The way she asks, she means business, daring me to say anything different from what she expects.

"No, they didn't—" Vic starts to say, but the woman cuts him off with a sharp glare. There's a threat in her gaze that she'll make good on if he so much as tries to speak for me again. This instills in me a new fear and respect. I can't lie to her.

But I have to.

"Mika," she says, her fingers probing gently around my nose. There's no outward, physical pain. I remember the cracking of bones in my face when I was sucked into the abyss. Maybe the serum they injected me with also healed me because Sahara definitely broke my nose when she took me.

Jacqulyn says my name again, pulling me from my thoughts.

"No. They weren't able to." I say each word as if I'm tiptoeing around a sleeping beast.

Vic gives the woman a wary look, jaw clenched. Both our pulses race as we wait to see if Jacqulyn believes the lie.

She breathes deeply, letting her hands fall to her bag. She digs around. "Your nose isn't broken, but I imagine you're going to have a killer headache for a couple of days."

Yeah, no kidding. She has no idea.

"Anything else hurt?"

I shake my head. Nope. Nothing. I should hurt. I should hurt all over, but I don't.

"Get her out of here," she commands Vic. Then she's on her feet, stepping over bodies of henchmen on her way over to Devon and Jonah. The older boy's sobs are quieter, but still inconsolable.

Shouts echo down the hall, coming from both sides. I

jump to my feet, hands curling into fists, but I notice Vic deflate with a swear under his breath.

He glances at me. "The emergency services and investigators are here."

We share a look, and I realize what he's saying. With this new team here, we're too late in retrieving any evidence of their experiment on me.

CHAPTER FORTY-NINE

I AM YOU

They know.

Why else would they have tossed me in here as soon as we got back, and asked me to wait?

I pace the short length of Hogan's office. My stomach is in knots so tight it feels like internal damage. Every slight noise has me on edge. My muscles stiffen at each sound: a creak of a door, a scuff of shoes, the *plop-plop-plop* of a leaky faucet, the hum of technology. A muted din of voices in discussion.

They're going to kill me. Their responsibility is to kill monsters. The pictures of OSE students who have won trophies for their skills line the walls. Their smiling, winning faces taunting and gruesome.

I risk taking a seat in front of Hogan's desk, hoping to find some semblance of calm. My leg instantly starts to bounce, hands clutched together in my lap. I relax my fingers long enough to pull the sleeves of the oversized black hoodie over my hands and think back to when I first arrived.

Dr. Castillo checked me over. I was terrified the whole time that she'd draw blood to examine. She didn't, but her expression was serious, grim, making her look a decade older than the seventy years she probably is.

Granted, we have a dead EON, a friend, a sister, on our minds. Then the woman cleared me and sent me to the showers. Jacqulyn stood vigil outside the door the whole time, and she gave me the sweats and hoodie I wear now. I twist the sleeves in my hands.

Footsteps echo in my head, like the beat of a death drum. *Thump, thump, thump.* My heart picks up speed and my skin flushes with a sickening feeling. The door creaks open. I jump out of the chair and whirl to face my doom.

Vic enters, hunched against himself. His eyes meet mine for a second before he looks away. Hogan is behind him, more ragged than when I first saw him on my return. His expression wan and exhausted. Despite the bags under his bloodshot eyes, he's serious. Deadly serious. I want nothing more than to disappear.

Vic stands next to me, staring at the floor.

Hogan shuts the door with a barely audible exhale through his nose. Vic and I both turn and take seats as the man passes us and sits down at his desk. He taps on the keyboard, movements stiff and mechanical.

Oh, god. He knows. I'm dead. They're going to kill me.

The click of keys reverberates in my ears. The world

swims and blurs together in a watercolor mess. The demon chuckles and drags her nails along the forefront of my mind. I dig my nails into my palms to keep myself from flinching at her touch.

"No worries," she coos, her grim words composed of silk. *"You're stronger than both of them. You could use the trophy to bash the old man's skull in."*

She goes on, detailing how the blood and brain matter would feel, the texture and the smell, the way the splatter would improve the décor.

"I have a dead student." Hogan's voice pushes the demon's musing away in a brisk, daunting sweep. My gaze flicks up at him. The look he's giving me and Vic has me collapsing in on myself. Vic shifts in his seat, as if he can maneuver away from the man's stare.

"And..." Hogan's features harden, but he doesn't resume his statement. A different voice, a little distorted and muffled, takes over for him. Coming from the speakers of his computer.

"I thought you were dead." Vic's voice, strained with a sob. *"I thought I lost you."*

"I'm not me. I'm not me. I'm dangerous." My voice. Stiff and afraid, but it is me talking, and I realize this is an audio recording of when Vic found me after I tried to chase down Sahara. I guess it didn't matter that he tucked the communication device away.

"No, no!" Vic again, his voice tight with panic and determination. *"No."*

"You don't understand!" Me, sounding like an animal on the verge of attacking, scared and not wanting to face the threat. *"I wanted to kill you just then!"*

"But you didn't." Vic, so sure of himself as he speaks. *"You didn't."*

"You're all going to kill me. That's what you're all trained to do." I clench my eyes shut. The color, long drained from my face, tries to drain even more, leaving me lightheaded and cold.

"No. They won't kill you. I don't know what they'll do. But I won't let them kill you."

God, I wish I could find solace in my best friend's voice, but his words are like the first nail in the coffin. My coffin.

"But how?"

"Lie. We're going to lie." There it is, my death sentence. As if my being turned into a tainted freak of nature wasn't already a death sentence. *"You hear me? I don't know what they'll do with you. What they'll do to you. We have to lie. We have to hide it."*

Hogan taps a key and the hum of the recording stops. If there are other sounds, they're drowned out, for the ringing of panic and defeat in my ears is loud enough to silence even the demon that's screaming at me to murder them.

How did I think this was going to end? If Vic and I got away with the lie, the complications of what they did to me still remain. What did they inject me with? How long will it take for the demon to take over completely, and before I kill everyone? Not just the EONs, but my sisters and parents as well.

Perhaps. Yes, perhaps it would be better for them to kill me. It would be better for everyone involved if I were dead.

"I take complete responsibility for this," Vic says, voice bold with an authority that doesn't match his fearful pallor. I fully see his lawyer mother in him now. I've always seen him more like his jovial, ready-with-a-joke father.

"As you should and will," Hogan says, the words curt, making Vic flinch. "Of all the foolish and idiotic—" The man takes a breath. "You're suspended until further notice. Your mother is here to take you home. You owe your family a Thanksgiving. We'll discuss your future when you return."

My best friend doesn't move to stand right away. From the corner of my eye, I see that his resistance is stark in how he holds the man's gaze—a silent argument, a battle he loses. He stands, places a hand on my shoulder, and gives it a gentle squeeze before he exits. The door clicks shut behind him.

Hogan taps on his keyboard, then lets out an almost inaudible breath before commanding, "Tell me everything. This is being recorded."

I remain silent, staring at the floor. I'm not as brazen as Vic. I never will be. You can't be anything when you're dead.

"We can't help you if we don't know what happened," he says, voice softening. An inflection of hope in his tone.

They're not going to kill me? I wonder if it is possible for the brains of the AIO to come up with a way to reverse what happened. Get rid of the monster that now resides within me.

A little glimmer of hope sparks in my heart, just like the warm glow voice, and I tell Hogan everything. Starting from when I found Sahara in my home, how she discovered who I was. The doctors and scientists in the watch box along with Dr. Clive Davis, the serums injected into me. The dark place I went to, the glow voice, the excitement of the doctors over the success of merging Monarch with a human. The power I felt in almost killing Dr. Travis, Sahara injecting herself. The demon in my mind, Elizabeth dying, me trying to avenge her death. Sahara's capture/escape, me with the demon wanting to kill Vic, and the fact that every sound is battling for conquest of my ears.

I tell him all this because I want hope. I need hope. The thing taking over my mind—I can't let it take over me.

"Mika, sweetie, host of my malignant form," the demon purrs. *"You can't get rid of me. How many times must I say it?"* Chills creep down my spine. *"I am you."*

ACKNOWLEDGEMENTS

People I'd like to thank:

Firstly, my wonderful and very supporting husband. Thanks for accepting my crazy.

Secondly, Hanna. This story wouldn't exist without you. Funny how it went from being a goofball fanfiction to a fully fledged novel for all who care to read.

Thirdly, for my family and friends for being so supportive and encouraging. You are all the best!

Fourthly, to my beta readers, editors. You all gave me the most invaluable insight. It would have been impossible to turn this into the polished kickass story that it is without you.

Fifthly, to all the readers, current and future, thank you so much! Go and create your own worlds. Get up on out there and do it.

Last, but not least, I'd like to thank myself for not giving up and shying away. This is by far the scariest and most stressful thing I've ever done in my life. I loved every single second of it.

That must be what passion is.

Thanks again.

About the Author

S.E. Sharp has been composing stories since she first learned how to write. From short stories about horses and dolphins, to Star Wars and Supernatural fanfiction, to fully fledged novels that just need some extra TLC before sharing with the world.

When she's not writing or working, she likes to binge watch procedural cop shows, paint gradients/silhouettes with watercolors, go for hikes, and long runs.

She currently resides in Alaska with her husband and her Shih-Tzu/Chihuahua mix.

For updates on novels in progress, dog shenanigans, Alaska scenery, and laments of an author, connect with her on Instagram at: sesharp_author

Check out her website for new and upcoming novels at: www.sarahesharp.com

www.ingramcontent.com/pod-product-compliance
Lightning Source LLC
Chambersburg PA
CBHW021441310726
48971CB00005B/1460